In Arcadia

Andrea K Höst

All characters in this publication
are fictitious and any resemblance
to real persons, living or dead,
is purely coincidental.

In Arcadia
© 2017 Andrea K Höst. All rights reserved.
ISBN: 978-1-925188-14-1
EBook ISBN: 978-1-925188-15-8
www.andreakhost.com
Cover art and map: Andrea Hösth

ACKNOWLEDGEMENTS

With thanks to all the fans of the Touchstone Trilogy. Your love of these books made it impossible for me to not want to revisit Muina.

AUTHOR'S NOTE

This book is in Australian English. It can be read as a backstory-heavy stand-alone, but with inevitable spoilers for the *Touchstone Trilogy*.

When expanding a couple of paragraphs from a novel into a story of its own, errors come to light. In writing *In Arcadia*, I had to correct a season and a date in *Gratuitous Epilogue*, but any other variations are simply the filter of Cass vs Laura.

Map of Arcadia

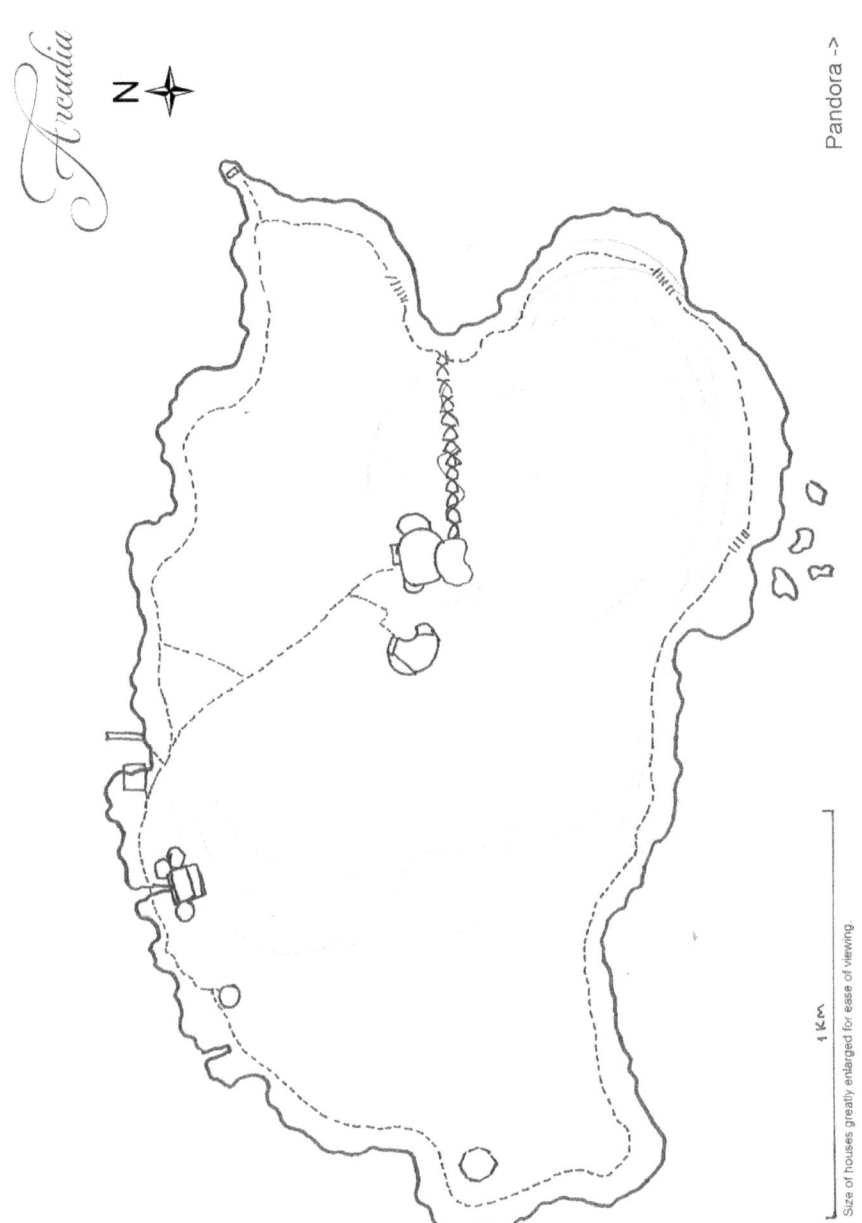

Arcadia

N

Pandora ->

1 Km

Size of houses greatly enlarged for ease of viewing.

CHAPTER ONE

Laura Devlin's first two months on her new world were full and hectic. There were a great many people to meet, particularly a son-in-law and five grandchildren. There were inoculations, medical examinations, and the injection of a nanotech computer interface that was followed by a dictionary download into her brain. After that came tours to view the grand wreck of the planet's original civilisation: ruins that were quickly being overshadowed by technically advanced cities supporting the more than two million people who had migrated to the planet of Muina in a scarce few years.

In between, Laura fit in some infant-level virtual schooling, a generous dose of gaming, and a good dollop of time prodding at the empty garden beds that came with her brand new house. Most of all, she reaffirmed, over and over, the fact of Cassandra. Cass. Never Cassie. Her daughter, alive, safe, and happy.

None of this had eased Laura's nightmares. Far too often she would wake from endless scenes of all the worst that could have happened to her funny, sweet, uncertain child after she had vanished on her way home from high school. It had been three months before Cass had been able to reach her family with a partial explanation of her disappearance, and that strange apparition had been in a large amount of danger, so Laura hadn't truly deep down relaxed until a surprise package of detailed diaries allowed her to finally accept that Cass was alive, safe, but never coming home.

Thankfully, after three and a half long years, Laura had had the chance to make Cass' new world her own home, and finally been reunited with her daughter. But messages and reunions and many hugs could not erase the indelible mark left by those first months of despair.

Rising in the pre-dawn, Laura left the latest nightmare tangled in her sheets and pulled on a light dress and sandals before venturing outside.

To a lifelong Sydney resident, the Muinan summer around the city of Pandora was mild and pleasant, but Laura had maintained her habit of walking in the cool of early morning, tracing the paths of the island that was now her home.

An island! With all her daughter's strange powers, large new family, and uncomfortable level of fame, for some reason Laura kept stumbling over the fact that Cass owned an island.

This was something less of an enormity than it would be on Earth, since the planet of Muina was going through a resettlement rush, and large plots of land were being portioned out to all manner of people. Cass had gained hers because she'd been key to unlocking the planet to habitation—along with some incidental saving of the galaxy. She'd named the island Arcadia, and built a secluded house that allowed her some privacy from several planets'-worth of crowds fascinated with her every move.

Then she had built a place for her mandatory guard detail to stay.

When Cass had learned that she would finally, after more than three years gone, be able to bring her family to her new planet, she'd added houses for Laura and Laura's sister, Sue. They were rather impractically large, and felt empty and strange to Laura, lacking the crammed bookshelves that she had left behind. But the island itself was magnificent.

This morning was particularly still, and Laura paused on the north patio to drink in the hush, then started along the whitestone path that led past her sister's matching mini-mansion, down the slope to the main path that circled the entire island. Left would take her to

Cassandra's house, with a stop on the way for the guard house where a pair of Setari—'psychic space ninjas'— would be stationed to watch over the island's valuable inhabitants. To the right, the path traced the island's eastern and southern shore: a part of Arcadia still completely free of buildings.

Laura inhaled deeply, the stillness entering into her. The lake was rarely so glass-flat: a mirror to drink the sky. She followed the path to the north-eastern point of the island, where a stone bench was set on a small spit, commanding an unimpeded view east over the vast freshwater lake to the city of Pandora. The new capital of Muina, a barely visible whiteness on the horizon, picked out in the rosy tints of dawn.

A bird sang sweet, fluting welcome, and Laura sat and listened, absently turning over the question that had been growing over the last few weeks.

What was she going to do with the rest of her life?

Part of the answer was obvious. Her son, Julian, was still only sixteen, and not quite ready to set up house on his own. And Cass, all of twenty-one years old, had become mother to five children: a little found family of four she had adopted, with an addition born seven months ago. There was a lot of grandmothering in Laura's future.

As rewarding as this had already been, Laura felt the need for something more. She had gone from school to a career in IT support. When her marriage had fallen apart ten years in, she'd supplemented her income by selling handmade dolls and jewellery, and she'd worked hard to make time for the people she loved and the things she enjoyed. Now, there was no mortgage, no debts. Instead there was a strings-free house that generated its own electricity, and a formidable chunk of money gifted to her by Cass to cover any other bills, leaving Laura free to enjoy Paradise.

Was it taking too much for granted to do nothing but game, garden, and play with the grandkids? Or did she need to earn this futuristic happily ever after?

A ship lifted above the distant city. A sleek wedge of a thing rising on blue impellers. Laura watched with awe and appreciation. Inter-dimensional spaceships. Teleportation platforms, psychics, and cities that grew themselves. A computer in her head. An expected lifespan of a hundred and thirty years. And Cass.

No, she wasn't taking any of that for granted. She was grateful every day.

It was such a lovely morning that she decided to do a full circuit of the island: a trek that took just under an hour and a half at Laura's standard walking pace, but stretched to more than two hours because she kept stopping to collect unusual leaves and the occasional flower. And to take photographs using the 'interface' installation in her head, which did everything a smartphone could offer, and a great deal more.

The most marvellous thing, though, was that her knees didn't hurt going up and down the occasional steps. She felt like she could walk forever, with the easy energy of her early twenties. That was Muinan medical science.

"Unna Laura!"

Circuit almost complete, Laura was not surprised to be spotted as she paused on the bridge that crossed the natural pool below her daughter's house. She waved up at Sen, who was hanging rather far over the railing of the main patio balcony. But only briefly, before the girl was hauled unceremoniously back. Then Cass was looking down.

"Hey, Mum! Come up, we're having breakfast."

The sight of Cass, smiling and relaxed, still hit Laura like a blow to the chest. Not a bad sensation, but dizzying, and Laura took a deep breath as she circled the pool and climbed the broad, flat stairs to the partially covered patio Cass used as a breakfast area in summer.

She was greeted with a warm clasp around the thighs from Sen.

"Unna Laura!" the girl repeated. Unna was a word she used only for Laura, even though it didn't mean 'grandmother' in any of her languages. "We're making pancakes."

"Lira is, anyway," Cass said, heading indoors in response to a thin wail. "You're setting the table, Sen."

"Then I can help with that," Laura said.

"It's my job!" Sen said seriously, and tugged her toward a seat at the head of the table. "Unna Laura can be Guest of Honour."

That was another reflection of the strangeness of Cass' life: a great many people wanted to meet her, and she could not always wriggle out of the flood of official engagements. Sen, only six, had not been obliged to attend many of these, but they'd obviously still left an impression.

Sitting obediently, Laura absently twined her collection of leaves and flowers into a wreath as she watched Sen set the table with more enthusiasm than neatness. Once the last utensil was more-or-less in place, she dropped the wreath on the girl's head.

"There. A reward for being so diligent."

Sen crowed, and spun in a little circle of delight. She was a pretty child, with masses of thick black hair, very dark eyes, and a warm gold-brown skin that was set off nicely by the green, bronze and white tones of the impromptu crown. But it was this joy, a radiant happiness that rarely faltered, that made her so engaging.

"What is diligent?"

"Diligent means hard-working," Laura explained. "You had a job and you made sure it was done."

"You should do today's words, Mum," Cass said, returning with an armful of crotchety baby. She was dressed in the figure-hugging black nanosuit of the Setari, and frowning down at her youngest worriedly. "I think I might skip work and take Tyrian for a check-up. He won't settle at all."

"His mouth hurts," Sen informed her helpfully, and Cass brightened.

"Must be another tooth. I've got some gel for that somewhere."

She headed back inside, and Laura wryly reflected on the usefulness of psychics when baby-wrangling. Sen— like Cass' husband and their son—was a 'Tenlan Kigh' talent, which meant she had an ability to 'know'. 'Psychic psychics', as Cass put it. Tenlan Kigh—which translated confusingly as Sight Sight—was the rarest of the sight-related psychic talents, and tremendously convenient.

The oldest of the children, Ys, demonstrated a different ability as she drifted slowly down from the upper patio. Telekinesis, one of the movement category of talents, allowed users to fly, although Ys' talent was only strong enough to let her take short hops.

"Good morning, Unna Laura," she said formally, before briskly tidying Sen's table-setting efforts. She was a tall girl for nearly-fourteen, thin and bony, with short, somewhat wayward hair.

"So diligent," Sen said.

"What's that?" Ys asked, pausing.

"A new word. Ys is diligent. Rye is diligent. Lira is sometimes diligent. And I..." Sen skipped around the table and grinned cheekily. "I am a sweetheart!"

"Tokki," Lira commented, arriving with a plate of thick, American-style pancakes.

'Brat', the dictionary in Laura's head whispered.

"How long did it take you to do the work for the translation app?" Laura asked Cass, who returned as Lira began unceremoniously portioning out pancakes.

"It felt like centuries," Cass said, grimacing. "I started trying to get through it in a big lump, which was stupid. I should have just done a few words a day, like I do now, but I was worried it wouldn't be ready before you got here. I'm glad it makes a difference, though."

"Oh, absolutely—the auto-translate makes picking the language up quicker than I thought possible. Pronunciation is difficult, but I can make myself understood well enough, and don't have any problem listening to people. It's only when I hear a word where you haven't entered a translation, and this vague multiplicity of possible meanings washes over me, that I have trouble. In some ways the 'conceptual translator' is more confusing than simply not knowing what the word means."

"I keep finding words I didn't get quite right the first time around," Cass sighed, rearranging her nanosuit to incorporate a harness for the still-restless Tyrian. "There's a lot that I don't completely understand, even after three years. And 'Muinan' itself is changing: three planets' worth of language mixing together, with a bit of Earth's as well."

"Not to mention neologisms like 'Unna'," Laura said, and then had to explain what a neologism was to the three girls. "So when Sen decided to call her new grandmother 'Unna' she created a neologism. You copied her, and if other people hear it and use it, it might even end up in a dictionary itself one day."

"There's two words for today's lesson," Cass said, for learning three new English words was part of the family's daily routine. "Once you've got a better handle on Muinan, you and Aunt Sue and everybody can start adding words to the app as well."

"The pancakes will get cold," Lira said, grumpily. She spoke in Muinan, for she was the least enthused about the breakfast English lessons, though she seemed to follow the conversations well enough.

"They're nearly at the dock," Cass said, and explained to Laura: "Kaoren and Rye went out in the canoes. Kaoren says not to wait."

"I'm not sure I could, it smells so delicious. What kind of berry have you put in them, Lira?"

"It is one from Kolar: hithal, it is called," Lira replied, this time in English, adding: "Something to try," with an affectation of indifference even as she closely watched for reactions to first bites.

Laura was suitably complimentary, for Lira was showing considerable promise in the kitchen—anything that involved building or creating interested her. "I'm so looking forward to some of the spice plants I brought with me becoming available, just to see what you'll make of them," she told the girl. "Vanilla and cinnamon particularly, though it takes at least two years for cinnamon to grow into a useable tree. You'll have fun experimenting when the biotechs send back samples."

"For all we know, a version of them might be growing somewhere on Muina anyway," Cass said. "But, yes, the techs can hurry up and produce vanilla, cinnamon, and especially chocolate."

"Have there been any new theories about why Earth and Muina are so similar?"

"There's always theories," Cass said. "The official one is still that there was clearly a lot of back and forth travel and trade between Earth and Muina a really long time ago. After you six arrived they had some more Earth humans to do genetic comparisons with, and they still say we're all genetically from the same stock. I try not to get drawn into talking about whether people started on Earth and came here or vice versa: it's a bit of a touchy subject."

A step from below heralded the arrival of the last of Cass' new family: her husband Kaoren and older son Rye.

One did not perv on one's son-in-law, of course, so Laura merely made her regular intellectual footnote that Cass had married a very tall, very handsome and very fit young man. Rye, only recently turned thirteen, idolised him, and when they were both dressed in knee-length swimming costumes and loose tank tops, with their hair cropped in the same short style, they displayed a bond that did not require a strict blood tie.

Kaoren, Laura reflected, straightforwardly enjoyed being a father.

"I am sorry we were slow," he said to Lira. "We'll be ready as soon as we can."

Lira shrugged with exaggerated unconcern as the pair went to clean up, but then took the remaining pancakes inside to reheat.

"Diligent!" Sen proclaimed when the older girl returned, and stood on her seat so she could crown Lira with the wreath.

"Tokki," Lira repeated, but this time with a hint of warmth to the word. She touched the wreath lightly and then sat down, obviously pleased.

Cass and Ys had watched the exchange, but settled back to their breakfasts—and, in Ys' case, likely reading a dozen info-streams via the interface—without comment. There was undoubtedly a level of rivalry between Sen and Lira. Both of them possessed rare talents, had been much-cossetted in earlier years, and were consequently inclined to display temperament when denied coveted treats. The large difference between the two girls was Ys and Rye, who had always been there for Sen. Those three were all from a moon called Nuri, and had been bound together even before their world's destruction.

Lira, by contrast, had suffered a long isolation, and among the Devlin Ruuel family that had settled onto Arcadia, Lira was the one who struggled to believe she belonged, and was wanted for her Self and not just the powers of a Touchstone that made her, like Cass, so valuable. Undeniable beauty and a figure already maturing at thirteen added complication upon complication, and that did not even touch upon the media who watched her perhaps even more obsessively than it did Cass.

Laura had many thoughts on encouraging Lira, but was keeping them to herself. Her own role as parent meant trusting in her daughter and son-in-law, supporting without pushing. Being 'Unna' meant she got to follow their lead while focusing on fun treats, so she simply offered to teach them all how to make a wreath once they were back from school that day.

Hearing this as he and Kaoren returned, Rye said: "We can go to Middle Meadow. There are lots of flowers there I haven't catalogued yet."

Rye was a born naturalist, and Arcadia his personal project. Whenever he spoke of it he shed his natural diffidence and glowed with enthusiasm. Laura had brought a great many seeds and plantlets for him from Earth, and had thoroughly enjoyed stocking her new flower beds with his assistance.

The family began to discuss their day's rather complicated timetable, so Laura sat back and just enjoyed them, and marvelled at her daughter, who had survived a great deal, and was now proving to be not half bad as a working Mum-of-five. Of course her employer, the interplanetary defence force called KOTIS, made certain to accommodate Cass as much as possible, meaning she could take Tyrian with her for many of her current assignments. And Kaoren, who was easing back into his work for KOTIS as a Setari captain, could bring order to any level of chaos.

As the breakfast dishes were tidied away, a text box popped up in the 'screen' inside Laura's head. Standard English alphabet, which was another accommodation KOTIS had been careful to provide for Cass' convenience.

Cass: *Jules is still in bed, I suppose?*

Laura: *I expect so. He's found a new game he really likes.*

Cass: *Aren't you worried about him, Mum? He practically gets up at midday each day.*

Laura: *Well, so does your Aunt Sue. They're both night owls.*

Cass: *But Aunt Sue at least* goes outside *when she's up.*

Laura: *Don't worry, Cass. I make sure Julian's cave is aired at least once a week. But if you'd like to revisit the occasions when I couldn't get you up before midday on a Saturday when you were sixteen...*

Cass: *Blah. Okay, okay, whatever. I'm just...he isn't unhappy, is he?*

Laura: *He is blissful. But also learning a new language, and dealing with all the Earth things that aren't here. He puts in solid time in virtual school, and comes out of his cave when I ask him to. I think we can leave him to that, just for the moment.*

Cass sighed heavily, but turned her attention to getting her collection of children down to the dock for their trip to school.

Mildly entertained, Laura enjoyed any hugs offered, and then strolled back to her house, choosing not to mention to Cass that she was fairly sure Julian's withdrawal was related to visits to Arcadia by numerous pretty girls, combined with the presence of Sight Sight talents. The idea that Kaoren—not to mention Sen—could *see* his reactions to some of the island's visitors had clearly occurred to Julian almost immediately after their arrival.

Sight talent etiquette meant Kaoren was highly unlikely to ever show any sign of noticing anything Julian didn't say out loud, but Sen was still learning proper circumspection, and reticence didn't change the fact that they would *know.* Laura certainly wouldn't want to suffer teen pangs before an audience who could catch glimpses of what went on beneath surface composure. This was a dilemma Julian would have to resolve himself, and Laura would leave him alone to do it.

Setting aside the question of her own time, Laura spent the remainder of the morning wandering about her new garden, checking the growth of seedlings and thinking about what to do with the empty space out back. Her usual landscaping style was an enormous amount of mulch and a cottage garden denseness, but she'd never had an area so large: a long meadow rising a little way, and then sloping south and east from the little hill where her house had been planted.

This was an entirely pleasant aspect, and so she was tempted to just leave it be. But she also kept picturing it as a sheer mass of flowers, or all manner of complex garden rooms. Weeding wouldn't be the usual deterrent, since she'd been gifted with a specialised robot 'drone' that would take care of any plant she didn't 'permit', and so she could consider establishing a really extensive garden.

Her main challenge in planning anything was that she didn't know how to garden in a climate involving a couple of months of snow. She'd brought along a few ebooks covering the basics, but there would be considerable guesswork and experimentation involved in her garden, especially where Muinan plants were concerned.

So many factors. Unknown pests and diseases. A year that was forty-one days longer than Earth's. 'Weeds' that might turn out to be Muinan plants she would like to include.

Weeds that might eat you, given some of the things that had shown up on Muina.

A lifelong study of Earth-to-Muina gardening would no doubt be valuable, but gardens were something Laura simply liked, not something she wanted to devote every hour of every day to, so she hesitated to embark on anything really difficult. Perhaps for now she would keep the grassy meadow, and concentrate on the small beds around the northern patio, even though many of them would likely only work for shade-loving plants. Still, the strawberry runners she'd planted were doing very well in the sunniest spot, and she was looking forward to a small harvesting and sampling session before autumn kicked in.

A text message flashed onto her 'inner screen'.

Sue: *Clean up and come have second breakfast.*

Laura: *Sounds like a plan.*

Susan—named for a Narnian Queen—was the younger of Laura's two sisters. A photographer, Sue had always been the most adventurous of the family, and had happily upped sticks to follow Laura to a whole different planet. Laura, although she was enjoying Muina enormously, felt a little more whole to have Sue with her.

Out of habit, Laura greeted her sister with Auslan, even though Muinan medical science had effortlessly reversed the slow loss of hearing that had started in Sue's pre-teens.

Sue signed back absently, then said: "Hey, did your boobs perk up after our last visit to the medics?"

"I...you know, maybe a little?"

"I suppose it's hard to tell with those mosquito bites. I swear mine are sitting an inch higher. I was talking to Didi Senez about standard health care here and, unless they have a particular issue they just go once a year for 'damage repair'. That seems to have been what we got over the last two visits—it sweeps out obvious cancers and works on worn cartilage and muscular issues. That's why your knees don't hurt any more. And, apparently, it helps with boob sag."

"Both results to appreciate."

"Didi is going to something she calls 'skin treatment' next week, and says we should book in with her. It's more cosmetically-focused—wrinkles, jawlines—but much the same process. They squirt nanites into you and then direct them to specific issues. Scar removal, moles, cellulite—all the little lumps and bumps. Growing hair where you want it and not where you don't."

Laura thought for a moment, then shrugged. "Well, if it doesn't involve surgery, why not, after all? I'll think of it as a very intensive facial. Will it delay the trip to Telezon?"

"Not unless their nanites eat our noses off, or something. I swear, every second movie I've watched here involves nanites eating you."

"And the rest are about the Setari." The elite psychic soldiers Cass worked with were an interplanetary preoccupation.

"Hardly ever happens, though," Sue went on. "Being eaten by nanites. I looked it up."

"'Hardly ever' makes me suddenly far less inclined to see what skin treatment is like."

"I expect they could grow our noses back if they're eaten off. Speaking of which, don't wait for the kids. They're cleaning up after painting Maddy's room."

"How did it work out?" One of Sue's three house guests, Maddy Caldwell, had wanted real decoration in her room, not the projected images common on Muina, and her sister Alyssa had designed an Australian-themed mural for her.

"Not bad. I took a couple of very nice shots of them in-progress, too."

They chatted idly about the complications of Cass' fame, which spilled over on to the handful of Earth immigrants who had joined her on Arcadia. Not only did it mean Sue felt she couldn't publicly display her photographs, but jaunts like the planned trip to the region called Telezon inevitably required a security detail. Even a shopping trip required security.

Thinking this over, Laura began poking around the various options of the Muinan internet, and was deep in sub-menus when Sue said:

"Well, well. The infamous Tsur Selkie."

Laura looked out the door to the patio, but there was no sign of a visitor on the path leading down to the dock.

"Check your email," Sue murmured, and added: "I do hope he's as flinty as advertised."

"I don't think Cass meant that description as a positive," Laura said, checking her email. Tsur Selkie was a KOTIS officer Cass had described a number of times in her diaries. According to Cass he was short, abrupt, and 'like Clint Eastwood'.

The email was certainly short, simply requesting a preliminary meeting in a Muinan fortnight—the first of a series to gather background in relation to Earth.

"I'm almost disappointed he didn't just plonk an appointment in our calendars and expect us to show up."

Sue giggled. "If he's half as humourless as Cass made out, I'm positively going to have to be restrained from spreading some high grade nonsense."

"Psychic psychic, remember?" Tsur Selkie was another Sight Sight talent. "Chances are high he'll be able to tell when you're lying."

"Yes, but what will he do about it? Will he just write it all down, and thank me? Will he look cross? Call me out? This," Sue said, definitely, "is going to be fun."

Laura shook her head in resigned amusement. "Try not to annoy him too much. We specifically want to prod the Muinans toward opening a trade relationship with Earth. I don't really know how much influence Tsur Selkie will have over that, but alienating him hardly seems like a good idea."

"What is a 'Tsur' anyway? Starting all the military ranks with 'Ts' seems unnecessarily confusing, especially when Muinan uses 'Tsa' for a general civilian honorific, and..." There was a short pause as Sue researched her question, then she snorted and said: "It just means Sight Sight Advisor. Doesn't show where he is in the KOTIS hierarchy at all."

Shrugging, Laura sent an acceptance, made a note in her calendar, and turned back to her new project. "Check this out," she said, sending a link.

Munching on seaweed snacks, Sue reviewed Laura's work, then said: "Is 'Tiamat' supposed to be you?"

"Everyone needs an artistic alias."

"Because it makes so much sense to sell the things you create entirely anonymously, rather than cash in on Cass' ridiculous fame."

"Exactly."

"I was being sarcastic."

"Yes, I'm aware of your default state."

"I can understand not wanting to be dependent on Cass, but...well, no I do see where you're going. I suppose I could do something similar with my pictures, at least those that don't depict people. Unless I want to devolve into a paparazzi stalker of my own family, there doesn't seem to be a huge amount of money in photography, but there is a market for 'image sets' for room décor. Screensavers for walls. Going to tell Cass?"

"I might have to, to be able to arrange anonymous postage. I'll worry about that if I sell anything at the exorbitant prices I intend to charge."

They discussed possibilities until Sue's three house guests arrived. Unlike Julian, these were new Muinan residents that did cause Laura concern. Maddy, Alyssa and Nick had not been part of the original 'move to Muina' plan. Nick, who was Sue's technically-ex stepson, and Alyssa, Cass' best friend from high school, had known the true explanation behind her disappearance, and of Laura and Sue's plan to join Cass on her new world, but there'd been no suggestion of them coming along until Maddy, Alyssa's younger sister, had relapsed, and her parents had gambled desperately on stories of nanite technology and cures for cancer.

That had worked. Maddy had been released from medical care a week ago, and—while not yet robust—was no longer in danger. But she and Alyssa were both desperately homesick. Nick was more difficult to read. He clearly embraced all the wonders of Muina, but he had spent such a large part of his life keeping an eye on his alcoholic father that Laura very much doubted that it was simple for him to walk away from that tie.

Since the dimensional gate to Earth only opened once in a Muinan year, the three could not even send letters to ease the homesickness, not even a message to let Maddy's parents know that she had recovered.

Laura, who knew the struggle of waiting, simply said good morning, and suggested that they might like to join the wreath-making expedition that afternoon. Shadows inevitably crept into every paradise, and she would do her small best to lighten those touching these children, since it was not possible to just wave a wand and make them think of Arcadia as 'home'.

CHAPTER TWO

When psychic space ninjas retire from combat service, their formidable paranormal abilities can be turned to other pursuits. In the case of Maze Gainer—formerly Maze Surion—Telekinesis made him a landscape gardener who could rearrange your trees.

A weeping maple wafted overhead. It passed over the deep, whitestone-lined pit that had replaced Laura's back yard, and settled onto the middle level of the series of steep whitestone terraces that had been built up to provide a 'back wall' for a curving pool.

The drastic alterations were the result of a casual conversation on the day Laura had had breakfast pancakes with Cass. Although Maze had retired from Setari squad duty in order to concentrate on his family and his burgeoning business, he still participated in training and administration tasks, and occasionally rostered himself on for Arcadian bodyguard duty. Laura had been enjoying another visit to her favourite seat when he had jogged up on a training run and stopped to chat about the approaching autumn, and gardens in snowy climates. She had ended up giving him all her scans of Earth gardening books since, while the text was unreadable for him, there were countless pictures.

Laura had pointed out a few of the gardens she thought particularly lovely, and woken the next day to an email attaching a complete design for a Japanese-inspired water garden to be installed at her back door. Barely a week later a large chunk of the hill had been carved away, and whitestone nanotech formwork had been set to grow, while Maze sourced plants to match his vision. Eager to get the major work done before his small family went on a trip to their home world, Tare, he had taken only another

Muinan eight-day week before he was setting in place fully grown trees.

"I always say there's nothing like watching other people work," Sue said. "That goes for double when they look like young gods and bring their own shower of leaves."

"He would make a good Apollo, wouldn't he? Now I wonder how I can go about getting him to let me pay him."

"Won't work," Cass said, from inside the house. She wandered out onto the long back porch and gave the settling tree—and the man floating above it—a wry look. "Not if he's told you it's a gift. Besides, he's really in love with all the scanned books you gave him. Tare and Kolar's climates are completely different from Muina's, so he hasn't really had a good range of examples of all the things that can be done with gardens. Alay told me he stayed up all night, first trying to look at everything, and then excitedly plotting out things he wants to try."

"Well, if I do expand the gardens I'll make sure to hire him properly. You're sure you don't mind me working on the whole hillside?"

"Why would I? I didn't put anything out here because I figured you'd like playing around with it. Besides..." Cass nodded to the line of children sitting in a row further down the curving back patio. "Lots of free entertainment. Hell, this even got Jules to make an appearance. And Rye's not the only one excitedly planning other gardens for you. They've all been looking through those books too, and have mapped out something modest and easy to look after that's only twice as large as the gardens at Versailles."

"I might need more gardening drones for that. And the whole island. This will be more than enough for now: I think it's going to be beautiful."

Cass looked pleased, and then paused, studying Laura's face. "I can't get over how different you look. Do you see yourself in the mirror and not recognise yourself?"

Laura gave her a dry glance. "I just look more like the me in my head. Not quite the me in my early twenties, but closer than I have been for a while. You'll probably always think of yourself as how you look now." She paused. "And on this planet, I suppose, that will be mostly right for a long time. I get startled when I see Sue, though. She looks fabulous."

'Skin treatment' had not been entirely painless, but no noses had been lost, and the results had been well worth the long, moderately embarrassing session. It was no wonder Laura had so much trouble guessing the ages of people on Muina.

"Maddy's looking happier too," Cass said, watching the children cheer on the arrival of another tree.

"She's feeling better physically. It makes a big difference." Laura touched Cass' arm lightly. "You can't cure her homesickness. We all knew this was a more-or-less one-way trip. And she's alive."

"I guess so."

But Cass wasn't smiling as she went back inside, and would no doubt keep fretting about something she couldn't change. She seemed to feel personally responsible for the happiness of the little collection of Australians she'd imported.

It would probably help if Maddy could mix with a few friends her own age. Maze and Alay, like Cass and Kaoren, had brought their children over to watch the arrival of the trees, but ten year-old Maddy sat in between the collection of early teens and the two infants—and Sen was a couple of years too young to really be a peer. It was too soon by far for Maddy to begin attending school, but Laura thought she would suggest a few age-selected play groups. The neighbouring islands had been heavily settled by the families of the senior Setari—many of whom had also adopted Nurans—and Cass and Kaoren would know who to invite.

Trees in place, and any fallen dirt swept out of the bottom of the deep pit, everyone gathered to watch as underground pumps were switched on, and the artificial pond began to fill. Maze, after a brief consultation with one of his business partners—an ex-Kolaren installations expert—dropped down to join Laura on the rim, his eyes almost as bright as the gathered children's.

"No hiccups so far. Once it's reached the outfall we'll leave the circulation pump running, and the main pump will only be needed if you drain it."

"It's incredible, Maze," Laura said, sounding the Muinan words out carefully. "I can't thank you enough."

He smiled—a smile Cass had mentioned frequently in her diaries, and fully as heart-stopping as described. "For a day spent playing at something I love? Not necessary."

"Just agree to be mutually appreciative," Sue said, angling her 'scanner'—a very high-tech camera—to capture the sunken stair slowly being swallowed by the flow of lake water. "What happens in winter, by the way? A skating rink, or an ice-crusted death trap?"

"If the water flow is shut off, we expect the ice will be thick enough to walk on. What is 'skating rink'?"

As Sue explained the English term, the water reached the rim of the pool's primary edge, welled, and then flowed over the outfall. That took all the children with it, running down the hill along the snaking course Maze had designed, all the way to the lake shore. As 'drainage channels' went, this was a helix punctuated by sheets of falling water, and interlaced with two criss-crossing paths that allowed a walker to admire—or stroll through— endless cascades.

"Put in a nice water feature," Cass said, propping Tyrian against one of her shoulders.

That produced a doubly-brilliant smile from Maze, with an added glow for Alay, coming up behind Cass with their toddler, Katen. Kaoren, carrying a couple of towels in anticipation, made the last of the group and they walked down to catch the kids and admire the 'water feature'.

It would certainly not be out of place in Versailles, and gave Laura plenty to think about as everyone managed to get more than a little wet, and then trailed back to her house to enjoy the meal Cass and Kaoren had waiting. Factoring in nanotech formwork that could 'grow' itself even underground, and drones that could be set to weed and dig and water, it really wasn't such a great extravagance to expand down the hill.

Mindful that she had a meeting in an hour, Laura detoured first to change into something dry, and to have a good long gawk out of her bedroom window. Anything she did to the hillside would be visible here, for her room was semi-circular and strongly resembled a conservatory, with its curving outer wall and a third of its ceiling made of one-way glass. It gave her an unparalleled view of the eastern reach of the island, with the south-east aspect now dominated by 'the Braid', as everyone had immediately begun to call the ridiculously long water channel.

Feeling a little overwhelmed, Laura returned to the lounge and talked with Maze about monitoring the trees for transplant shock, and then took a glass of juice out to marvel once again at the now-tranquil pool. A single leaf of classic maple shape spun languorously in the centre of the broadest section of water, before unhurriedly finding its way to the drainage channel, and slipping away.

"Is it what you would have chosen?" asked a quiet, beautifully modulated voice.

"I doubt I would have been so ambitious," Laura said, turning. "But it has certainly started me thinking about other possibilities."

She found herself facing a man an inch or so shorter than her own five-seven, his colouring similar to Kaoren, Lira and Sen's—a type Cass called 'old Lantaren', with light brown-gold skin, and epicanthic folds to very dark eyes. There was no doubt to his identity, since he wore the dark blue uniform of KOTIS command personnel, but Laura managed not to say: 'the infamous Tsur Selkie' aloud. She very much hoped she was also succeeding in not gaping. In part it was because he was so suddenly there, like a magician who had conjured himself, but it was more that he...

"I wished to see the Gainers before their trip to Tare," he explained. "So came a little early."

"I think you've timed it exactly," Laura replied, struggling to pronounce the Muinan words clearly. There was no mystery or reason to be flustered: he'd obviously come up the path beside the house instead of through it. Or flown. She had no idea whether he could fly. "Everyone's just packing up."

She led him inside, and then retreated to one side to watch. Force. That was the word. Sheer force. She had never before met anyone whose simple presence added such weight to a room.

Sue: *I was expecting someone shorter. And less...less...*

Laura: *Indeed.*

Sue: *Everyone's standing up straighter.*

Laura: *Perhaps that's why Cass thinks he's short.*

Sue shot a brief, appreciative glance at Laura before turning her attention to her scanner. Laura just watched.

Cass' diary had described Tsur Selkie as a short, eternally abrupt man who reminded her of Clint Eastwood. Compared to many of the Setari, who averaged around six foot, Laura supposed he was technically short. Also slender, with the controlled grace of a dancer. It was difficult to gauge abruptness when he was specifically there to have a conversation, but he spoke with precision and certainly didn't run on. He maintained an air of formality, asked brief questions, and listened.

Nothing about him reminded Laura of Clint Eastwood.

Instead, he projected effortless authority. Almost everyone in the room really was standing taller, and the three Setari gave the impression of being liable to salute at any moment. Both Katen and Tyrian watched him with fixed fascination, while the older children became markedly more efficient in helping to tidy up lunch and find discarded items of clothing, even though they were eavesdropping shamelessly on a relatively unremarkable conversation.

The other thing that stood out to Laura was Tsur Selkie's separateness. He was careful in his movements, rarely coming physically close to anyone, and in response the people around him kept their distance. That was a trait he shared with Kaoren, for they were both primarily Sight talent psychics. Kaoren had all the identified Sights while Tsur Selkie had, at the least, both Sight Sight—knowing—and a particularly challenging one called Place Sight. Place Sight talents could see and feel 'the impressions living creatures leave on the world': ghostly auras, the memory of rage, the shape of a dream. Most particularly, Place Sight talents could sense people's emotions when they touched them, which explained why Tsur Selkie was wearing gloves on a warm day: the left fingerless and the right giving complete coverage.

Rather than stand staring, Laura put together a tray with some water and red pear juice, and took it out to the table on the north patio. This was a good spot for summer conversations: the high trees dappled the table with shadows, and the breeze from the north made them dance.

"Want me to stay and translate, Mum?" Cass asked, as departure moves began.

"I think we'll manage. Besides, I need more practice talking Muinan."

"Okay. Just open a channel to me if there's anything you want cleared up."

Cass and Kaoren departed with their brood down the path to their house, while Maze and his family rose into the air, waved cheerfully, and zoomed away, and really it was impossible to watch that without an urge to pinch oneself to make sure the world was real.

Curious about the practicalities of flying, Laura asked Tsur Selkie: "Can Telekinetic talents, when it's raining, use their talent to keep dry?"

"That would be exceptionally difficult. Tsee Namara might briefly succeed, with interface assistance to track the path of the rain, but it would involve catching each individual drop. Telekinesis works on objects: it cannot form a shield."

A 'Tsee' was a Setari squad captain—the same rank as Kaoren—and Zan Namara the strongest Telekinetic talent. She was stationed on the planet Tare, and Laura hadn't yet met her, though she had figured large in Cass' diaries.

"I will not take much of your time today," Tsur Selkie said, as Sue led him to the table. "In truth, my primary aim in this session is to gauge your ability with our language, so that I can schedule a longer debriefing. You do not have difficulty understanding me?"

"No, it's speaking that's the challenge," Laura noted, sounding the words out with only occasional long pauses. "We're working on improving our pronunciation and grammar."

He nodded, and Laura noticed how very upright he was sitting, his hands resting neatly on his knees. Relaxed, but with an innate good posture. As soon as Laura saw this she realised she and Sue had unconsciously imitated him, and she immediately leaned her arms on the table.

"The long-term aim is to decide what to do about Earth?"

"To assist the Triplanetary Council's decision regarding diplomatic contact with your world, given the limitations of access. The current position is that it would be unwise to commence overtures via an unstable gate that opens only once a year, and that formal contact should be postponed until an Ena ship course can be established. That, however, is the equivalent of 'possibly never', given the difficulties of locating a world and charting a course to it through the Ena."

The 'Ena' was a complex set of dimensions that sat outside 'real space'. The Muinans used it as a shortcut between planets, but it was both infested by monsters and as navigable as an Escher drawing.

"Today, we shall cover the dissemination of information about Muina on Earth. Clearly it was not known only to your family. How widely have the details spread?"

Laura, who had failed to keep matters as secret as she would have liked, searched his face for any hint of condemnation, but found only focused attention.

"It's very difficult to say how far the story's gone," she admitted. "At least now that a gate genuinely did open and more than one person went through and back. When Cass first disappeared, the police—Sydney law enforcement—were involved, of course, and it was a news item. Old news by the time of her birthday, when she managed to nearly reach us."

Her chest tightened with the doubled memory of watching Cass becoming a 'cold case' and then, when the family had gathered on Cass' birthday, looking up and seeing a ghostly outline of her daughter. Not dead. Cass, stuck in the Ena behind an intangible window, had used sign language to reassure them. Not dead.

"Sue..." Laura began, mouth dry, but Sue picked up the story, giving Laura a chance to take a drink and try to wash away a few memories.

"When Cass appeared before us, I recorded the scene, but though we could see her clearly enough, the recording only showed a grey blur."

Tsur Selkie didn't look surprised. "Scanners and other machines have considerable difficulty detecting Ena manifestations."

"What we were left with was a half-dozen of us sure that we had seen Cass, but with no real proof that she was alive," Sue went on. "We had an argument over what to do, because telling the truth seemed like a terrible idea, and spending years pretending to be looking for her even worse. Eventually we decided to say she'd called home for her birthday to tell us she'd run off with a boy. Pure slander, and totally out of character for Cass, and we're lucky Nick had a friend in a country called Thailand who could make a relatively untraceable call to Laura's house, because the police did check that. But it gave us a reason to no longer look for her."

"And brought me three years of people telling me Cass was a horrendous brat," Laura said, with a faint grimace.

"Over and over," Sue said, with remembered annoyance. "Outside those who saw Cass in the Ena, we only told Alyssa, as per Cass' instructions, and our sister Bet told her husband, but otherwise we stuck firmly to the 'Cass is in Thailand' story until her diaries showed up."

All of them in a thick parcel plastered in stamps, with Cass' so-familiar tiny writing sending a jolt of lightning through Laura, so that she'd sat right down on the front steps of the house and torn it open. Everything Cass had lived through for an entire year, three books worth of it, and *photographs.*

Even though Sue was still talking, describing how Laura had given photocopied extracts of the diaries to close family, Laura realised Tsur Selkie was watching her, quite as if he could see straight through her to the bittersweet joy that still welled up whenever she saw those photographs. Oddly, the sense of transparency didn't bother her. There was no sense of judgment from the man, only observation.

"Still not proof," she said. "Other than showing that she was still alive, and looked well. The diaries could have been fiction, and so we kept them in the family still...except for Julian excitedly showing a few school friends, who promptly started bullying him. It had all quieted down when the second letter came, and Cass told us when and where the gate would open, and asked if we wanted to come here."

She stopped talking to look down over the slope of trees to the lake, and then across the deep blue water to the far northern shore.

"That was an easy decision for me, Laura and Jules," Sue said. "Not for our sister, Bet, who is very involved in a community organisation, and who is married to a man with a large extended family that he couldn't imagine leaving behind. And Mike—Cass' father—was in a similar position, except his wife didn't believe anything we said." She paused, then added grudgingly. "Which I suppose wasn't that unreasonable a position to take. On Earth...you have to understand that on Earth there has never been any verified occurrences of dimensional gates, or psychics, or aliens, but there are countless stories about them. Stories that are complete fiction. If I hadn't seen the ghost version of Cass on her birthday, I'm not sure I'd have believed either."

Laura took up the thread. "Most people, being told this story, or even getting their hands on a copy of the extracts from Cass' diary, wouldn't for a moment believe it. Since we were sure, we pooled our resources and gave all our money to Bet. She bought the nearest house she could manage to the gate, while we put it about that we were going to 'move to Thailand'. The gate is on a suburban street, and was going to open around midday, so it would inevitably be a relatively public departure, but of the people who knew and were going to watch us go, I think most of them would have kept quiet. But then there were the Caldwells."

"More to the point, there was Maddy's doctor," Sue said. "The Caldwells arranged..." She stopped, then said: "Cass doesn't have a translation for this word...just looking it up...ah, palliative care. They arranged for palliative care at home, and then brought her to Bet's new house on the day we were due to depart. But they couldn't just claim Maddy 'got better', let alone that she had moved to Thailand, and so they arranged for the doctor to witness her going."

"And Doctor Jamandre is a person whose entire career revolves around trying to stop children from dying," Laura said. "She'll probably do what the Caldwells planned to ask: 'check up on' Maddy occasionally, and report some improvement. But I have no doubt whatsoever she will be waiting the next time the gate is open, to see what's on the other side, confirm that Maddy is still alive, and then to make firm representations on behalf of all her other patients."

Laura paused, trying to gauge some measure of response from this man who listened with so much attention and so little reaction.

"I do, very much, want to encourage the Council to open some kind of diplomatic exchange," she told him. "Even if it is sporadic, and complicated, it will mean a great deal to Earth."

"That is understood," was all Tsur Selkie said, exceptionally unhelpfully. "It is not clear to me for what reason the child's parents did not join her here."

Not quite able to bring herself to push him about contact with Earth, Laura let the moment go, and explained.

"Their two other children, mainly. They're both rather high-achieving, and Caitlyn in particular has a national profile—she's an Olympic hopeful in figure-skating—while Rory had just landed a small ongoing role in a drama series. Neither of them could up and vanish without causing comment, even if their parents wanted them to abandon everything they'd worked for."

While Sue explained ice skating for the second time that day, and then the Olympics, Laura reflected that at least she hadn't had to face such a terrible choice as Eric and Nina Caldwell's. Julian had been as enthusiastic about the move to Muina as Laura, and it was only Bet Laura would really miss.

"Do you have any imagery with you of this skating?" Tsur Selkie asked. When they both blinked at him, he lifted his hands and became briefly less formal, producing a faint, momentary smile and saying: "That is Sight Sight. It creates a need to know, to understand, far more often than it provides explanations. It is not important."

"Alyssa might have one of Caitlyn's competitions," Sue said. "Just a moment."

She gazed off at nothing for a minute, then said: "She'll convert and send you a recording of a world championship—the pinnacle of the sport."

He thanked her, then said: "With Cassandra's help we will be able to confirm whether conditions around the gate on your world alter. During our next meeting I would like to model probable responses from the people—the peoples—of your world. Would the next twelfth suit you?"

Laura double-checked her calendar and agreed, wryly reflecting that setting the next meeting a full Muinan month away revealed his opinion of their halting and inexact speech. She would have to make sure to spend more time in the virtual school.

Meeting done, Tsur Selkie rose, thanked them for their time, and departed down the path to the dock. Laura and Sue looked at each other.

"You were very subdued. What happened to your scheme for testing Tsur Selkie's credulity?"

"I know! I couldn't do it! Whenever I thought about being silly I got all tongue-tied. Tongue-tied, Laura. Me! And I was looking forward to this all week, thinking of all the things I could try to get him to include in his official reports. I was going to tell him that Maze is a beautiful cinnamon roll, too precious for this world, too pure. Just to see how he'd react."

"He'd probably agree with you. If you explained what that meant."

"But would he put it in his reports? In Cass' diaries, they're always putting everything in reports. I was hoping to introduce all the KOTIS stuffed-shirts to Tumblr-speak, and convince them that's how Earth people usually talk."

"At least until they work out you're really introducing them to trolling? I'd start with someone other than a Sight Sight talent, if you really want to make the attempt."

"The main thing I want to do right now is force Cass to watch Clint Eastwood movies until she can point out what part of any of them reminds her of Tsur Selkie. He is very much not Clint Eastwood."

"I suspect that he's being rather less commanding with us than he would be with KOTIS personnel on duty. But yes, I don't see it, other than a bit of a 'man with no name' vibe, which does fit Selkie's watchfulness, and the unchanging expression. I don't think Cass can have seen many Clint Eastwood movies, though. I wonder what she'd make of *Every Which Way But Loose*?"

"Most of Eastwood's roles are all about being the lone wolf, and this Tsur Selkie is...would you say 'authority'? A sense of being in total control, the one who gets to make the decisions, with acres of hidden depths. Perhaps a Napoleon?"

"You say that because he's short. Short-ish."

"Caesar, then—of the Julian variety."

"And that's the haircut."

"Machiavelli?"

Laura thought about it. "I don't actually know what Machiavelli was supposed to be like. As for Machiavellian...well, he was involved in a program that conscripted children. And got some of them killed."

"He'd make a terrific cult leader. The voice. The focused attention. That sense of looking right into you."

"I suppose all Sight Sight talents are a bit like that. I didn't get very far in my attempts at pushing trade with Earth."

"I wonder how much influence he has over the decision? Could you catch any impression of what he thought of the idea?"

"No. He's opaque and I expect we're open books to him." Laura sighed. "Is it possible to talk about Earth's history without making any sane civilisation want to avoid us like the plague? We stagger from atrocity to indecency, between bouts of hypocrisy. But where would trying to shade the truth get us with a Sight talent?"

"Pointless to fret about it yet. Have you decided what you're getting Ys for her birthday? Seems to me interplanetary trade negotiations aren't half as difficult as finding a present for a girl who just wants you to leave her alone so she can read. Especially when she has all the books already, and I can't find anyone to sell me a time-turner."

Laura laughed, and nodded, and turned her thoughts to more pleasant considerations. She had a month to decide how to be both honest and positive with Tsur Selkie.

CHAPTER THREE

Tyrian was the infant equivalent of a mood ring. Much of the time he would make an excellent stand in for a Midwich cuckoo: solemn and staring and grave. But if you picked him up when you were annoyed or angry he would react to that immediately, no matter how gentle your touch or voice, for he had inherited both Sight Sight and Place Sight from Kaoren. These were Sights that developed early, and so anyone holding Tyrian required a lot of personal discipline in order to avoid transforming quiet baby into squalling baby.

On the up side, he responded very well to positive emotions and one of Laura's new favourite things was to try to make him laugh. Lying on her back out by the pool, she hoisted Tyrian up above her, blew out her cheeks, and goggled her eyes. He let out a delighted squeal and waved his arms. Dropping him down on her lap, she tickled him, and then hoisted him up again and puckered her mouth like a fish.

Tyrian giggled, all happy smiles, burped, and vomited milk over Laura's face and neck.

"Urk!" Laura had only barely managed to turn her head in time to spare her mouth and eyes. She sat up hastily, then tweaked her grandson's chin as he briefly wavered on the edge of shock, and fortunately he laughed merrily in response. "I'm glad you find it funny, kiddo." She wiped her face with the back of one hand, and smiled down at him. "You look like your Mum when you laugh, you know."

"He does," a voice agreed, and she turned, steadying Tyrian, to find that Tsur Selkie had once again arrived early for his appointment. "I will watch him if you wish to clean up," he added.

Laura hesitated, then thanked him and climbed to her feet. "I won't be long," she said, handing Tyrian over and relaxing fractionally when the KOTIS officer demonstrated that he at least knew how to hold a baby.

Even so, she showered and changed quickly, reflecting that he'd understood what she'd said to Tyrian, even though she'd spoken in English. Cass' translation app worked both ways, but Laura hadn't realised Tsur Selkie was using it. At least she'd grown better at speaking Muinan, though her pronunciation remained far from perfect.

Still a little damp, Laura returned to find him sitting sideways on the broad rim of the pool with Tyrian on his lap, propped against partially raised knees. Playing pat-a-cake. Tyrian had returned to solemnity, but was managing to bat at Tsur Selkie's hands with reasonable accuracy, and appeared pleased each time he managed it.

"You have children, Tsur Selkie?" Laura asked.

"Two daughters," he said. "Allidi and Haelin. This is a game they enjoyed at this age."

"He almost looks like he's moving before you do."

"He is reacting to my decision on which hand to move."

Fascinated, Laura sat down cross-legged beside him, watching as Tyrian continued to almost appear to anticipate which hand Tsur Selkie held up for him to pat. "So guessing games are good for Sight Sight talents?"

"At this age, very simple ones only, preferably those where the correct choice is known to you. Two to three choices, and never continued if his Sights don't trigger and he fails. Until Muinan age three or four he will switch between a state of strong certainty about his immediate environment, and occasions when Sight Sight isn't triggering, when the world will feel threatening, and unknowns or new developments will upset him." He raised his right hand, and Tyrian again batted at it.

"As he grows older, more capable of abstract concepts, Sight Sight will trigger less and less, unless he is trained to focus it. That will be a difficult time for him, especially in combination with Place Sight. At the moment, Sight Sight's certainty mitigates the distress that Place Sight often brings."

He paused and dropped his hand when Tyrian yawned mightily. "Games that trigger Sights are also tiring, so this is best played before a scheduled nap."

"When do the other Sights usually manifest?"

A discussion that expanded to the wide array of known psychic talents nicely filled the time until Kaoren returned Sue from an expedition to the northern shore of the lake. While Tsur Selkie managed to maintain an air of formality even with a baby falling asleep in his lap—and still threatened to steal the air from the room through sheer intensity—he was also a superlative listener, and Laura found talking to him paradoxically relaxing.

"Do Sight Sight talents tend toward careers like psychiatry?" she asked, as he handed the snoozing Tyrian up to her.

"It's been known," he said, standing. "But it is rarely successful. The talent might offer extra insight, but insight also tends to bring a self-belief that mixes poorly with the delicate negotiation of someone else's psyche." His flicker of a smile surfaced. "We are, as a group, too arrogant."

Laura glanced down at Tyrian, imagining him growing up too insightful to be wise.

"What does it involve, exactly, being a Sight Sight advisor?" she asked, moving inside as she heard Kaoren and Sue's voices.

"During this settlement phase, it has primarily meant construction projects."

"Construction?"

Kaoren, hearing this, grimaced. "That is something I avoid as much as I can: assignments to look over large buildings, power generators, ships, checking for hidden flaws. Physical faults like that do tend to trigger Sight Sight, but we cannot guarantee safety—and it is exceptionally dull work."

"I thought Sight Sight talents went around solving mysteries," Sue said, clearing a bottle from Tyrian's carry cot so Laura could put him down.

"Occasionally. It's rare that there is criminal investigative work that cannot be better addressed by science," Tsur Selkie said. "Assignments like this are more common—gathering information toward large decisions."

Reminded that Tsur Selkie had not visited just to teach her about psychic infants, Laura gathered the inevitable scatter of baby toys and clothing, and saw Kaoren on his way. Sue, in the meantime, set out snacks and drinks on the northern patio, where they could fully appreciate the first few motes of gold, red and orange. Autumn in the Pandora region looked likely to be spectacular.

Tsur Selkie sat exactly as he had before: very upright, hands on knees, formal but without the curt, no-time-to-waste attitude Cass' diaries had suggested. Laura had not seen him as Cass originally had—in a command environment during a crisis—and she could not decide if this innately formal but relaxed version of a KOTIS officer marked the change from a period of extreme danger to the current peace, or if he was attempting to put her and Sue at ease.

"In this session, I would like to cover probable reactions on your world, should a delegation be sent—or a ship locate your world. I understand there is no designated 'leader' of Earth. And the gate is located in a non-central part of the world?"

Laura produced a map of Earth from among her mass of scans, and gave him a short history of Earth's major political divisions, and Australia's current position.

"So at first you'd be dealing with the Australian authorities. Who will be bemused, but then..." Laura grimaced. "Well, they're politicians. They will insist on many photo opportunities, but they're likely to be extremely enthusiastic about any kind of trade negotiations."

"No, don't forget you'd be dealing with whoever is waiting on the street, first," Sue put in.

"I suppose so," Laura said. "Our family and the Caldwells and Doctor Jamandre. But if word of the gate has spread to enough people, there might be press waiting."

"A circus," Sue said in English, then added: "Chaos and excited shouting. Which would continue without end, really. A bit like how Cass is treated here—so many people painfully eager to meet her—but rather worse because on Earth the Muinan delegation would represent two of the seven great villain motivations."

Sue was obviously feeling less tongue-tied today. Laura, who rarely failed to be entertained by her sister, had to admit she also wanted to know how this man would react to some high grade nonsense.

But Tsur Selkie took the opening volley without blinking. "Which are?"

"Money and living longer." Sue took a long drink of juice, watching him with immense interest. "The other five are revenge, saving or bringing back a dead loved one, world domination, good intentions, and 'just because'."

"Would Muinan technology not also represent the potential for world domination?" Tsur Selkie asked, taking 'villain motivations' entirely seriously. "It is an important consideration for us—that we might destabilise your planet's political balance. Would other nations, for instance, make war upon your Australia to gain control of the gate to Muina?"

The question was a reminder that this was a conversation of consequence. Not that Sue would be easily quashed: she firmly believed that humour opened the mind to unexpected viewpoints.

"An attack on Australia isn't likely," Laura said. "Too many allies with big guns. But control of any delegation is a different matter. The knowledge, the power they would represent is immense. And..." She hesitated, but there was no point hedging around something so obvious. "There might be attempts to kidnap them, to force them to share everything they know."

"Lots of aging billionaires out there," Sue muttered.

"Lots of aging government officials, too." Laura stared down at her hands, and then out at a lake framed in gold-specked green, before meeting the eyes of the patiently waiting KOTIS officer. "While I'm still very keen to have Muina open relations using the gate, I could not say that a delegation could visit in complete safety."

He nodded, as if this was only what he expected her to say. "The same problem occurs for the Caldwell children. They have the interface installation, which represents a large advance for your people. Could we allow them to return, and not be concerned with their safety?"

That was a depressing consideration, but neither Laura nor Sue could deny that anyone returning would likely be intensely studied.

"The possibility that we will locate your world through the deep space of the Ena has increased, however," he continued. "I would not care to predict an imminent discovery, but I now consider contact to be an eventual probability."

"What's changed?" Laura asked, surprised and pleased.

"Exploration in the Ena's deep space has long involved expensive drone losses, but we have recently been trialling sending out large groups of much smaller and simpler units. Their instruments do not have the same range as our original explorer units, but we are gaining data far more quickly than ever before."

"Finding Earth is still in the possibly never category, though?" Sue asked.

"It remains a matter of chance, but the use of drone shoals greatly increases the odds. To that point, we are beginning long-range planning for ship-based contact. Cassandra previously stated that if there is a rift opening from Ena's deep space anywhere on Earth, it will be located in something known as the 'Bermuda Triangle'. Would you agree with that?"

"The Triangle's a story, nothing more," Sue said, firmly. "Earth is a heavily-travelled planet, and I think we'd have seen a whole lot more disappearances in recent years if there was an enormous invisible gash in the sky so close to a major continent. Unless not all rifts to deep space are so large as Muina's?"

"Those we have observed all have similar proportions."

"Then, if there's a rift into Ena deep space at all, it's got to be somewhere completely outside the travel routes. Somewhere completely away from people, where even light aircraft don't fly."

"Antarctica?" Laura guessed.

"Best option. Otherwise, I don't know, northern Russia?"

They went through the likely locations, and the closest nations to them, and then moved on to the probable world reaction to a spaceship turning up and asking to chat.

"There's plenty of precedent for that sort of thing in our fictions," Laura said.

"Oh, boy, is there," Sue said.

"Extra-terrestrial contact stories fall into a few distinct groups," Laura went on. "Aliens show up, and the people of Earth are brutal and cruel to them. Aliens show up and try to annihilate us. Aliens show up and make peaceful overtures, and..."

"And it's all fun and games until the plasti-flesh masks come off." Sue grinned and mimed lifting away her face.

"Plasti-flesh?" Tsur Selkie repeated, sounding out the English carefully.

"I suppose Cass would know by now if Muinans were really lizard people in disguise," Sue added.

Tsur Selkie's flicker of a smile made an appearance, but he only said: "We must account for a precedent for deception?"

"Trojan horse aliens," Sue said, and then explained Trojan horses.

For the remainder of the session, they told him alien contact stories. *ET*, *War of the Worlds*, *Independence Day*, *The Thing*, *Space Battleship Yamato*. Aliens drawing the people of Earth into intergalactic wars, aliens testing the 'worthiness' of humans, or simply being mystic and vague and incomprehensible. It was an involved conversation, because Tsur Selkie would always ask for explanations when they fell back on English terms and phrases.

"Does all this fiction really help you, Tsur Selkie?" Laura asked, after they had explored a dozen different flavours of First Contact disaster.

"It gives me a frame for the psychology of your world. It appears that, while there are smaller groups that would react negatively, those who have weaponry that could reach us at a considerable distance are not likely to use it immediately, unless some major misstep occurs?"

They agreed that the chances of missiles being launched were low, with some caveats depending on exactly where the Muinan ship revealed itself.

"So then you'd need to decide which country to *land* in..." Sue said. "How complicated this all is."

"The language barrier is another factor. You speak one of the most widely-spread languages, but not the most spoken?"

"English is, ah, second or third," Sue said. "Mandarin is the most-spoken, but we don't speak it. Laura could teach you Japanese, thanks to far too many years of anime, but I only have bits of French and German."

"I brought along a few English-other language dictionary apps," Laura said. "They're very basic things compared to the one Cass has been working on, though."

She stopped as Mimmit, the cat she'd brought with her from Earth, leapt onto the table. Tsur Selkie, like more than half of Muina's population, was originally from Tare. Taren visitors, raised on an island world of densely populated, hive-like cities with little open land and few animals, often flinched from sudden contact with small creatures, so Laura shifted in readiness for whisking Mimmit away. But Tsur Selkie merely looked down at the striking tortoiseshell, with her harlequin mask of black and orange, then lifted his partially gloved hand from his knee and rested it on the table.

"Perhaps you can set out for me the divisions of Earth by primary language," he said, as Mimmit briefly scented his fingers, then strolled down the table to Laura.

That task more than filled the remainder of their session, with Tsur Selkie concluding the discussion by setting their third appointment for a mere week away.

"Well, you have your answer," Laura said, after Tsur Selkie had once again politely taken his leave and departed. "Positively unflappable."

"I didn't try anything really silly on him," Sue said. "But, yes, I don't think even cinnamon rolls would have gotten more than that brief 'ah yes, humour' smile. Sad."

Sue didn't look sad. She looked smug, which always meant trouble. Laura eyed her sister thoughtfully, but was distracted by a vehicle strongly resembling a flying car zipping across her line of view and dropping toward the dock area. She sighed with unabashed envy, for personal vehicles were strictly controlled in an attempt to prevent citizens from joy-riding right out of the safe zones around the settlements, and into Muina's still very dangerous wilds.

"Tsur Selkie travels in style. If they ever open those things up for civilian use I am absolutely going to get one, and I will refer to it constantly as 'my flitter', and pretend that I'm in an Andre Norton novel."

"Norton novels always seem to involve arduous journeys through abandoned alien ruins," Sue said. "Cass has done enough of that for all of us."

That was entirely true. And Laura thoroughly hoped that no-one she knew would ever endure such a thing again. Firmly putting Cass' trials aside, she continued to poke at the large and unwieldy prospect of Muinan-Terran trade.

"I wonder how much of their technology they'll be willing to bring to the table? The Tarens are the ones who had all the advanced tech, and when they started trade with Kolar they deliberately kept them several steps behind so as not to lose an advantage. It might have become more relaxed now that they've settled Muina, and allowed nanotech on Kolar, but what if they take the same 'we'll only give you so much' approach to Earth?"

Sue, while continuing to smirk obnoxiously, said: "Just confirming the existence of non-terrestrial life is huge."

"So daunting to consider all the ways this could play out. Even if this doesn't start any wars, think of the impact on the world economy. The interface would devastate mobile phone providers. Medicine—*old age*— would never be the same. Factor those vat-food factories into food production for drought-afflicted regions. And infrastructure that grows itself will alter so many things. Even gardening robots. All these wonderful things that will either lift Earth to a post-scarcity state or..." She shook her head and looked at her sister. "The Luddite rebellion multiplied by...everything."

Sue was now attempting to channel Spock, one eyebrow scrunched down and the other canted to her hairline.

"Are you going to sit there pulling faces? Because if there's a shoe waiting to drop, you'll need to untie the laces."

"You didn't even notice, did you?"

"Notice what?"

"That he's dying to get into your pants."

This was so completely outside Laura's line of thought that she said blankly: "Who?" Then: "Tsur *Selkie*?"

"You are so oblivious where men are concerned."

Laura stared at her sister, then shook her head. "No. I was paying attention. He was entirely professional. You're imagining things."

"I'll give you the entirely professional. He was on duty, after all. But only you would fail to notice that you had ninety percent of his attention, and he only looked at me when I was speaking."

"I did talk more, didn't I?" Laura said, dry now. "Really, Sue, are you ever going to stop trying to set me up with people?"

"Next week when he comes back, dress up a little."

"*Sue.*"

"That whole most intense person in the universe thing he's got going *doubles* when he's looking at you. What's a good name to call him? Is there a non-negative word for a black hole?"

"...gravitational mass?"

"'The Pocket Event Horizon' is a bit long—but it kind of works. It certainly feels like an event when he shows up, and you can see the whole room being reshaped around him. And he is too so totally hot for you, Laura."

"Now you're just making things up."

"Okay, tell me this. How long had he been here before I showed up?"

"I don't know. Maybe half an hour."

"And it's not as if I was late back. This guy, by all accounts, is incredibly busy. Military big brass who gets chauffeured around to the point where his ride arrived to collect him the very moment he walked down to the dock.

And yet he's shown up early twice now so he could sit around waiting to start. With you."

"He hadn't even *met* me last time. He wanted to talk to Maze and Alay. And today...maybe he wanted to look Tyrian over?" Laura thought back over the afternoon, and saw only a reserved but comfortable-with-himself man helpfully making sure she understood the complications of her grandson's talents. She had enjoyed the talk, but had noticed none of the pressure she usually felt when someone was trying to chat her up.

Admittedly, she had occasionally felt breathless, but that was only to be expected talking to a man of such concentrated presence. A Pocket Event Horizon.

"Well, well. Who would have thought a serious soldier was your type? Always something new to learn."

Laura was not blushing. She was just annoyed. "The conclusion you're jumping to is a mirage."

"Yeah, yeah. Stop playing 'oh no, not me'. Let's look at some pros and cons instead. First pro, he's a total hottie. On the negative side, military man, might make you wake up at dawn and do push-ups."

"I already wake up at dawn."

"Pro: gainfully employed, and the job comes with a 'flitter'. Con: minimal evidence of a sense of humour. But I suppose that might go with your tendency to be painfully deadpan."

"Isn't playing straight man of one comedy duo enough?" Laura said. "This is silly, Sue. Let it drop."

"But you're thinking about it! You're picturing him naked. You're remembering all those stories you've heard about Sight Sight talents and Place Sight talents and just what that means for sexytimes."

"Well, you've certainly now succeeded in making me self-conscious about talking to him again," Laura said, collecting their glasses and taking them back inside.

"This is awesome," Sue said, following her with the half-eaten snacks. "You hardly ever bite when I dangle man-bait. I'm going to have so much fun."

With considerable forbearance, Laura ignored this last and said, as she placed the glasses carefully on top of the cleaning unit: "Besides, I think he must be married. He has two daughters."

"So look him up. The man's semi-famous—he's sure to have an entry in the Muinan version of Wikipedia." Sue put her tray next to the glasses, and made good on her own suggestion. "Here we go...Gidds Selkie. Widely regarded as the architect of the Setari program. Does that mean he's the one who had the bright idea of conscripting children? I'll put that in the 'con' column. Even if it did lead to saving this corner of the galaxy."

Laura, who had not been able to stop her thoughts from following through on the 'picturing him naked' part of Sue's suggestions, found this titbit a functional cold shower. While there had been opportunities to leave the program, and none of the Setari saw active service before adulthood, there had still been accidents in training. Children had died.

Could she ever really want to be with a man who had set that in motion, no matter how successful the program had been, or how many lives it had saved?

Turning the cleaning unit on, she listened far more equivocally as Sue continued: "Born, urgh, Taren, Earth and Muinan years require too much maths to convert. He's around, oh, not quite forty. I didn't expect that. Looks thirty, acts fifty. If he helped set up the Setari he must have started just out of school. And...here we go, divorced from someone called Elezin Zadel. Involved in early Ena scientific projects. Hm. 'Survivor of the Tasken Outbreak'. What's a...oh, one of the bigger ionoth-monster killing sprees, back when incursions from the Ena first started getting serious on Tare. I'm not sure if 'tragic backstory' counts as a pro or a con."

They both paused, as the glasses, jug and plates began to be pulled into the surface of the cleaning unit. Laura did have a sink, and still ran the occasional dish under the tap, but the nanotech cleaner—basically a vat of nanite goop connected to the waste system—was a true wonder. She could put anything dirty—dishes, clothes, jewellery—on top, and the goop would absorb the object, remove 'foreign particles', and then spit an astonishingly clean object back out. It had been designed for the water-poor planet of Kolar, but Cass said it had quickly spread to Muina and Tare as well. Laura loved it with a passion that she would not normally direct toward kitchen appliances.

"I wonder if people on Tare stand around gawping at their dishwasher?" Sue asked.

"I bet they do on Kolar." The glasses, which had barely been dirty, were already emerging—Laura's favourite part of the process.

"They should add a little 'ta-dah!' sound effect for when they come out again," Sue said. "Kaoren, by the way, says that Selkie didn't come up with the idea of conscripting children. Yes, yes, I know you'd rather have a reason to put the scrummy soldier out of your head, but then I'd miss out on you at the next meeting, sitting there with a Sight Sight talent, trying not to picture him naked."

"I think," Laura said judiciously, "that I'm going to go for a nice dusk-time walk."

"Exit our heroine, stage left, in a state of some confusion? At least admit you're thinking about it."

Laura rolled her eyes, and went to find a light coat, then took a stroll down to her favourite bench. To think about Tsur Gidds Selkie, naked.

CHAPTER FOUR

"Laura! Laura, listen to this." Sue made disbelieving faces as Laura stepped carefully over the pool's outfall. "They have uterine replicators and *they don't use them!*"

When Inika Senez, one of the 'Setari extended family', laughed, her riotous gold and black curls sparkled like fireworks. "Is it so strange to choose to experience in-body gestation?"

"Yes," Sue said firmly. "I particularly can't believe it of your daughter, and these other highly trained senior Setari who have been filling the islands with infants. Why in the worlds have they gone and put themselves through all the things that pregnancy does, if there are functioning uterine replicators?"

"Oh, Mara wanted to know what it was like." Inika wrinkled her nose judiciously. "I doubt she'd do in-body again, even if she wasn't now sufficiently supplied with children, since it was a difficult pregnancy for her. Me, I enjoyed all but the last month or so of mine. But all the Setari—anyone with strong talents—also have to weigh the impact for inheritance."

"What do you mean?" Laura asked, settling on the grass beside the two women.

"Children of machine-supported gestation gain many advantages—their nutrient balance is much better managed, and medical issues more easily addressed—but they rarely have quite so strong an immune system, and they never gain the full strength of their parents' talent set."

"They're weaker psychics?"

Inika nodded. "That is a large decision to make. Though in the last few decades it is a factor that has pushed many toward machine-supported."

"Because of the Setari program." Sue glanced at Laura, but she wasn't in such a teasing mood today—perhaps was reserving her ammunition for when Tsur Selkie arrived for his appointment that afternoon.

"Yes. It is not an enjoyable thing to see your child only on holidays. Although..." Inika raised a shoulder. "I would still choose in-body, and have Mara be the woman she is, even though I had less time with her as a result. I could not deny her the things I relish being able to do, let alone the chance for greater wonders."

She lifted one hand, and the air in front of her glimmered, and formed into an elaborate snowflake—which immediately melted in the muggy heat that had sparked an impromptu picnic around the cooling waterfalls of the Braid.

"Are the replicators expensive to use?" Laura asked.

"Not overwhelmingly. For a first child, costs are kept moderate so as not to prevent those on base level from accessing the option. Additional children, yes, the cost would be high—at least on Tare, where much was done to discourage us from multiple children. Didi and I were thinking of maybe a third child, now that we're on Muina and don't face the same restrictions. I am tempted—although with so many grandchildren, perhaps we will delay a while longer."

Sue glanced at Laura, but did not pursue the subject, simply saying: "You have to tell me what it is you've done to your hair to make it sparkle when you move. I am completely envious."

They talked lightly of high-tech cosmetics, until Inika headed down the slope to help her wife corral a few of the children chasing each other around Braid Meadow.

"Thinking of cooking up a few?" Laura asked, watching Sen and Maddy run shrieking through a line of cascades.

"I've too much world exploration to do at the moment," Sue said. "But...it's quite something to completely dismiss any phantom ticking of biological clocks. Not to mention that I could do it in a civilised and entirely sensible manner that doesn't involve barely being able to bend over for months at a time.

"And you could probably get them custom-designed into the bargain."

"I wish Mum could have seen all this."

Laura glanced at her sister's profile, then sighed, and lay back on the grass, gazing into the brilliant blue of the sky. "Mum would still be alive if she'd had a chance to see this," she said, because if the Muinans could get Maddy running down hillsides in three months, they'd certainly be able to handle breast cancer.

"And she would absolutely get herself a flitter," Sue said.

Laura laughed, because it was true. 'Redoubtable' was only the most common word used to describe their late mother.

"Mum would want to do the wandering through abandoned alien ruins, too. We are but weak echoes."

"And she would be totally on board for some Serious Soldier seduction."

"I expect she would."

Sue leaned over and looked at Laura's face. "That didn't sound nearly hot and bothered enough. Only a few more hours until the Event Horizon. Where's the anticipation?"

"You're determined to make something out of nothing, aren't you?"

"I bet you're not even going to put on any makeup. Not that your failure to dress up is going to hide anything. He's still going to be able to see that you think he's tasty."

"Let him," Laura said, serenely. "I expect he's used to people finding him attractive. But I, for one, did not see the slightest hint that he was dying to get into my pants, or any other item of clothing."

Sue frowned at her, then wrinkled her nose.

"I don't believe this uncaring act for a moment, and I point out, again, that he won't be fooled. Really, I can't decide if Sight Sight is a pro or a con."

"You could consider it a convenience. No need to flutter eyelashes, or shake curls, or whatever counts as flirtation here. But even if Tsur Selkie notices any secret blushes, I guarantee he'll be perfectly correct. You forget he's working, and the sort who would consider romance a conflict of interest—at least until this report is done."

"You are so dull. And after that?'

"After that, well..." Laura shrugged. "For all I know, I'll never see the man again."

They dropped the subject as Maddy and Sen raced up and insisted they join them in a race to the pool at the very bottom of the Braid. But Laura was not truly sanguine about the meeting, and did spend an excessive amount of time picking out a simple dress to wear that afternoon, while shaking her head at her own lapse into nerves.

Sue, returning shortly before the appointed time, peered about, then sighed exaggeratedly: "He didn't show up early? And here I was trying to give you more alone time."

"I'm surprised you denied yourself the entertainment," Laura said, turning up the air-conditioning and putting some glasses on the dining table. "The patio's not so tempting today. There's still not a speck of wind."

"Are you disappointed? I think you're disappointed."

"I think—." Laura paused as the Muinan equivalent of a doorbell sounded in her head. "Right on time."

She triggered the front door and turned, saying out loud: "We were just talking about staying inside today."

Tsur Selkie, as impeccable as ever, drew breath to reply, paused for a moment, and then said: "Yes. An over-warm day."

Laura flushed. She wasn't even fully certain why she did it, because there could not be a more innocuous subject than the weather. It was, she decided as she turned quickly back to the table, the pause—a moment of complete stillness—before he spoke.

Sue: *Told you.*

Ignoring her sister, Laura poured cold water while he crossed the room, then said: "What would you like to cover today, Tsur Selkie?"

"Resolute opposition. Any groups who would have strong reasons to reject any contact from Muina—who would violently oppose a Muinan presence."

That was a complicated topic. On the whole, Laura thought the people of Earth would be cautious, but very interested, and keen for trade. She didn't know of any specific 'anti-extra-terrestrial' organisations or countries, and most religions were very adaptable. There were always extremists, of course, but which of these in particular might take against a Muinan envoy was difficult to predict.

"Race will probably be a factor," Laura said, a little reluctantly, and then had the uncomfortable task of explaining white supremacy to this very serious man. The vast majority of the inhabitants of Muina, Tare and Kolar appeared to have descended from Asian stock—though with an admixture of other races—and she could not pretend that this would have no impact.

Tsur Selkie, as usual, listened without commenting, and then asked a lot of questions. So they took a tour of Earth's races, with a pass through evolution, a side-order of sexism, and a history of conquest, slavery, and cultural imperialism.

This was certainly not a conversation that lent itself to thoughts of romance, which made the session triply uncomfortable for Laura. She could not put Sue's suggestion out of her mind, and had to keep fighting off thoughts that were extremely inappropriate to the topic of the conversation. All while trying not to feel disappointed to see in him only a very professional man conducting an interview. She couldn't gauge how much of this his Sights made clear to him, but she felt transparent and foolish, and wondered how Cass and Kaoren had survived months of this IknowheknowsIknow business.

It was remarkable, though, how inadequate Cass' description of Gidds Selkie had been. How could she not have mentioned his poise? The fine delicacy of his temples? And that incredible, mesmerising voice?

Laura's session of muted mortification finally ended, with Tsur Selkie saying: "I think that will cover what I need. Thank you for being so open."

"We've made Earth sound thoroughly awful," Laura said, glad for the moment that he was keeping his opinions to himself. "But we...strive, I suppose I want to say."

Before Tsur Selkie could respond—or Sue point out that Muina's chequered history involved mass sacrifice—a clatter and thumping on the stairs warned them that Julian had emerged from his 'cave'.

"I just can't work out how you make so much noise on whitestone," Laura said, turning to smile at her gangling son. "That sounded like the descent of several wardrobes."

Julian ignored the comment, bouncing over to the north patio doors. "Check out the storm that's coming! We're going to get smashed!"

The glass doors slid open as he approached, and a low-level gale cut through the air-conditioned stillness of the room.

"You'd think the kid had never seen weather before." Sue stood and followed Julian, saying to him: "We watched one of the storms of Tare. You really think this is going to compete?"

"Tare's storms aren't as interesting 'cause there's nothing to blow away. You're lucky the patio furniture's heavy, Mum."

The trees did look thoroughly wind-tossed, so Sue murmured apologetically to Tsur Selkie and headed out to make sure she wasn't about to donate any possessions to the lake.

"The forecast said rain, not a storm," she said, discovering not so much a bank of clouds as a solid wall rapidly approaching from the west.

And yet, this was not nearly enough to distract her from an overwhelming awareness of Tsur Selkie following her out, of an Event Horizon just behind her. The paradox of the man was how everything he did felt at the same time momentous, and yet calming. Laura kept finding herself holding her breath as she waited to see what he did next, and then relaxing in the face of his complete composure.

"There is a theory that overuse of the teleportation platforms causes meteorological side-effects," he said, making an extended survey of the western sky.

"Sounds like an excuse for when the weather people get things wrong," Sue said, then shielded her face as what felt like half a tree's worth of leaves pelted them.

"*Awesome*," Julian said.

"There will be hail," Tsur Selkie said, with the quiet certainty Laura had learned to recognise from Kaoren's Sight Sight pronouncements.

"*Double* awesome."

Muinan-language text appeared abruptly on Laura's internal interface 'screen'.

Pandora Region Alert: Strong Winds. Hail.

"Hey, did you do that?" Julian asked, turning to Tsur Selkie. "You can message the whole city?"

"Kaoren reported the storm's severity," Tsur Selkie said. "He and the guard detail are securing the boat house."

"Speaking of which, I'm going to run home before this hits," Sue said, and was as good as her word, dashing down the path toward her house.

"Your strawberries are going to be mush, Mum," Julian said. "Let's move the table over them."

Laura wasn't entirely certain how much Tsur Selkie had followed of a conversation that had bounced between English and Muinan, but he moved without wasting time on questions to help them prop the formidable whitestone table over the tiered strawberry bed.

"The chairs may be best indoors," he said, with another glance at the sky.

That said something for how severe he expected the storm to be. Nanite-grown whitestone furniture had a honeycomb structure and was not nearly as heavy as natural stone, but it was still solid stuff.

"Is Mimmit inside?" Julian asked, as he brought in the last chair.

Along with immunisations, Mimmit had had a sensor installed, and so her location could be tracked via the interface. Earlier in the week 'cat plus storm' wouldn't have been a concern, since Mimmit had taken a firm 'house cat' view on life as soon as the days had started to cool, but the unusually warm day had seen her out and about, probably engaged in her ongoing flirtation with Cass' two cats.

"Moving very rapidly in this direction," Laura said, after the briefest pause. She turned and stared down the path to the boat house. The world was disappearing into greenish-black gloom, but the wind had dropped, as if the storm was holding its breath.

A parti-coloured streak shot into view.

"Go Mimmit!" Julian called, and cheered as the cat hurtled between their legs and disappeared into the house.

Other movement caught Laura's eye, a flutter in the grass, and for a moment she mistook it for another cat. But then it repeated, again and again, and something struck the repositioned table and shattered.

Laura sent the command to close the door, and shook her head in faint wonder as the slope was replaced by a popcorn-hopping cascade of chunky balls of ice.

"*Wicked*," Jules said reverently.

"The islands are a useful location," Tsur Selkie said, watching the scene with an analytical air. "But comparatively exposed."

Laura's response was forestalled by a text from her sister.

Sue: *Not quite a cabin in a snowstorm but it'll do in a pinch. Ask him to dinner.*

Laura: *Just he and I, a roaring fire, and my teenaged son? Nice story you're writing, Sue.*

Even so, she turned to the man beside her, refused to be distracted by the interesting combination of strength and delicacy in his profile, and said:

"It certainly isn't weather for travel. Would you like to stay for dinner, Tsur Selkie?"

CHAPTER FIVE

It took the full measure of Laura's fortitude to stand shoulder to shoulder with a Pocket Event Horizon as he turned his head and looked directly into her eyes. His expression didn't change: he simply stood there, holding her gaze for far longer than was necessary.

Sue was right. Sue was very very right.

"Mum! Come see! The pool's turned into a giant slushie!"

Laura couldn't help but laugh, just a little, and won a flicker of a smile in response.

"I would be glad to," the Event Horizon said. "If you would call me Gidds."

"And you can call me Laura," she responded, and found it quite easy to say, nerves dropping away. An unspoken acknowledgement had been made, and everything seemed uncomplicated. He was attracted to her. She was attracted to him. They would have dinner.

"Winter here is going to *rock*."

They would have dinner with her teenaged son. Entertained, Laura went to look at her hail-filled pool.

"When it snows I'm going to sled all the way down the slope into the lake," Julian informed her.

"I'm sure there's a reason why that would be fun," Laura said.

"Well, it would be if I went down on a big inner-tube...though getting out of the lake might be a bit rough. Here comes the rain."

'Rain' was an inadequate word. 'Sheets'. 'Vertical flood' rapidly becoming 'horizontal flood'. They watched in appreciative silence.

"Living on top of a hill in the middle of a lake certainly tends to the dramatic," Laura said eventually. "Did you take a land grant in the islands as well, Gidds?"

"I haven't yet been released for Muinan emigration," he said. "Even though I spend the majority of my time here. But after my daughters transfer to Pandora Shore, they plan to view all the possibilities of Muina before deciding how my grant is to be used."

"Are they starting soon?" Pandora Shore was the special Setari-linked school that Laura's grandchildren attended.

"After the Thanksgiving Ceremony." He glanced at her, then added: "I return to Tare tomorrow to make the final arrangements."

"How long will it take you to finish this report thing?" Julian asked.

"As much as possible I prepare reports as I go along—else I would never keep pace. I can't predict how long it will take for a decision to be made, since there's a great deal of disagreement on the political side, but my part is done."

Laura processed this very deliberate communication, then carefully corralled her scattering thoughts. More practicality, less palpitations. Dinner.

"Is there anything you prefer not to eat, Gidds?"

"I avoid non-cultured meats."

Julian's eyes went wide. "Is that because if you eat animal flesh you can feel what the animal felt when it died?"

"It's possible," Gidds said, unfazed by the question. "Or, occasionally, impressions of an animal's life. Vat-grown meats don't come with such complications."

"Cheese would be okay, right? We can have fondue. I'll make the goop, Mum. You never do it stringy enough."

Julian was an excellent cook so long as it involved cheese, for which he had an inexhaustible enthusiasm.

Nothing had delighted him more than confirming that the Taren dish 'nymoz' was indeed indistinguishable from fondue, even if the milk was vat-cultured.

"Fondue three days in a row strikes me as excessive," Laura said. "And we have quiche already. Set out something for us to drink."

"Okay." But Julian was not to be distracted, asking: "What about eggs? Are eggs a problem?"

"Not usually."

"And it was vat-cultured egg, anyway," Laura murmured. Much of the Muinan settlements' food supply was artificially grown, since the new farms were not established enough to provide for millions.

Laura heated and cut slices of quiche while Julian, apparently unaffected by Event Horizons, set out glasses and continued to pepper their guest with questions about the impact of Place Sight on food. Gidds responded with unimpeded calm, even to speculation about the emotions of bacteria.

Would he have answered in the same manner, if she weren't a factor? Laura wasn't certain, but she liked him for his patience. And it was a real pleasure to see Julian's natural effervescence at full flow. He'd faced his own challenges following Cass' disappearance—not least of which had been the week Laura had almost entirely shut down, when the Police had started winding back their investigation. That and several years of bullying had meant unexpected walls had gone up around the chatty, gregarious child Julian had been, but Muina was undoubtedly a dream come true for him. He was flourishing.

And helpfully moving on to questions Laura was thinking of asking herself, such as: "Did you come up with the idea of the Setari?"

Gidds shook his head. "It would be more correct to say I was one of the first Setari. I was recruited into KOTIS by Isten Notra, who found drones inadequate for experiments that required entering the Ena. That was a very controversial program, since we only risked travel through deep space at the time, and had lost almost all knowledge of the other aspects of the Ena, which were considered too dangerous for living personnel. But the need to learn more had become a priority."

"When it became clear the number of tears into real-space were increasing?" Laura asked, hoping he wouldn't find the continued interrogation annoying.

"When it no longer became possible to deny," Gidds said. "There had been a great deal of opposition to official recognition of the problem. And, then, all in a month, Isten Notra's proposals for direct action were authorised, and an Ena exploration team assembled."

"Were you Captain?" Julian asked, between quick mouthfuls of quiche.

Gidds sustained a wry smile for several seconds, and Laura realised that rather than resenting the inquisition, he found Julian's enthusiasm amusing.

"I was forty-seven—in Taren years," he said, "and my presence barely tolerated."

"Why so young?" Laura asked, startled. There were three Taren years for each Earth year, so forty-seven meant he'd been not quite sixteen. Younger even than the Setari, who hadn't been permitted to participate in missions until full adulthood at 'fifty'.

"Because I was the strongest known Combat Sight talent at the time. That, along with my Place and Sight Sight, made it worth the risk of bringing me on expeditions."

"Strongest on the whole planet?" Julian asked, gleeful. "Are you from, like, a super-powerful family or something?"

"Strong enough. But I had simply trained myself to a higher pitch at a time when talent training was not encouraged in pre-teens. Developing the elemental talents at a young age was regarded as highly dangerous.

Pushing development of Sights considered simply cruel. But we have now learned that without early training, it is far more difficult to increase the strength of our talents— and that early training for Sights means more control to combat their difficulties."

"Why were you trained young?" Laura asked.

"I spent most of my childhood attempting to achieve Precognition," Gidds said, and though his voice was as unruffled as ever, Laura immediately remembered Sue's 'tragic backstory' comment, and regretted her question.

Gidds made a small gesture with his left hand, something Laura read as a combination of comprehension and absolution. Sight Sight again, and she did not know whether to feel uncomfortable or relieved that, to this man, people were often transparent.

"When I was very young, and Ionoth had started to come through tears into the Ena and kill widely, it seemed to me that the only way to prevent this was to know beforehand where a tear was about to open."

"But it didn't work?" Julian asked, having entirely missed any by-play. "I didn't even know Precognition was a real talent."

"It has never been confirmed, but is unofficially regarded as a seventh Sight. Although there are also theories that it is Sight Sight at a strength not achieved since the days the Lantar ruled Muina, or even that it is gained through all six Sights operating together. If it exists, I did not achieve it."

"So you gave up?" Julian asked, pecking the crumbs of his demolished slice of quiche from the plate.

After the most minute of hesitations Gidds said: "I am still training my strength. But when Isten Notra made her proposal—that I join the scientific expeditions into the Ena, and also train KOTIS members—I began to see an alternate path, one where professionals cleared the ionoth in the Ena near-space immediately adjacent to our cities, rather than unprepared citizens dealing with them in their homes."

"I haven't heard anything about pre-Setari Ena exploration," Laura said, as Julian went to fetch slices of nut pie. "Was it successful?"

"In that we made progress, and did not all die, yes."

Over dessert he described the early days of KOTIS. Soldiers walking through invisible dimensional tears and learning the rules of the Ena. Dealing with attacks from an endless array of monsters. Mapping pocket dimensions, and discovering how unreliable the geography of the Ena could be. Carrying out experiments while refining strategies that would one day become Setari daily routine.

Laura watched him, and did not drop her gaze when he met her eyes. His were steady as he kept to a factual and unemotional recounting of what had almost certainly been a grim and difficult time. KOTIS personnel had died, in far higher numbers than the powerful and extremely skilled Setari.

"And after all that you got stuck being a teacher?" Julian concluded.

"I am still assigned Ena missions," Gidds said, with another transitory smile. "And will join Kaoren in the site investigations here, once I've been permitted to relocate."

"Can you beat Kaoren in a fight?"

"Sometimes," Gidds replied. "But on the whole he has surpassed me."

"Do—?"

"I suspect that's enough interrogation for one day, Julian."

"But I've barely started," Julian said, and added to Gidds: "I was only going to ask if you played *Home* or *Five Ends* or any of the other big online games."

"I vet them occasionally," Gidds said, as unperturbed by this question as any other. "In order to decide whether they are permitted for the Kalrani. Virtual experience games sometimes trigger Sights in odd ways. For the most part I do not have the time—and would be unlikely to enjoy playing a game that involves fighting Ionoth."

"Ha." Julian grinned. "I bet Kaoren's playing *Home* just because Cass likes it." He bounced up to avoid Laura's eye. "I'll do the washing up, Mum. See you Mister—ah, Tsur Selkie."

Grin widening, he took their plates to the cleaning unit, then bounded back upstairs, and all of a sudden, Laura was alone with Gidds, with every scrap of her relaxed acceptance somehow vanished.

What was she thinking of doing? This was not like the time Bet had set her up with 'Darvash from Accounting', nor the odd dates she'd gone on with Sue's vast circle of acquaintance. This was a man of considerable influence, one who made decisions about Cass' life, and Laura simply didn't know enough about him to be sure that he would take a lack of follow-through, or a waning of interest, gracefully.

No. No, that wasn't true. She was quite certain Gidds Selkie would behave impeccably. It was more that he was such an overwhelming man. Formal and polite and restrained. *Mild*, even, and yet...an Event Horizon. So intense that whenever Laura looked directly at him she could almost see the world warping around him, and could feel herself being inescapably swallowed up.

"What was it you called the first dish of our meal?" he asked—a completely innocuous question no doubt in response to her glass-clear fit of nerves.

"Quiche," she said. "The Muinan spelling for that...ah, it's a little difficult. It's a French word and dish." She spelled it phonetically, and then explained 'French'.

"You are perhaps missing the foods of your own planet," he said, rising from his chair and turning to gauge the sheets of water outside.

"Oh, a few," she said, standing and following him to the north patio doors. "Cinnamon particularly. But mostly it's been a fun game trying new foods, and reinventing Earth dishes with Muinan ingredients. Some items aren't available at all, but there are very many similar ingredients. The flour I used is from a Kolaren grain and has a different taste, but I think it works well. And it's shocking how many vegetables are tremendously similar to Earth plants. The botanists who have been playing with the seeds I brought from home tell me more than a few are almost identical to Muinan plants—just different cultivars."

She paused to consider the storm, which hadn't eased significantly. "I'm afraid this looks like it's going to continue for quite a while. I hope it hasn't thrown your plans off too much."

"If I had an urgent appointment, there are craft that can travel in these conditions. But I have enjoyed the opportunity to talk to you while not on duty."

Inordinately pleased by this, Laura couldn't help but smile, but then told herself not to overreact. She needed to be sensible.

"I would enjoy kissing you as well."

Quiet words. They stole any notion of 'sensible'. Once again she turned her head. His gaze was unwavering, his eyes inky-dark.

"I'd enjoy that too."

They weren't standing far apart. She leaned a little forward as he moved, and their mouths found each other without awkwardness. Just a touch, and then an exploratory kiss.

Laura plummeted. Could such a simple thing really make the world spin? She held on to him for balance, and his arms curled around her waist. Just kissing. It was nothing much, really. Kissing, and hands sliding over a blue uniform. Not nearly reason enough for the stars to slip from their courses, for time to slow down.

She was leaning into him now. The muscles of his arms tensed, relaxed, tensed again. Did this uniform have any seams, any opening to allow a hand to slip beneath, to find bare flesh? Her own shirt was far more obliging. His gloves stole a large amount of her fractured attention: one fingerless, the other complete, they made a maddening contrast as his hands moved over her back.

This had become far more than a kiss. Her heart was racing but there was no panic, no sense of being trapped. A kiss, a touch, a coming together. A thing she had no interest in escaping.

"I think..." Laura hesitated a moment more, but knew she wanted this. "I think we need a different room."

CHAPTER SIX

Gidds drew back, but it was only so he could look into her eyes. His expression was utterly serious.

"I would like that. Very much."

Men with voices like Gidds Selkie should not use them to say things with such a depth of sincerity. Laura supposed her tiny gasp in response had been audible, and didn't really care if Sight Sight gave away the faint shiver that ran through her as she slid her arms down and found both his hands, extremely aware of the gloves he used to protect himself from touch. She kept hold of the left hand, the one covered only by a fingerless glove.

A short walk to her bedroom. It was easiest to make it without looking back at him, though she kept imagining what he must be able to sense from her, through the hand she had taken, with the Sights that he had trained to their highest pitch.

Rain dominated the room, pounding in gusts against the curving window. Laura paused, since she liked watching storms, but she didn't want the distraction and so triggered the polarisation function and shut away the world. In a house where even the roof was made from stone, the storm reached them only as a muffled hiss.

Though perhaps shutting away all distraction was a tactical error. Looking into the calm face of the man she'd brought to her room made Laura feel very young, rather nervous...and more than a little impatient. She dropped her gaze to the hand she still held, and deliberately peeled off his glove.

Even over the murmur of rain, Laura heard his intake of breath. She liked that, liked that he sounded a little shaken, that the 'serious soldier' was working on his composure behind an appearance of calm. It took concerted effort to not look up, to resist checking his expression, but rather to simply reach for his other hand.

He presented it to her, prompting her to glance up after all, in time to catch that fleeting smile. As she drew the second glove off she stayed watching his face, but that wasn't a good idea, just as she had suspected, because the man was simply *mesmerising*, and Laura really did feel like she was being dragged forward, that the stars were slowing down around her, and quite possibly she would have stood there for an immeasurable amount of time, holding a pair of gloves.

He took them from her, moved, and this time there was no reason to stop kissing.

oOo

Muinan-Taren-Kolaren literature was full of stories about Sights and sex. Sight Sight talents would discover things you never knew you wanted. Place Sight talents... Place Sight was far more than empathy, but that was the facet that came to the fore with a naked Gidds Selkie and a bed. An immensely controlled and measured man who was intuitive and responsive to a degree that kept Laura gasping. He could feel her reaction to his every movement, and whatever she disliked he stopped immediately, and whatever she enjoyed, he improved.

He stunned her, left her trembling—and would be perfectly aware of the fact. Laura would have felt at a disadvantage, but his shaking breath matched her own, and for several minutes all they did was lie tangled together.

"I'm finding I'm glad of the weather," she said at last.

He shifted a fraction, fingers brushing her flank. "Yes. I was not enjoying the prospect of returning to Tare without a reason for another meeting. Although...what is it that changed? Between this week and last week?"

Sight Sight need to know, Laura guessed. "Sue told me you were attracted to me. I didn't believe her. But I thought about the possibility. A lot."

"I will have to thank your sister," he said. "And remember that she is observant."

"Could—could you really see a difference in me, right away?" So disconcerting.

Instead of answering her directly, he sent her a visual link over the interface. An image of herself, standing by Sue, surrounded by a delicate tracery of light: a shifting forest of semitransparent, curling fern fronds. She would have had no idea what the sudden alterations in the ghostly patterns meant if not for her own memory of nerves, anticipation, and then a sudden flush of awareness.

The image changed. Her face now, closer, brown hair falling across her forehead, surrounded by transparent curlicues.

"That really is a very...complicated way to exist in the world," she murmured, not quite able to resist reaching out and touching his cheek, just so she could watch the ghostly tendrils shift about her own face. "Though being able to see through another person's eyes is just as remarkable a thing to me."

His response was to kiss her once again. After that came a slow exploration, and she watched herself as he saw her, and was fascinated by the sheer complexity.

"You spend the whole of your life surrounded by this?" she asked, and then sucked in her breath as he trailed fingers across her lower stomach.

"I can modulate the visual component," he said, pausing to show Laura her face as if through a series of strange filters. Patterns, shadows, and a haze of coloured light. And, finally, just Laura without any added complexity, wearing an expression of pleased wonder. "Sights can never be 'turned off', but there is no effort in maintaining a particular visual mode. The other aspects of Place are not so easily managed."

All the slow exploration had become too much for Laura's restraint, so she began touching him in turn, and that led to another demonstration of the impact of Place Sight, and then a shower, and a slightly-damp return to bed.

"When is your flight tomorrow?" she asked, to cover that she found sleeping together in some ways more challenging than the sex.

"Dawn." He shifted beside her, arranging himself at a comfortable proximity, and curling his fingers through hers, but clearly avoiding touching her otherwise. "I have arranged to be collected a quarter-kasse before. There's no need to get up—I will breakfast on the flight."

Laura studied his face, feeling grave and unsure and yet pleasantly enervated. And wryly aware that every doubt or flutter of excitement would be clear to him.

"I like getting up early," she said, and carefully lifted their linked hands to kiss the back of his fingers before dimming the lights and settling down to at least attempt to sleep. Gidds squeezed her hand in response, then let go, and lay still.

Giving her privacy, she realised. Or, perhaps, simple self-preservation for a busy man who had a dawn flight and, if he maintained contact, would be unable *not* to follow the emotional rollercoaster that was now boarding for a ride through Laura's head.

After Mike had walked out on their marriage, it had taken Laura a few years to give in to her sisters' insistence she try dating. Sometimes that had worked out, but she'd never brought men home, or stayed the whole night at their place. That was down to the complexities of children, and also because her bedroom had been her workroom, and a sanctuary to her.

Laura glanced across at the door to her new workroom, firmly shut, and wondered if Gidds' Place Sight had plastered the sliding panel with large 'keep out' signs.

She was getting ahead of herself. Occasional dates followed by dinner and sex had been relatively simple things. They should be even simpler on Muina, where contraception and a lack of STDs were a near-certainty. But Laura had to admit she did suffer from what Sue called 'ambivalence in the afterglow'. Or, at least, had not in all of the last decade found a man who had inspired her to more than a few dates, and some strictly limited physical activity.

She already knew that Gidds Selkie wouldn't fit this pattern. In part because the last hour had left her simply...stunned. And definitely keen for a repeat performance.

Or fifty.

But in other circumstances, without the storm, she doubted she would have been quick to spend the whole night with the man. He attracted but outright confused her: so overwhelming, impossibly intense, and yet somehow quiet, comfortable.

She hadn't quite intended that last gesture. Kissing his fingers. An odd combination of affection and comfort, and she was not sure what she'd intended to convey with it.

Not sure at all.

oOo

Laura woke, surprised at herself. Instead of spending an hour or two turning over the wisdom of leaping into bed with technically-alien military officers, she must have dropped off almost immediately. And now was arranged along said military officer's back, with an arm slung across his ribs.

Mindful of Cass' comments regarding the sensitivity of sleeping Sight talents, Laura removed the arm, so he wouldn't be woken by a continuation of her internal debate, then slid out of the bed and took herself off to her bathroom.

Wasted effort. She heard him shift before she shut the door. Although, since it was a little over an hour before dawn, perhaps he was responding to an alarm.

And, in truth, she'd hopped off her rollercoaster before the first drop. There was mutual attraction, and hopefully would be more sex, and she would get to know him better. It hadn't really bothered her at all to have Gidds spend the night. Of course, the bedroom was quite empty, almost impersonal, for her carefully arranged art supplies and current projects were safely locked away in her workroom.

When she emerged, after a considerately brief period, she found him partially dressed, standing in the now-open doorway of the bedroom patio. Impossible not to give into the temptation to slip her arms around his waist and kiss his shoulder, and kiss him more when he turned around, but then she was distracted by what he'd been looking at outside: a little sea of mist, ineffectually lit by the spill of light from the doorway.

"This island certainly has weather," she murmured, before adding: "Is there a way to avoid accidentally waking you?"

"It's not worth trying. Anyone with strong Combat Sight will react to the movement of living creatures. We grow adept at falling asleep again after establishing there is no threat, but it is one of the reasons Sight talents often have shielding on their rooms."

He let go of her with a satisfying reluctance, and took himself off into the bathroom. Laura visited her cavernous walk-in wardrobe to pull on something warm, and then went out to the kitchen to make a couple of mugs of an herbal tea that was a popular Muinan breakfast drink. Then she opened the patio doors to interestedly consider the mist. Her house had become a ship on a sea of white.

"Do you drink this?" she asked as Gidds joined her, and handed him the second mug when he nodded.

They sipped, and there was a not-quite-awkward pause where they were both very clearly deciding what to say next. But then Gidds, with a hint of amusement leaking into his voice, said: "I would like to see you again, when I return from Tare."

"I would enjoy that," Laura said, smiling at the echo of their exchange last night, before adding: "Do you have a role in the Thanksgiving Ceremonies? Cass seems to have a long line of commitments."

"Not the Ceremonies. The week has become a time of review for the Triplanetary Council, and I have multiple reports to go over with Committees. My schedule is very full for the rest of the month."

"Come to dinner on the first, then."

"I will do that." Gidds was being extremely serious again, and in that voice. Laura managed to keep her mug upright, but it was a near thing.

A rising hum gave bare warning that they were out of time. The mist billowed, and a small flying vehicle rose out of the filmy sea to hover above the north patio. A woman in a green uniform, her face almost entirely obscured by goggles, brought the machine to a stop a precise four feet out from the door—and two feet up.

"Until then," Gidds said, handing Laura his mug. He took three steps, and another onto the landing strut, climbing effortlessly into the seat beside the pilot.

Holding two near-full mugs, Laura did not wave, but she watched with considerable envy as the flyer zipped away, glowing blue impellers marking the machine's wake.

"I don't know what I want more," she murmured eventually. "The man or his military har...no, I'm not going to make that pun."

Retreating indoors to tip away the drinks, she fetched herself a coat, and then went on an earlier-than-usual walk, delighting in the novelty of such a thick mist—and grateful for the interface, which told her where the path was even when she couldn't see it.

It did not take long at all to reach her favourite seat. She was there in plenty of time to watch the morning flight pass by, not quite overhead and barely visible through white.

Then she settled down to think.

oOo

"You're going to wear an imprint of your ass onto that seat."

"That would only make it more comfortable," Laura said, miming astonishment at the sight of her sister, not only up before midday, but before breakfast. "So you're a morning person now?"

"I was photographing the mist," Sue said, tapping the box hanging from a strap over her shoulder with a show of conscious virtue. "These scanners pick it up pretty well—I got a few nice shots."

Since Sue didn't have the red-eyed and wired look of one of her all-nighters, Laura assumed that she'd succeeded in waking thanks to an early alarm—and not for the weather. Nor was she inclined to beat around the bush.

"Spill. Did he break out the witty repartee? Bore you witless? Were there push-ups?"

Laura couldn't keep back a helpless snort, and Sue bent to peer into Laura's face.

"Wait. Are we talking Tab A, Slot B?" She added a highly direct ASL sign, and Laura's expression in response prompted a crow of delighted approbation. "Fast work, big sis! *And?*"

"Oh, he's ruined me for other men, certainly." Laura managed a coolly detached voice, but then shook her head. "I'm not even sure I'm joking."

"*Wicked*," Sue said, demonstrating where Julian sourced his vocabulary. "But...is there a reason you're sitting out here wearing the Pensive Face? Please don't tell me this was a one-off."

"Well, he's gone back to Tare. But he is coming to dinner again, after the celebrations are over next week. And no, he wasn't boring to talk to. Given he was describing the creation of the Setari, it would be an achievement to be dull, and he was simply matter-of-fact and unfussed by Julian's flood of questions. I'm...I'm not altogether sure that witty repartee is his thing, though."

"No-o," Sue said, judiciously. "Serious Soldier to the core, that one. Intelligent, not entirely without humour or sympathy, but don't expect snappy patter. Most definitely the type whose life revolves around his job. But that would suit you, I think: you like your alone time. So, fantastic sex, not intolerable to talk to, at least willing to put up with Julian. And yet, Pensive Face."

"Name one thing we have in common."

Sue's eyebrows shot up, then her eyes narrowed and she said: "Cass."

"In that my daughter's part of his job? Very funny. But think about it, Sue. Do you think he's a reader—of any sort of fiction, let alone my sort of fiction? I've never pictured myself with a man who doesn't inhale at least one book a week."

"He's a psychic space soldier. I'd call it an ideal match myself. You love science fiction and he *is*..."

"But that's exactly it. It's not fiction to him. It's not entertainment. His whole life has been..." Laura paused, and then sent Sue an interface link. "Read that."

Sue's expressive face made it easy to follow her progress through the linked article. First simple interest as she saw that it was a detailed record of the 'Tasken

Outbreak'. A grimace as she watched the first short video of the Ena-born monsters that had poured through a tear in the walls between dimensions. A crease between her brows as she read statistics, details. And then stillness, as she reached the description of the aftermath. Of the recovery of a small boy from an apartment with no other survivors.

"Partially *eaten*?"

"If I have a regret about yesterday, it's not researching Gidds a little more before letting Julian loose on him. How he ended up working for KOTIS, why he'd trained himself so intensely, those aren't entertaining things. He side-stepped the details, but there's no way that can be something he likes talking about."

Sue was frowning, still reading. "So you're saying...what? You like fiction and he's too real?"

"No. There...there just seems to me a vast disconnect between someone who likes to read about SF-nal universes, and someone for whom those plotlines are anything but entertaining. An inherent mismatch."

Sue looked at her. Then, apparently struggling to control her expression, she pronounced a single word.

"Twit."

"Very helpful."

"You're not usually so silly. Yes, he really does have a tragic backstory, and I vaguely regret putting it in those terms. But he's not a child, he's pushing forty. He's taken what happened to him, set out to prevent it happening to others, and succeeded. You're not going to traumatise him because you can deconstruct a trope at twenty paces, and Ellen Ripley is how you relax."

Laura had known all along that was true, but it helped to be told. She was so lucky to have Sue with her.

"Is there anything you regret, coming here?" she asked, impulsively. "You had a reputation, on Earth. A professional network, and so many friends,

Sue shrugged. "I don't miss my hearing aids. I miss Bet. I would have missed Nick, but since he ended up coming along, I get to enjoy being semi-parental with him again. He's such a good kid and, worrying about his father aside, this is the happiest I've seen him. As for my reputation, I'm building a new one, and have even sold some photo compilations."

"Really? I haven't sold a thing."

"I've made almost enough to buy a cup of coffee, if there was coffee to be had. Coffee, now, that I'm going to miss. I'm down to hold-out rations of what I brought with me already. But watching you tie yourself in knots over Serious Soldier almost makes up for that."

"It is my honour to serve."

"And I thank you for sacrificing yourself on the altar of hot sex and quality cuddles. So try not to go overthinking things."

Laura saluted, and then they paused appreciatively to watch another flight lift over the distant city of Pandora, and waft past for their consideration.

It was unlikely that Laura could put doubts aside entirely, no matter how often she told herself it was all really quite simple. She didn't think Gidds was a simple man, even if his approach had been very straightforward. The break before seeing him again would probably be a good thing, so long as she followed Sue's advice and didn't work herself up into knots. Five days until the Thanksgiving Ceremony, and ten until...until another night of Gidds.

CHAPTER SEVEN

"Mum, are you two ready—oh, hey, Princess Leia!"

"Who?" Lira asked, suspiciously.

"The person I'm modelling your hairstyle after," Laura told the girl, then paused, frowning over at Cass standing in the doorway. "Wait. You haven't shown them *Star Wars*? Are you sure you're my daughter?"

"I haven't subtitled anything since Tyrian was born," Cass said. "Between him and working again, I hardly ever find any spare time, and KOTIS is always pushing me to do more BBC nature documentaries anyway. You should do it for language practice."

"I will," Laura said, and then shared with Lira a still of the Cloud City escape, so she understood who they were talking about. "It's a style that only works for people with such long, thick hair as yours, Lira."

"Why does she have a weapon?" Lira asked, interestedly.

"Her group was betrayed, and she's fighting her way free." Laura made certain the looped braids were even and added: "There, you're done. Do you like it?"

Lira considered her image in the mirror. She was a beautiful girl, and normally confident in her appearance, but the Ruuel Devlin family had a rare public engagement that day, and everything they did, said, and wore would be minutely discussed by their millions of fans and critics. Nearly-fourteen—in Muinan or Earth years—was a difficult enough time for any child, without the added pressure of such intense scrutiny.

"It is...yes, I like it," Lira said. "Thank you, Unna Laura."

"You're welcome," Laura said, giving the girl a tiny hug. "Is it time to hurry, Cass, or is it more of a leisurely stroll?"

"Stroll," Cass said. "When Kaoren's involved, we hardly ever get to the hurry stage." As Lira headed out of Laura's bathroom, Cass lingered for her own hug. "Thanks Mum. She really needed something extra today."

"All the time I put into helping your aunts cosplay certainly is coming in handy. Does Lira find public appearances harder than the rest of the children?"

"There's a lot more focus on her. I think she could handle that well enough, but there's always discussion about whether she's visibly aged, and...and how long she'll *last*. Not being 'real' is a genuine nightmare of Lira's, and they practically have betting pools about it."

"That talk isn't dying down, now that it's been a couple of years?"

"Oh, a bit," Cass said, switching to interface conversation as they headed out to the patio. "And she is at least an inch taller than she used to be—but I think it's going to be with her her whole life. The Ionoth girl."

Lira—unlike Ys, Rye and Sen—was not a survivor of the moon world of Nuri. Instead, she had been born on Muina, centuries ago. The last recorded Touchstone before Cass, she had been kidnapped and used as a power source for a giant, reality-distorting machine—and had not, technically, survived the experience.

Exactly how Lira came to regain a physical form, and how long it would last, was a subject of much debate and scientific study. To all tests and scans she was as human as Cass, but there was no way to prove that she was not a creation of the Ena, just a different sort of Ionoth monster.

Lira had paused with Rye to examine the strawberries, and Laura promised them that tomorrow they could harvest the ripest. Then Julian, neatly dressed, with his hair combed flat, arrived with only mildly dragging feet, and they headed down the hill.

"*Cass,*" Laura continued, over their private interface channel, "*when you say Lira is nearly fourteen, do you mean fourteen in Earth years or Muinan years?*"

Cass produced an expressive grimace.

"*Both, sort of. They told me the kids' estimated ages in Taren years, at first, and I converted that to Earth years, and we picked rough birthdays for them. But I should have converted them to Muinan years, and when Ys realised and pointed out that most of them were really a year younger in Muinan years, none of them—not even Ys—were willing to actually change their supposed ages. Since we don't have official birthdates for any of them, we let them have their way.*"

"*I, on the other hand, have embraced being thirty-nine instead of forty-four,*" Laura said. "*Don't the school officials and so forth object to incorrect ages?*"

"*They're letting it slide. A lot of the things you can and can't do under the laws here are based on passing tests rather than a strict age cut-off anyway.*"

To Laura's delight, there was a large version of a flitter waiting for them at the docks, hovering patiently beside the bank. Only Tyrian, and Kaoren's sister Siame—who was visiting to play babysitter—were skipping the Thanksgiving ceremony, and Arcadia's residents had six additional Setari along to play bodyguard. Mostly for Cass and Lira, who weren't actually allowed to travel without at least two guards each.

"*Does it still bother you?*" Laura asked Cass through the link, after they had boarded. "*That you can't go anywhere alone?*"

"*It's bothering me more for the kids, now. Lira's the only one that has a mandatory guard, but there's no way any of them could go wandering about Pandora on their own. We're lucky that guard duty is usually rostered to Setari we consider friends.*" Cass glanced pensively at the rest of the occupants of the flitter. "*A lot of them have much the same problem, anyway—they're heroes, and plenty of people will always be completely obsessed with the Setari. I'm sorry you all get stuck with it, though."*

Laura had tried to avoid becoming too caught up in the notoriety of being "Kaszandra's Mother", but she had certainly been left disinclined to wander about the city after reading a few of the interface sites frankly discussing everything from her appearance to her known purchasing choices. All the Terran transplants were the focus of great interest, and not even Sue particularly enjoyed it.

Today, that interest was at highest intensity. First a Thanksgiving Ceremony held in the vast Moon Piazza, where an audience of thousands—not even counting those watching over the interface—cheered constantly, either at Cass or the Setari. Next came a family-oriented, VIP-only picnic lunch in a park area, where a truly formidable number of people asked Laura what she thought of Muina, and told her how proud she must be of her daughter.

Cass herself was a small revelation. She had not become a chatty social schmoozer, but the day was clearly within her coping abilities. She gave a short speech, politely if briefly responded to the questions of various dignitaries, and constantly tag-teamed with Kaoren and their Setari escort to keep an eye out for her family and guests. Laura had never expected to be rescued by her daughter during social situations, but Cass very neatly extricated Laura from an extremely intrusive man, and deposited her with Alyssa, Nick and Sue instead.

"We're clustering for protection while we wait for the signal to leave," Sue said, cheerfully. "If we all stand frowning seriously at each other I figure it'll be at least five minutes before someone butts in to ask what Cass was like as a child."

Since she'd been asked exactly that at least two dozen times, Laura could only smile thinly, before saying to Alyssa: "I wasn't sure how Maddy would cope with the crowds, but she seems to be enjoying herself."

"That's Sen. She always works Maddy into a silly mood. Does it deliberately too. For a six year-old, Sen's an uber-manipulator."

"So long as she never turns her powers to evil..." Nick murmured.

"Have you decided whether to go ahead and send Maddy to school?"

Alyssa nodded. "I was against it a few weeks ago, since she's well behind the rest of us in language because of the delay in installing her interface. But the other kids do seem to distract her from missing home. Once she's there, we'll move on to what the heck now for us."

"I'm concentrating on passing the adulthood exams," Sue said. "I find it oddly disturbing not to be legally classed as an adult. My first few attempts were shambolic, but I'm determined."

"It's not that they're difficult—it's that you can't use the translation program in the exam environment," Nick agreed. "We have to push our comprehension skills. After that..." He and Alyssa exchanged glances. "We're going to join KOTIS."

"For serious?" Sue said, surprised. "This is the first I've heard of this."

Alyssa nodded. "When Nick says 'join', he means 'do a lot of work so that we can qualify to apply', but yeah, I'm sold on the idea. I'm not sure we would have thought of it ourselves—we started out asking Kaoren whether anyone would object if we went and got jobs in a store or restaurant or something. We can't just sit around on Arcadia living off Cass' money, after all. And even though they have this 'base level' concept here, where everyone gets necessities for free, it's always going to be more fun to have more of an income."

"You can live reasonably comfortably on base level," Nick said. "Free housing, food, clothes, toiletries, interface access and the equivalent of free-to-air TV—but I want to travel."

"Not to mention watch that hilarious show about those kids trying to get into the Setari-linked school here in Pandora," Alyssa added. "Anyway, Kaoren's...interestingly honest when you ask him important questions. And he told us we'd be giving KOTIS a massive headache if we worked somewhere KOTIS couldn't easily control access to. That we're too close to Cass not to be a potential security risk for her."

"I get that whenever I try to take off alone," Sue commented. "Someone might kidnap me and try to use me for leverage, blah, blah, blah."

"Kaoren actually suggested setting up a smallholding," Alyssa went on. "Farming, with a couple of KOTIS greensuits to guard us. Which...no. I've never met a plant I couldn't shrivel within a month, and I get too anxious about sick animals to want to be looking after a few thousand of them. We also wanted something where we're in easy reach of the Setari islands—Maddy's only just started making friends here. I'm not going to move her."

"When Kaoren suggested KOTIS next, it didn't seem like any better of an idea," Nick said, with a faint sigh. "Guns, saluting, even killing monsters—that's not my kind of thing. But Kaoren pointed out that now that they've figured out a better way of exploring the deep space of the Ena, KOTIS is transitioning from 'Organisation for saving us from dimensional destruction' into 'planetary exploration, security, and settlement'. NASA on steroids. They've only just started using drone shoals in the Ena, and have already catalogued five hundred planets. It can't be long before they stumble across more habitable ones."

"Suddenly this becomes understandable," Sue said. "So KOTIS is going to transmogrify into a combo of Space Patrol and Galactic Survey? That sounds so completely awesome I'm almost tempted to sign up myself. Do you think they need official photographers?"

"Do you think dawn push-ups would be involved?" Laura put in.

Sue grimaced. "You're right. I wouldn't last a week. But I can live in hope of forming my own rag-tag band of misfits. You up for 'acquiring' a ship and skirting the near side of the law with me Laura?"

"Running risky trade deals in the face of KOTIS disapproval?" Laura suggested agreeably. "Having tense confrontations over the rights to alien ruins, but helping our antagonists out occasionally with pesky space pirates and first contact situations?"

"We can be the thorn in KOTIS' side," Sue said, with enthusiasm.

Almost on cue, Laura received a channel request over the interface. Her heart thumped, hard, and she felt just a little ridiculous as she silently answered.

"*Gidds.*"

"*Laura.*" The interface-transmitted voice—a combination of mental projection and sub-vocalisation—struck her every bit as deeply as it did in person. "*I hope you're well?*"

"*A little overwhelmed,*" Laura said, only a touch ironically.

"*The session I'll be attending next is one of the first public discussions of the Triplanetary's approach regarding Earth. It can be viewed on this channel.*" He sent her a link, paused a moment, then added: "*These are preliminary sessions, to allow those who wish to contribute to air their views. They are not those who will make the decisions.*"

"*I—thank you for letting me know.*"

"*I'll see you next week.*"

"Turns out there's plenty of jobs in KOTIS that are a lot more interesting than guarding and/or shooting things," Alyssa was saying as Gidds cut the link—reminding Laura that he was famously abrupt. "Some don't have a chance in hell of getting—we're way behind on the science track—but even with all their tech, they still need administrators, quartermasters, cooks, that kind of thing. On ships. That'll be going to brand new planets."

"Qualifying for which is going to take us long enough, from the sounds of it, that we'll be able to stick around Pandora to be with Maddy at least until she starts university or something," Nick added.

"First stop adulthood exams, next the final frontier!" Sue said, lifting an imaginary glass in a toast. But with her usual flawless instinct, she was studying Laura keenly. "What's so distracting?"

Laura sent them all the link, and that killed amusing side discussions and turned the trip back to Arcadia into an uncomfortable shared viewing session. The people of Muina had found quite a lot of reasons not to open any kind of relationship with Earth, even if a way to it was found through the Ena. Earth was violent. Earth was complicated. Earth had more than twice the population of the entire Triplanetary.

"Nothing particularly unexpected," Sue commented late that night, over a glass of their latest random sample of Muinan alcohol.

"Gidds said this was a public opportunity to participate—the decision-makers would come much later."

"That did have an air of angry windbags about it, didn't it? Not that a lot of them don't have a point. So Serious Soldier has been in touch?"

"Just to point out the session."

"He looked tired."

"Yes." Gidds had been sitting next to the session convener, but if he'd contributed, it had only been on private interface channels. His posture had been as perfectly upright as ever, but there'd been shadows sketched beneath his eyes.

"If anything, it made him even more fanciable."

"Yes," Laura agreed, and wondered if she could survive another week of only thinking about Gidds Selkie.

CHAPTER EIGHT

Laura had not slaved over a hot stove for hours, but she'd taken more care than usual with the evening meal, and was just heading for a quick shower when she received a channel request from Gidds—and had her mood killed by a last-minute cancellation. After a fortnight of anticipation, Laura could not quite avoid a noticeable pause before she managed a light: "*Another time then.*"

"*I am very sorry, Laura,*" Gidds said. "*I know this must mean wasted time and effort for you.*"

Laura glanced back at the kitchen, mentally shrugged, and said: "*Julian will enjoy it. Can we reschedule?*"

"*I'm assigned to Arenrhon for the rest of the week—a location outside the teleportation network.*"

Of course he was. "*Tell me, do you have the concept here of a 'nightcap'?*" She'd used the English word, and so added: "*That is a late evening drink, before retiring.*"

"*Duzig,*" Gidds said, and then took one of the Sight Sight tangents she was coming to recognise: "*What is the relevance of headgear?*"

Laura laughed. "*We're going to go down a lot of side roads if you want to get into English etymology.*"

"*I would enjoy that,*" Gidds said, perfectly seriously.

"*I expect I would too,*" Laura said. "*As for 'nightcap'...*" She paused, checking her e-dictionary for confirmation, and then said: "*Nightcaps were worn in cold places when going to bed—it seems the name transferred to a warming drink taken before bed.*"

"*I see.*"

"*Anyway,*" Laura said, brisk now. "*I usually go to sleep around an hour—around a half-kasse before midnight. If you finish your meeting in time, come by for a nightcap. Otherwise, another day."*

"I'll do that," he said, and she could hear the warmth in his mental voice. *"Thank you, Laura."*

He cut the channel, and Laura sighed, because it was clear the man's life was not his own. Then she shook herself, and called Julian down for dinner.

"So what have you been playing today, kiddo?" she asked, as he obligingly demolished a large portion of a carefully prepared meal. "Anything you'd recommend?"

"Red Exchange. I wanted something that doesn't revolve around Setari and psychics, something more fantasy based. Since everyone here is at least a tiny bit psychic, it's pretty rare for a game to have no people with talents. But in *Exchange*, the people in the game go around collecting contracts with nature spirit things. They get powers in exchange for blood, but the spirits aren't, like, demons, or anything considered bad. It's pretty cool—as much puzzle as combat based—and it's only just released, so everyone's not a million times stronger. Here."

He sent her a link. Laura read through the details, and thought it a good option for a distraction. Diving into a virtual world would spare her several hours of waiting hopefully for Gidds to show up.

"Another thing I like about the game is it has this weird accent modulator thing depending on which island you start on, which is good for hiding mine," Julian said, collecting plates. "Most games I just don't talk, since I can't speak Muinan well enough. You know, there's actually people who pretend to be me, and put on bad Aussie accents?"

"Cass said there are several people playing *Home* who have completely convinced a large number of players that they're her—or Kaoren, or one of the other Setari."

"It's so stupid. The accent modulator is good, though— I even joined a band. That's what they call player teams or guilds in the game. I started on Zylat—message me if you need anything. My character's called 'Space Ninja'."

"You think a name in English is a good way to hide your identity?"

"Everyone's doing it. Cass' translation app got sort-of hacked."

That sent Laura off for a brief tour of current news, and the reflection that she'd best not assume she wouldn't be understood having a conversation in English. Then she plunged into character creation, discovering that all the people of *Red Exchange's* world were different shades of blue, and had one less finger on each hand, and that the island of Zylat was wonderfully fantastical.

Thoroughly engrossed, Laura had in fact almost forgotten Gidds altogether when he messaged her with a brief "*On my way,*" and she had to hurriedly redirect her thoughts.

Laura: *Are you forbidden alcohol, like Kaoren?*

Gidds: *No. That ban operates only for those with elemental talents, and the higher Telekinesis ratings. But I avoid anything that confuses my senses.*

Laura: *Name a favourite drink, then.*

He named several, showing a preference for light, energising flavours, and Laura settled on bennen, a gingery infusion. Since she'd remembered to turn on the proximity alarm, the interface warned her of Gidds' approach, and it amused her to meet him at the door, cups in hands, and pass him one.

A flicker of a smile showed he recognised the symmetry, but instead of drinking he took her cup as well, set them both on the nearest flat surface, and slid his arms around her waist. For a moment he simply studied her, and she considered him gravely in return: clearly fresh from a shower, with his hair still damp. Then he kissed her very thoroughly, and only after a good five minutes let her go so he could retrieve the cups and give one back to her.

Entertained, Laura accepted her bennen, and headed for one of the lounges: "Do they always overwork you, or just on special occasions?"

"This week has been excessive. There are meetings where I can usefully contribute, but too often I am being used to shift responsibility. If I—if my Sights—raise no objection to a proposal, then arguments against it are weakened. It is not a good use of my time, or particularly sensible. Sight Sight triggers too unpredictably to ever be considered a guarantee."

"Is that what happened tonight?"

"No, the Ormon of Nent accused the Southern Ancipars of attempting to undermine his rule. They have Place and Sight Sight talents with them, but have taken to using me as a neutral third party during disputes." He grimaced. "A lie detector. Not a role I enjoy, although I was at least able to defuse this particular crisis."

He'd stopped the two major political regions of Kolar from...what? Squabbling? Going to war? After a week without any time for a break. No wonder he looked hollowed out, more than tired. But he was also incredibly focused, watching her unwaveringly as he drank. The gravitational effect seemed to double, triple, with every moment that passed.

The man could make it hard to breathe. To think. Laura set aside other considerations, and did what she'd been planning ever since he'd vanished into the mist. This time, she took his gloves off last. It was an act he clearly found highly erotic, and Laura began to hunt for other things that would make him catch his breath that way. She wanted to leave *him* stunned.

A suitable interlude ensued, and Laura thought that she'd at least partially achieved her goal. She was learning this man.

"Do you have another dawn start tomorrow?"

"Mid-morning." His eyes were heavy-lidded, barely open.

"Good," she said, firmly, and he smiled, then promptly fell asleep. Very tired indeed.

Laura took her thoughts to the shower.

She had wanted the man back in her bed, and that's where she had him, but she knew perfectly well she didn't have the temperament for an ongoing, purely sexual relationship—and she would be surprised if Gidds did either. They were finding their ground with each other, feeling their way toward whether they wanted more, and Laura was discovering a streak of coward in herself whenever she started to frame that answer.

It was not simply that he was so overwhelming, this precisely correct Event Horizon. Nor that he spent his days doing things she suspected she'd need a higher security classification for him to fully share. Laura had never been easily awed by people with political or social power. It was more that she still could not readily name things they had in common. When the edge had been taken off their mutual attraction, what would they talk about?

And, despite herself, when she imagined conversations, she kept positioning the things that were central to her life—stories and her own creative response to them—as trivial in comparison to the Serious Business of Gidds' packed schedule. She had no patience for the dismissal of Art as a valuable facet of life, but she also saw little evidence that Gidds spared any time for it. No doubt he would demonstrate a polite interest in whatever she was doing, and...

Annoyed at herself, Laura abandoned her overlong shower, and went back to the bedroom. They'd kept the lights on dim, so she could see him, curled a little in his sleep. On the far side of the room, the door to her workroom stood firmly closed, and she thought about the symbolism of that, and wondered again whether his Place Sight would plaster the door with big 'keep out' signs, and how that would make him feel.

Sue would say there was no need to kick-start an angst generator—the important thing was to enjoy the moment. But Gidds made Laura want to think about her future, and his place in it—and she knew there was a tediously simple reason why she kept reacting with an instinct to back away.

She'd opened her life once, to someone she'd thought was exactly the right person for her. She'd been mistaken. On paper, Gidds was a far worse match, and perhaps it was foolish to get close to someone so utterly different from what she thought she wanted. But she'd do the man the courtesy of giving him time to prove her wrong.

She owed herself that much.

oOo

Gidds, with only occasional distracted pauses, was able to keep his job at bay during a relaxed morning in bed, and then made up for a need to respond to several messages by preparing breakfast while he did so.

While he worked, Laura went out to the south patio and sat on the wide double rim surrounding the pool, appreciating autumn, and the fact that safety fencing in technological futures involved force fields that activated only at the approach of unaccompanied children. This allowed her to enjoy Maze's gift without obstruction. The trees had survived without notable transplant shock, and their reflections in the water were entirely beautiful, inviting daydreams. Laura drowsed.

"What are you thinking about?"

"Oh, the game I was playing yesterday," Laura said, interestedly inspecting the tray Gidds carried. "What are these called?"

"Toshen." He set the tray down between them. "A favourite of my daughters."

It resembled fried cornbread flecked with herbs and vegetables. Laura sampled a corner, and found it crumbly and delicious, with a zing of the radish-like Taren vegetable called vut.

"Your daughters are at Pandora Shore now?"

"Yes. They wish to continue on as Kalrani, but now that the Setari program has returned to a voluntary and less intense curriculum, I will be able to see more of them."

"More? But...if you were in charge of Setari training, wouldn't you have seen them often?"

He shook his head, gaze focused on ripples on the pool. "No. It would have been unfair to allow myself more access than the families of other Setari in training. I had them for Sights sessions, which gave me more time than most parents of Kalrani. Otherwise, the holiday breaks, the same as everyone else. It will be very different now—I will have them every long rest."

'Long rest' was the weekend of their eight day week: two days, the same as Earth, although Muina also had 'short rest' which was a half-day in the middle of the working week.

"Presuming you're ever given rest days of your own."

"That is a difficulty," he agreed. "But I expect it to be manageable—and to allow me to see more of you. I've added you to my schedule group, so you will be able to see how my time is blocked out."

"I've added you to the house permissions," Laura said, with a faint laugh. "Perhaps we can try dinner again when you get back." She hesitated, then continued: "Or a rolling series of nightcaps. Whichever works."

He reached across the tray and brushed the fingers of his partially gloved hand over the back of hers. Not, she thought, to check how she was feeling, but simply to show pleasure.

"Tell me about the game you were playing," he said then.

Laura resisted the temptation to ask why, and described *Red Exchange*.

"I haven't progressed very far," she said. "I'm supposed to be finding out what the spirit—the teszen—I'm trying to make my first contract with most desires, but have spent most of my time wandering about looking at things. A very pretty world."

"You enjoy the exploration?"

"Yes, although the plot and collection aspects seem interesting as well, and I generally enjoy puzzles. It's like a combination..." Laura stopped, because *Pokémon*, *Final Fantasy* and *Myst* were all going to be meaningless for him. "Like a combination of a few Earth games I liked, but with all the amazing aspects of a virtual interface environment as well."

"I would enjoy playing that with you."

Laura didn't quite hide a moment's surprise.

"Free time would still be a difficulty, of course," he said. "But it is something we could share when I am in a remote location. And, if it is suitable for Sights, perhaps Allidi and Haelin will appreciate it."

"Well, schedule a time," Laura said, not sure whether he was doing exactly what she'd feared, but acknowledging that he had never said he didn't enjoy games. "Starting island Zylat. My character name is Angharad."

He tilted his head. "Does the name have a meaning for you?"

Laura wondered whether the ghostly ferns that surrounded her had unfurled into new patterns, or if he was just guessing. "It's the name of a favourite character in a favourite book."

He asked her to describe the book, so Laura talked him through the plot of *The Blue Sword*, and they ended up in a side discussion of whether the ability that triggered the plot had any resemblance to Sight Sight, and the difference between magic, 'powers', and talents.

The man, she reflected after he had departed, would discuss almost anything with the same focused attention.

Collecting information about Earth, satisfying his Sight Sight need to know, and...learning Laura Devlin.

Restlessly, she did some minor tidying, reviewed Julian's school progress, and promised herself that she'd do some more of her own lessons, since he'd passed her again. Then she broke out nearly the last of her hoarded share of the coffee supplies and made two mugs.

These she carried out of the house, down the path, and around the side of Sue's house, to where a rounded room looked west to complement Laura's eastern view. Since Sue and Laura had freely given each other a full set of security permissions, there was no problem triggering the external door—and then changing the glass polarisation so that the light could get in.

Sue lay sprawled with her usual abandon, as if unconsciously trying to take up the maximum surface area of the bed. The Pikachu onesie was a new development, however, and made Laura smile as she set the mugs on a bedside table. Then she fit herself Tetris-like into one of the gaps left by her sister, and waited.

It didn't take long. The smell of coffee had long ago carved a direct route into Sue's synaptic depths, and very soon there was a groan, and an elbow in Laura's shin.

"I don't know how I'm going to get you up once I've run out of your chemical alarm clock."

Sue groaned again, and rolled onto her side. "They promised me they'd prioritise growing the seeds you brought."

"Unless the techs have some sort of time-accelerator, that's still going to be three or so years."

"Urgh. Well, they've found all sorts of Earth plants here—if Cass is right about this place being an actual idealised copy of Earth, then there's got to be coffee plants somewhere. Ooh, and Bet will definitely have a care package next time the portal to Earth opens. Coffee and Tim Tams and copies of all the stuff we've missed. So, did you break out my lifeblood to celebrate something, or is this just more wibbling about whether the hottie is a good idea?"

"Wibbling. Or...not wibbling. I keep thinking over the reason why Mike and I divorced."

Sue sat up, Pikachu hood sagging over her eyes as she frowned at Laura. "Somehow I can't see Serious Soldier screwing around with snazzily-dressed lawyers. What haven't you been telling me?"

Laura sighed. Things that hurt her were things she didn't talk about, even with Sue. But she needed her sister's common sense.

"When Mike finally told me why—which was a week after he walked out, mind you—he started out blaming himself, calling himself an idiot, undeserving. You know that self-deprecating Hugh Grant impression of his. But he couldn't keep it up, and started running on the way he does when he's nervous, and ended up telling me what he really thought."

Her hand still clenched whenever she thought back to it: holding the phone receiver in a grip she could not ease, listening to someone she knew so well, and so little, talking on and on.

"He was bored. I was boring. The things I cared about meaningless, embarrassing, childish." Laura lifted a hand at Sue's outraged inhalation. "Don't worry—I never spent more than...well, a few of the harder days thinking it was about *me*. But it recast everything, the whole of the time I'd known him, into a different light. Mike met me at uni, and I was part of the roleplaying club, and he took up roleplaying. And he read Asimov and Lem, and also the books that I loved. And he went to WorldCon and DragonCon with us, before the kids came along. Because those were the things that I liked."

"Are you saying Mike was, like, a *fake geek guy*?"

"Not exactly. It's more...you remember Pete Filson? After he met Amy?"

"And became 500% evangelical?"

"Yeah. He wasn't putting it on. But I guess you could say that Pete was drawn to the things Amy cared about. Mike fell for me, and so he was naturally more interested in the things I cared about. Just like you used to be very into beat poetry."

"I am still into beat poetry, thank you very much—or at least appreciate some of it. Jean-Yves simply *introduced* me to it."

"And I introduced Mike to fandom, and he enjoyed himself a lot, really and truly, but then he met Margaret, and she was very much *not* into swords, sorcery or spaceships. The more he wanted her, the less he liked the things that she disdained."

Laura paused, watching her sister collect one of the mugs of coffee, and drink deeply.

"So, *unconsciously* a fake geek guy?"

"Cass did something similar to me a few years later, you know. Found a 'cooler' Mum and suddenly stopped liking the things I liked. But she deep-down enjoys SF, and eventually recovered."

Sue drained her mug of coffee and swapped it for Laura's. "So, if I'm understanding you right, you're worried that Serious Soldier is suddenly going to buy a bunch of miniatures and start painting them? Borrow all your ten-sided dice? In order to impress you? Oh, gods, if he starts roleplaying, can I be game master? I will pay you. I'd even let you have the rest of my coffee stash."

"Somehow, I suspect Gidds' idea of roleplaying would involve being exactly himself in any given situation. No, I don't expect him to go quite so overboard, but he's following the same pattern: he's attracted to me, so he's 'showing an interest' in the things that interest me. He even wants to meet up in the latest game I'm playing."

Sue made several faces, shook her head, climbed to her feet, and then ceremoniously bonked Laura on the forehead with her mug.

"You find the oddest things to get worried about. Look, do you want me to argue you into this, or out of this? No, don't answer that. It's no fun for me if you give up at the start. But do you remember back when Bet and I finally convinced you to let us set you up on a couple of dates, and you told us what kind of guy you'd consider?"

"Someone who likes the things I do," Laura said. "Someone who gets me. And someone who is honest enough not to have affairs."

"Yeah, it sounded so simple, but I think going and scaling a few mountains looking for the teeth of the Phoenix would have been easier. At least Serious Soldier strikes me as hitting point number three. Terminally upright. As for the rest...well, first, I don't think he's doing the same thing as the putz, and unless he starts pretending he's been a tru-fan all along, finding something you can enjoy together is a good and logical thing to do—and you totally need to tell me exactly which game, and when you're meeting, so I can stalk you."

"Only occasionally collapsing into helpless laughter? I'll pass. If that's first, what's second?"

"You're never going to find anyone here who really has all that much in common with you. You had a hard enough time on Earth. Sure, you could find yourself a creative Muinan who likes gardening and reading, but even if they learned English, or we translated everything we'd ever read or watched or meme'd, they'd never form quite the same cultural touchstones—not even Cass, who is literally a touchstone, but no-one here will see her as we do—or have their sex lives sabotaged by her in quite the same way, for that matter."

"*What?*"

"Do you have any idea the number of people who've propositioned me purely because I'm 'Kaszandra's' aunt? Talk about a mood-killer. I've hooked up in the past for any number of reasons, but faint family resemblance is a step too far. Anyway, you don't exactly have the same relationship to geekdom here because you're living the sci-fi fantasy. If Serious Soldier is actually capable of taking on the concept of 'fun', then roll with it." She drained the second mug and set it down. "Enough. Instead of sitting around coming up with silly roadblocks because you're starting to think the guy's a keeper, you can come into the city with me and Inika. It's all arranged: Mara's going to be our mandatory security, and we're doing lunch and then getting smuggled into the back of an exclusive salon, and we'll catch the school shuttle back with the kids. You could even get a trim yourself, Ms I-Like-Ponytails."

"I suppose I could get the split ends cut out. Are you going as Pikachu? Where did you get that anyway? I thought there was no room in your backpack for anything but chocolate and coffee."

"I had one made up for each of the kids—and me—as a cheer Maddy up exercise. I anticipated much breakfast hilarity, but haven't yet managed to get up in time for breakfast. Did you know Nick and Alyssa have actually started *jogging*?"

"Part of their KOTIS preparation?"

"They're very serious about it. After dropping off Maddy for her first day of school, they're going on a KOTIS orientation tour today. I'm not a thousand percent convinced the military life is what they want, but can understand the attraction of exploring other planets. Presuming KOTIS doesn't just station them somewhere harmless and dull."

"Have they told Cass yet?"

"Have you told Cass you're starting a little crafting empire?"

"I might if I ever sold anything." Laura glanced automatically at her mail as she did so, and said: "And it looks like that particular conversation's upon me. That dragon quartet."

"Nice! At the original price, or did you drop them?"

"I put them up, actually, in a fit of stubbornness. Art gallery prices." Laura found her cheeks had gone hot, and shook her head. "I'll go package it up while you reassemble your humanity."

"That went years ago, darling. Just don't ask me questions about turtles in deserts—or was it a tortoise? Anyway, pack, dress, lunch, go."

Chapter Nine

Muinan hair technology had moved well beyond dyes, and while Laura had truly not intended to have anything done, she hadn't been able to resist a simple treatment that changed how her hair reflected light—but only when there was a static build-up. Which meant that when she brushed her hair it turned a deep hunter green, and then slowly faded back to its usual mid-brown. She loved it.

"I wonder if we could use you as a storm detector," Sue mused. "*Laura's looking pea-green: better bring an umbrella.*"

"I'd enjoy that," Laura said. "A useful talent with no negative impacts so long as no-one strings me up to use as a weathervane."

"I'm more inclined to decorate you at Christmas. Does Cass do a tree here, do you know?"

"I think she said something about Year's Turning?" Laura glanced over at Inika and Mara Senez, returning from a treatment that would make their riotous curls more manageable, and then at their second Setari escort, the truly spectacular Zee Annan, who had not felt the need to have anything done to the long, silky braid she wore down her back. "That's the right name, yes? Year's Turning, for the celebration at mid-winter?"

"Yes," Zee smiled and lifted a long, elegant hand. "It's not something we track on Tare or Kolar, since there is not such a marked seasonal shift, but we've commemorated mid-winter and mid-summer these last two years."

"And because Cassandra decorates a tree in winter, much of Muina now does the same," Mara said, plopping down on the nearest chair. "In summer we give gifts of fruit and flowers. The years are so long here, so these mid-points are good to mark, and the small rituals make us feel we are honouring Muina."

The Muinans believed their home planet was a living being, and Laura was about to delicately delve into the question of whether they honoured Tare and Kolar similarly, but was distracted by an instant message.

Sue: *Check this out.*

Laura followed the link accompanying the message, and found herself watching the World Figure Skating Championships, with muted English commentary overlaid by a man excitedly speaking in Muinan.

"I wasn't expecting Serious Soldier to share it around," Sue said.

"I expect Gidds attached it to a report," Laura said. "And from there the world, it seems."

In the periphery of her vision Laura noticed Mara and Zee lift their heads and then exchange a brief but significant glance. Laura felt caught out, and then shook the reaction off. Gossip was inevitable. Gidds' first stay had probably been dismissed due to the weather, but there was no way he could have himself delivered to Arcadia before midnight and picked up the next day without someone putting two and two together. And whichever Setari had been assigned guard duty that night surely would have done so.

Laura would absolutely not be happy if her sex life was the next thing to show up on Muinan news channels.

"What is it shared around?" Inika asked.

Sue provided the link and, while the three Muinan women gazed into the middle distance, settled back to allow the hairdresser to make some final adjustments.

"Is it good?" the hairdresser—a man named Teffin—asked, tweaking a last stray hair into place.

"It's brilliant," Sue said positively, eyeing herself with satisfaction.

"Blue lemonade," Laura said. "With silver cachous floating in it."

"Yes!" Sue ran her fingers through what had been her blond-brown hair, and was now deep blue at the scalp, gradually lightening to a white-aqua. Whenever she moved, tiny white motes shimmered and faded. "Or stars reflected in the surf running up a beach at night, which is what I was aiming for. I love it."

"I do not at all understand what these people are doing," Anika commented. "They look like they're dancing on knives."

"Is this common on Earth?" Mara asked. "It looks very difficult."

"More common in colder countries than Australia," Sue said. "There's only a couple of ice skating rinks in Sydney."

"The floor really is ice? You walk on ice with knives?"

Sue explained as they finished up at the hairdressers.

"You can do this?" Zee asked, sounding fascinated.

"Me?" Sue laughed. "You won't ever catch me doing anything so athletic. I can stay upright on skates, but stopping is enough of a challenge."

"I've never tried," Laura said. "Alyssa's quite good, though I suppose she's out of condition at the moment. She never reached elite competition level, but her younger sister is trying to qualify. For ladies' singles, though, not ice dancing, which is what they're showing at the moment."

"If Cassandra had told us that Earth people dance on knives, I wouldn't have believed her," Mara said. "Although most of the other things she said turned out to be true. The 'volcano' and the 'tsunami'."

"We ended up believing her about the psychics and the Ionoth, too," Laura said, amused.

"Ignore her if she starts talking about drop-bears, though," Sue said, but then her eyes widened and she said: "I wonder if drop-bears would turn up as Ionoth on Earth, if there were tears into the Ena there."

"I'm not sure it would be the highest-priority nightmare. Though, who knows?" Laura remembered all too well the single Ionoth she'd seen 'in person': a thing that looked like it had been made of nails and old tyres, attacking Cass and Kaoren.

"Only a small number of the Ionoth that come through have any relation to the local environment," Mara said. "Shall we get going?"

"Can we walk to the school?" Laura asked. "It's not far."

Mara paused, eyes going distant, and then nodded.

Laura: *I will never be comfortable with the fact that they have to ask permission for us to take a ten-minute walk.*

Sue: *A twenty-minute walk, Long Legs. But yes, they're over-the-top. The vast majority of people here love Cass, or are at least grateful to her, and have no reason to attack us. And kidnapping us to try to get hold of a Touchstone just isn't going to work. The most that they'd achieve is upsetting Cass if we got killed.*

Laura: *Which is exactly why KOTIS guards us. What a quelling thought.*

Sue: *Worst of all, having hot bodyguards involves far less sexytimes than the movies would have me believe.*

Laura just managed to keep herself from laughing aloud as she followed their hot bodyguards out of the building and onto Moon Piazza, which was the ritzy section of Pandora, rimmed with buildings that could well have been modelled on the Royal Crescent in Bath—and featuring a statue of Laura's daughter, sitting at the feet of Muina, which was never not going to fill Laura with complicated feelings.

Pandora was a wonderful city to walk through. The Tarens and Kolarens had approached building their first city on their home planet by constructing an extensive subway system at the outset: a simple matter when reinforced tunnels could be directed to grow themselves. Most of the residential buildings were submerged into the hills, so that the 'suburbs' were miles of landscaped slopes with windows, and since air and hover transport was in common use, there was no need for paved roads. Instead the city featured walking paths alongside winding 'roads' of grass and flowers.

Since walking through fields of flowers—especially flowers she'd never seen before—ranked high on Laura's list of favourite things, she enjoyed herself thoroughly, the trip only mildly marred by the small but increasing number of people who trailed along behind them. Fans of Mara and Zee, Sue blithely informed them, and repeated a few choice pieces of the running commentary that was apparently lighting up the interface.

"It's difficult now that there are so many devices that do not have the same restrictions regarding image capture," Zee said. "The interest has always been there, and we knew it would inevitably include our children, but the spread of scans makes it feel more invasive."

"Speaking of which," Inika said, with barely a glance behind them, "do you have any more scans from the water picnic, Sue?"

They descended into an agreeable exchange of pictures as they walked through the most built-up section of Pandora, directly south of Moon Piazza. Here were large, blockish buildings, their stark white mass softened only a little by decorative patterning and the curving shapes of balconies. Pandora University, segueing into KOTIS headquarters, and then, at the edge of the lake, Pandora Shore School.

The school grounds were surrounded by a high, patterned wall, and it was necessary to pass through a checkpoint to enter, which at least rid them of their travelling audience.

"Nicely timed," Inika commented, as they strolled between playing fields and an auditorium. "The shoreline is lovely and peaceful here when the children are still in class."

These were words to inevitably summon trouble, and were rewarded so splendidly that, as their route took them to an unbroken view of the lake, Laura could barely take in what was happening.

Rocks. Boulders. Perhaps a dozen of them, ranging from the size of a suitcase to a small car. They spun in a wobbling double circle around the crouching figure of a young teenaged boy, and seemed to be picking up speed. A group of children on the far side of the scene broke and ran, but one boy—Laura recognised him as Shar, the older of Mara's two adopted sons—stepped neatly between the circling rocks and knelt beside the central figure, even as one of the larger stones spun out of formation and tumbled toward the scattering children.

Knowing who stood a foot to her right, Laura only half-choked, and then let out a relieved sigh as the stone lifted directly up, and then planted itself gently away from anything. In rapid order, the other rocks were similarly dealt with, four at a time. Zee was an extremely strong Telekinetic.

As soon as all the floating stone had been dealt with, Mara strode forward, not looking particularly surprised by the incident, and knelt beside her son, who was still talking gently to the apparent cause of the scene.

"I don't understand why, if he lost control, the rocks didn't just all fall down," Laura said to Zee, before realising that the second member of their Setari escort had moved a few feet away, and was gazing into the distance with the abstract expression Muinans adopted when talking over the interface.

"Because the stones were held up by Levitation, not Telekinesis," said a young, female voice helpfully. "Levitation is a manipulation of mass and gravity, and if that mass returns unevenly the result can be dangerous."

Laura turned to find at least two dozen children in the brown and black uniforms of Kalrani—trainee Setari— crowding out of the door of the auditorium to stare interestedly at the scene...and Sue and Laura.

"Thank you," Laura said, not sure which of the Kalrani had spoken. But then, meeting a pair of steady eyes, she was quite certain.

It was the modelling of the skull around the temples that gave it away. That very morning she'd traced a mirror of those delicate hollows. The girl was regarding her with complete calm, and offered her the faintest of nods in apparent acknowledgement of Laura's recognition. Then she turned away in response to a teacher's summons, and Laura was left blinking after her.

Since she had learned by this stage that Allidi was nearly thirteen, while Haelin had just turned nine, it was easy to guess identity, but Laura still confirmed by activating the interface function that allowed her to see people's names. Allidi Selkie.

Sight Sight talents. That added a daunting layer of complexity to the whole 'he has kids' situation. Laura doubted Gidds had told them that he'd embarked upon an affair, but that brief nod of Allidi's had been an outright signal of awareness. And children, no matter how self-assured, or psychically talented, or how much of the year they spent in military boarding schools, deserved care and consideration. Even if what Laura and Gidds had started faded away after a few more weeks, the relationship could be confronting or upsetting for Allidi and Haelin—and Julian and Cass, Laura supposed, though being older she expected them to be more sanguine.

Wondering if the girls' mother had also moved to Pandora, Laura trailed Inika and Sue down to where a small crowd of adults had descended from the air to take charge of the still-trembling Levitation talent—and a rather grey-in-the-aftermath Shar Annan.

"I know well enough that you won't have been encouraging that scene, Shar," Mara was saying. "But what possessed you to do anything but evacuate those nearby?"

"I was hoping I could keep him calm until there was a response to my alert," Shar said, rubbing his forehead. He was a deeply reserved boy, nearly sixteen by Earth metrics, and a rare survivor of Nuri's ruling class: a fact that—much to Mara's dismay—led many Nurans to treat him as an authority.

"Do you mind if I stay with Dezar a while longer?" he asked Mara now. "I can catch the next shuttle."

"So long as you're back in time for dinner," Mara told him, and watched with an expression caught between pride and exasperation as her son returned to the younger boy.

"Send him to Tare," Inika said, unexpectedly.

"What?"

"You're never going to get them to stop turning to him to settle disputes, and he's the kind of boy that will step forward if he sees someone in need. Bringing him out to the islands means he has some time away from it, but he's still too in reach of the Nuran community. Send him to Tare."

"I want him to have some peace, not exile him," Mara said, frowning after her son.

"There's that seniority gap on Tare," Zee said, coming up for the last of the conversation. "They were looking for some of us to rotate back there. If you and Lohn transferred for every second Taren year, Shar would have a few months at a time free to be himself, instead of the heir-presumptive of a destroyed world. And if he follows the science stream, well Tare's an excellent place for higher studies."

Mara looked irresolute, and further discussion was forestalled by the end of lessons for the day, and streams of students emerging—most heading past the auditorium to the security gates, but several handfuls drifting down to the waiting island shuttles.

"Unna!"

Sen, head of a small crowd of her age group, raced down for a hug, and then caught sight of Sue's hair and squeaked with delight.

"Looks awesome," Nick said, following in Sen's wake. "Like the ocean."

Sue beamed approvingly at him, and then lifted her eyebrows as Maddy came up, looking a little drawn, and obviously engaged in some sort of argument with Alyssa.

"Mrs Devlin," Maddy said to Laura, "Cass could make me a pair of skates, couldn't she? She can make anything."

"And everything she makes like that goes poof," Alyssa said, firmly. "Not to mention there's no rink."

"Ice is easy," Maddy said definitely. "Half the people I've met here can make ice. And Cass' projections don't vanish right away. I only need ten minutes to show them all I really can skate."

"If Cassandra creates a projection of one of those bladed boots, we can scan it and have a stable copy manufactured," Zee pointed out helpfully. "So you can dance on blades, Maddy?"

"It's easy."

"You haven't recovered enough," Alyssa said.

This, naturally, descended into a mild squabble. Maddy when healthy was headstrong and adventurous, and not at all inclined to treat her older sister as an authority. Sue did not technically have any more standing, but as head of household stepped in...and came down firmly on Maddy's side.

"With the proviso that there's no attempts at any jumps," Sue said. "Spinning in a circle, and zooming backward with your leg stuck out is surely impressive enough for any disbelieving crowd. Though where this little demonstration is going to take place, who is going to produce the ice and manufacture your boots, I leave to wiser heads." She sent a conspiratorial glance in Zee's direction. "You'd like to try it yourself, I suspect."

"If Maddy would consent to show me how," Zee said, very solemnly.

Alyssa's objections faded in the face of her sister's bright affirmation, and she agreed that Zee might look into arrangements.

Rye, Lira and Ys arrived at the tail-end of this discussion—along with the Kalrani girl who was Lira's designated protector for the day. Her duties ended at the dock, however, and Laura looked back to see her climbing the slope to join another girl in the brown and black uniform, one with a delicate frame, and short hair feathered close to her skull.

Allidi Selkie again, watching with quiet calm. Laura did not need Sight Sight to know she was being evaluated. It was a reminder that Gidds came as a package deal. Psychic daughters. Doubly daunting.

Resolutely, Laura put that issue away for later. She and Gidds had to first work out if there was a solid foundation beneath their attraction, something they could build upon. Whether they would enjoy sharing daily trivialities, and survive arguments, and open up to each other as they really hadn't yet.

She wished she didn't have to wait until next week to get him back into bed.

Chapter Ten

A white bird, trailing plumes of silver light, trilled a song that shaped words at the edge of hearing.

Ramara is dead. Zathar's heart breaks. The seams of the world divide. Bring light. Bring night. Bring life. Stitch the world together.

More than a few of the people around Laura paused to watch the bird disappear over the town's sloping roofs, but the majority ignored it, for the Messengers of the Weaver were a regular occurrence.

Non-player compared to player characters, Laura wondered. *Or newbies versus higher level?*

It really was very difficult to pick out the players from the computer-controlled characters. The Muinans didn't have true artificial intelligence, but their simulations were so sophisticated that much of their basic schooling was conducted by a pair of complex programs. Standing on the bridge into Tekan Town, Laura gazed at travellers heading in every direction and could not pick out the kind of set routines that would give an NPC away.

Then she wondered whether she would be able to spot Gidds without turning on the names display.

Would he have made a character that looked just like himself, except blue? Or simply have gone with a default model, and not wasted his time on customisation? Laura usually chose chibi models herself—she was always entertained viewing a game world from the viewpoint of chubby little gnomes or tarutaru—but *Red Exchange* did not have the range of races she was used to, so she'd made herself someone who rather strongly resembled Romana II from *Doctor Who*. A blue English Rose.

Laura sighed, and briefly opened her eyes, the game world receding to a square on her internal 'screen'. She was in her window seat, which was actually a tiny room all of its own, built into the roof level of her house. It was only accessible via a spiral stair from her workroom, was the one room that had a view of the southern reaches of the lake, and featured the most ridiculously luxurious adaptable couch. Filling its own glass-walled nook, the couch was very similar to the ones used on the interplanetary ships, and could be raised and adjusted to all sorts of sitting and reclining positions. Cass had certainly had a lot of fun thinking up things Laura would like in a house.

Although interface games could stimulate the other senses, allowing players to touch, taste, and smell virtual worlds, they did not remove players from the real world, and it had taken time for Laura to grow used to the sensation of being in two places and two people at once. Today it was doubly difficult, because she'd fallen ingloriously while exploring the rocks on Arcadia's northern shore that morning, and the resulting bruise was making its presence felt.

At least being in the game world didn't involve any actual effort. Closing her eyes again, Laura thought about walking, and Romana-Angharad obligingly strolled along the street, looking around.

Tekan Town was most definitely worth looking at. It was built across a series of very perpendicular hills, with most of the structures up near the peaks, while the valleys beneath were narrow and filled with fast-running water. Everything was connected by bridges: arches of stone, enormous tree branches adapted for walking, and even the occasional swaying rope construction. In a non-game world, Laura expected such a place would be frighteningly windy, but Tekan Town was a balmy haven, the branches festooned with flowers, the stone bridges decorated with great urns of greenery, and even the rope bridges wound through with vines of what smelled very like jasmine.

Between the bridges, many of the hilltops had been neatly lopped off to provide a flat surface for construction, while others had been hollowed into pointed mountain cathedrals where traders gathered to set up market stalls. The whole place was dizzying, not least because of the layered floral perfume, and made Laura wonder if there were swamp regions in *Red Exchange,* and whether the programmers would focus on scent to the same extent there.

There was certainly plenty of potential for too much reality in a virtual game, and Laura could readily imagine others where immersion would be a bad idea. She certainly would never have lasted through *Resident Evil* if she'd been able to *smell* the zombies.

The arrangement with Gidds had been to meet at the fountain on Porphery Mountain—the centre point of Tekan Town. Laura had been aiming to arrive a little early, but had misjudged her path, and quickened her pace in order to reach the broad plaza almost precisely on time.

Wouldn't want to be late for our first date, she thought, smiled at the idea, and then looked around for her Serious Soldier.

Gidds had not chosen a default model—at least not from Laura's memory of the various selections—and there was no distinct resemblance, but the young man sitting on the rim of the round central pool was still unmistakeable. Upright but relaxed, his hands resting on his knees, ineffably himself.

Laura did turn on the names display, just to be sure, and saw 'Ruvord', which was the name he'd told her he'd use. He'd chosen a similar build to his own, but with a squarer face, and longer hair, which was caught back into a high, short ponytail.

"Gidds."

He turned to her, his brief smile surfacing as he stood, and they clasped hands. No kisses this time, which Laura suspected would have been not quite comfortable for both of them, in their blue-skinned guises.

"Not too tired?" she asked, for while it was midday on Arcadia, it was close to midnight halfway around the world where he'd been stationed.

He shook his head. "Now that the Conclave is over, I've much more control over my timetable, so I simply slept for much of the afternoon and evening, making this functionally mid-morning for me. I have only just started, however, and haven't yet completed the first contract of the game."

"Neither have I," Laura said. "Since we were going to travel together, I haven't been playing. I found out the game's based on a long series of books, and read the first one of those instead."

"Background research?"

She laughed at the approving note in his voice. "It helped me understand the system a little more, but not the particular teszen that is supposed to be my first contract. They're all very individual."

Gidds hadn't even spoken to his yet, but since both of the spirits were located on the White Plateau, they decided to travel to meet his, and then work on solutions to both contracts.

"Is the name Ruvord significant to you?" she asked, as they climbed the intricately worked ramp-bridge that led up to the Plateau.

"A famous Taren explorer. From the Caverns Era."

Tare was an extremely unhospitable planet, all oceans and storms, and the early Taren settlers had lived almost entirely underground. A lot of Tarens still weren't at all comfortable with concepts like 'outside'—let alone animals or insects.

"I hope he didn't end up meeting a grue," she said lightly, and then explained the game ZORK, and the Great Underground Empire, and monsters that attacked only in the dark.

That conversational tangent was the result of long deliberation. Sue was right: even if he tried, Gidds could never catch up, just as Laura did not expect to ever be really well-versed in a thousand years or so of Taren-Kolaren-Muinan history, literature, and social conventions. She could build new experiences with Gidds, true, but simply leaving out of their relationship all the things that made Laura her very own self did not seem to her any better an idea than ignoring things that were important to him.

There was no way she could ever have a conversation with him like those she shared with Sue, but she had decided the only way to bring him into the frame of reference through which she habitually viewed the world was simply to explain as they went along. He gave ZORK the same focused absorption he'd brought to her description of Earth's political complications.

"It doesn't sound a very enjoyable game," he said, after she had outlined one of the first computer games she had ever played: a text adventure puzzle that required hundreds of replays to solve, and forgave not a single misstep.

"I'm not sure I'd have the patience for it now," she agreed, as they began following a rutted road across the broad, flat plateau that functioned as farmland for the town. "But back then...computers are less than a Muinan century old on Earth, and computer games only started to become widely available when I was in my teens. Everything was fascinating. And though they were far less complex, and often a good deal harder, they still involved a lot of things I really enjoy: puzzles, exploring new places, experiencing incredible stories. Even just the idea of what they represented fascinated me. I spent endless hours in *Elite,* a space merchant game that involved very little story, simply because I loved imagining myself with my own ship, flying from planet to planet." She glanced at the unfamiliar, square-cut profile of his avatar. "What part of these games causes negative reactions for Sight talents?"

He side-stepped a large puddle before answering. "For Sight Sight, the layering of false on real. Enhanced reality games are the most problematic, perhaps because they usually attempt to make the projections of the game seem true, but this sort of game feels more like watching an entertainment so long as interactions involving touch are minimised. Touch can still lead to a sensation like vertigo, while sight and sound are not so difficult. And it's a very bad idea to try to eat anything."

"I tried to eat a piece of fruit and didn't need Sight Sight to think it a bad idea," Laura said, grimacing. "It tasted exceptionally odd. Of course, it was glowing green, so possibly it was meant to be a bad idea. What about Place Sight?"

"Place Sight is in some ways easier, since for the most part there is no difficulty touching virtual objects or people. But Place can react to the ideas or intentions of the game's creators. Someone, for instance, was inordinately proud of the design of the bridge up to these fields. And games which include depictions of torture or suffering, or other very negative extremes, can be more than unpleasant. This...I will need to evaluate it longer, but I think I will be able to safely approve it for the Kalrani." His brief smile surfaced as he glanced at her. "And I also enjoy exploration and puzzles."

He's well aware that I'm *evaluating* him, Laura thought, as she smiled back.

"Did your daughters inherit your Sights?"

"Combat and Sight Sight," he said. "And Path Sight from their mother. Neither has Place."

"Do you regret that?"

He hesitated. "A little. Place Sight has many challenges, but it is also the most profound Sight to experience. It adds so much richness to my life."

They had reached a signpost, and Gidds paused to fish a card from the pocket of the simple tunic his avatar wore.

Laura had received a card of her own during the game tutorial, and been instructed to follow it to her first teszen.

The four-way signpost was decorated not with words, but with simple pictures. Gidds' compared the sketched symbols on his card, and turned in the direction of 'sheep'. Then he glanced at her, and she suspected that he had caught the sudden flash of hilarity she'd experienced, at the idea of him making a contract with some kind of sheep spirit.

"Does it feel limiting to be in a virtual environment?" she asked, to cover herself.

"For Place Sight, it is a matter of constantly reaching for something that isn't there. Sight Sight, which is more subtle, does not feel so absent—and also triggers more reliably on images alone. Although I don't need any talents to tell me you've hurt your leg in some way."

"Really? How can you tell?"

"You keep limping. The impulse controls for your avatar are responding to the pain you feel outside the game."

Laura hadn't noticed. A little embarrassed, she explained her excursion onto Arcadia's rocky southern bank. "It's nothing serious: a bruise."

"Would you find it intrusive if, for instance, Kaoren visited in a few kasse? Not entirely coincidentally."

She laughed, pleased that he'd been upfront instead of just trying to organise her. "He'll be doing that anyway— I'm having the whole family over for dinner. And then Cass will probably try to mother me, which I find wholly disconcerting. She's matured so much."

"She has grown into herself," Gidds said, considering another signpost, and then turning in the direction of the painted outline of a house.

The road took them past a number of the 'hairy' sheep clearly based on those found on Muina, and into a tidy farmyard. Here Laura was entirely distracted from hunting spirits by Zylat Island's version of a chicken:

banded brown and white feathered creatures that reacted to their arrival by scampering up trees and the sides of the farmhouse, and filling the air with excited 'glock' noises as they goggled down at the intruders.

"These were in the book I read," Laura said. "They're called goo-glucks."

And the thought of Gidds making a contract with a spirit representing the excitable climbers produced another jolt of hilarity, followed by a second glance. No matter how muted his Sights, he could definitely tell when she was being amused at his expense.

"Perhaps a contract with their teszen would offer speed," he said, unfazed. "Or claws."

He turned over the card, checking for further symbols, but—unsurprisingly for a newbie quest—they'd already arrived at their destination, and so he held it up in accordance with the instructions given by the representative of the Weaver. Nothing happened.

"How long did you wait?"

"It only took a moment for me. I was led to a pond, and when I held the card up there was an immediate ripple, and a voice that managed to be both very wet and very crotchety snapped 'No talking until you give me what I want most'. I'm not even—oh, I think something's happening."

Around Gidds' feet, motes of dust stirred and lifted. A fragment of straw whirled upward and stopped directly in front of his eyes, spinning gently.

"*...is a man?*"

The words were barely audible, a whisper on the wind. Gidds tilted his head ever so slightly, then said: "It is."

"*...what does man want?*"

"Your strength." Gidds was just as serious talking to a piece of straw as he was with anything else Laura had seen him do. "The land of Ramara has fractured and fallen beneath the ocean. We are gathering allies to heal the damage that has spread from her fall, so the land of Zathar does not share her fate."

"...*don't care. Ramara, Zathar, not here. Only care Zylat.*"

"If Zathar falls, Thetis will follow. And after Thetis, Mris, and Kaztar and Zylat. In return for your aid, I offer my blood."

"...*eat man?*"

"Yes," Gidds said, with perfect gravity. "Blood in exchange for your aid."

"...*eat man,*" the wind repeated, and the piece of straw whirled faster, slashing Gidds' avatar's face and leaving a tiny purplish line. A dark droplet of blood escaped the line, and a mote of light bloomed, burning it away. The light lifted, circled Gidds once, and then dropped to rest upon his hand.

It vanished, along with the wind, and Laura stepped forward to study the mark it had left behind. A tiny spiral of pale blue, slightly raised.

"Like a brand," she said. "Did it hurt?"

"Momentarily."

"Well, I don't think that was the teszen of the goo-glucks. You seem to have done some background research of your own."

"I asked many questions when I joined the Path of the Weaver." He looked around the farmyard thoughtfully, and his brief smile surfaced as he glanced up at the dozens of climbing birds still sporadically letting out their signature call. "I do wonder what their teszen would be. It is an interesting idea, to give every part of the world a motive force."

"A bit like Shintoism," Laura said, and explained that as they started back toward the route to her starter teszen.

"This isn't one of the belief systems you described in our briefing sessions."

"Earth has a lot of religions," Laura said, shrugging. "I'm surprised the Triplanetary has so strongly kept to planet-spirit reverence, especially when it only seems to be Muina herself that has ever responded in a verifiable way." She hesitated, aware that while there was some debate among Muinan descendants as to what exactly the spirit of Muina constituted, most treated the planet quite factually as a living creator entity.

"Which of Earth's beliefs do you follow?" Gidds asked.

"Oh, well, I'm an atheist.   I'm sure—have had demonstrated by coming here, in fact—that there are powers that Earth's science hasn't yet come to understand or acknowledge, but Earth's gods have always seemed to me to be explanations that developed into complexities."

"And so you don't believe that Earth, like Muina, lives?"

"I believe it's a living planet, and deserves our care for that reason alone. I've never seen any sign that it's a *thinking* entity." She sighed. "Of course, I'd say the same thing about Muina if it weren't for the fact that there appears to be a place in Kalasa where people can experience some form of communication with...something. Do you believe that it's really the planet?"

"Yes." He was direct, firm. "I had never been certain before visiting Kalasa.   But I could not say whether the same core exists for other worlds."

As they followed the route on Laura's card, they discussed the theories around Muina's resemblance to Earth—one of which was that it was a 'created' planet.

"Does the possibility bother you?" she asked. "I know that Cass was originally very worried how people would react, but she seems to have been far from the only person to think of that explanation, and I've seen some heated debates on the newsnets."

"I would like to know, but it is more an abstract question for me. Rather than clinging to a preferred truth, I will accept whatever is proven—in the unlikely event that a definitive judgment is ever made. Fortunately Sight Sight is not inflicting a strong *need* to have an answer."

"Do you —" Laura began, but then spotted the lone, overhanging tree that had been her second symbol. "Here's my demanding pool."

No ripples disturbed the water when they reached the rock-lined rim. It was an eerie spot, tucked away in a little hollow, and very still.

"I tried to ask it for more information, but it didn't react any further. Admittedly, I didn't try for very long, since, well..." She paused, turned, and met his eyes. "I stopped for a nightcap."

Even through an avatar, the doubled-intensity effect hit her. He reached for her hands, and squeezed them tightly.

"Your assignment is still due to finish in two days, right?

"Yes." One word that said a great deal, and most of it involved being naked. "After that, I will have a month primarily working with Kaoren at Kalasa, and can travel from Pandora via the teleport platforms."

"Does touching things in this game really give you vertigo?"

A small grimace. "Yes, unfortunately." But it was a moment more before he let go of her hands. Then he asked: "Would you like me to tell you the probable solution for the teszen?"

She blinked at him, saw that he was—of course—perfectly serious, and let out her breath in laughing exasperation. "Now was it your Sights that gave you the answer, or simple observation?"

"At times it is difficult to separate the two. But in this case, a thing you will be able to see."

"Well, that's something at least. If I can't figure it out, I'll ask for a hint, but it's heartening that there's something apparently so completely obvious you spotted it straight away."

Making an effort to avoid preconceptions, Laura looked carefully around, not initially seeing anything different than before. Tree. Rocks. A few little ferns. Water that was clear, though in the shade, so it looked quite black.

A tracery of silver.

"There's a lesson in this about looking beyond the surface," Laura said, kneeling so she could better peer into the water. The silver was not a fish, but a line, a slender chain dropping deep into the centre of the pool. Its end was fastened to a spur of rock almost at her feet.

Laura lifted the fine, chilly links. The chain was thin, but not so fragile she couldn't begin drawing it from the water, handful after careful handful. Ten feet. Twenty. A little pile of silver began to mound beside her.

"How deep can this pool be?" she asked, leaning forward. "I think I can see something coming up."

Gidds had knelt beside her, steadying her against the possibility of impromptu baths, but there was no difficulty pulling the last of the chain from the pool, and with it a small metal cage. Inside, was a sodden ball that, as she set the cage down, partially unwound into something scrawny and distinctly feline, grey hair clumped into wet spikes.

"Now this is just cruel," Laura said. "What a place to keep a cat."

Cat? Cat? The voice was just as crotchety as the first time she'd heard it, though rather less wet. *Woman is blind.*

"I certainly haven't been winning any points for observation," she agreed, examining the fastening of the small, square cage, and then trying to get a grip on the pin that was holding it in place. "What should I call you, if 'cat' is so very wrong?"

Kirr-tut! Woman knows nothing.

"Well, I'm new around here. But learning fast."

Gidds offered Laura a small stone, and she used it to knock the pin free, then watched with fascination as the kirr-tut slithered out the moment the door opened. It was as much marten or weasel as cat—a long and snaky furred animal—but with very cat-like high pointed ears and a wedge-shaped skull. It stretched, and shook itself, and made a sound like an exasperated sneeze.

What woman want?

"Your strength," Laura said, with a quick smile across at Gidds. "To prevent all the world from following Ramara beneath the waves. In return, I offer you blood."

Ramara drowned. Disdain shot through the kirr-tut's annoyance. *Yes. Will help.*

Before Laura could respond, it nipped her—the pain sharp and unexpected enough that she jerked and briefly opened her eyes onto the view from her window seat.

The brand that sealed her first contract was a paw print on the inside of her wrist. Laura regarded it with disproportionate pride for how little effort it had cost her.

"Not that I'm altogether sure what I've gained, unless it's a grumpiness mode. Somehow cross, damp not-a-cat will help me heal holes in the world."

They walked back to the city, discussing the similarities in the game to the crisis that had nearly seen the destruction of Muina, Tare and Kolar.

"And yet with no Ionoth," Laura said. "Forming contracts and healing damage, and so far as I can tell any combat is with nodes of 'corruption'."

"I like it," Gidds said, definitely. "I will have a second evaluation made by another instructor, and if they pass it, approve it for the Kalrani."

And then perhaps they would take another considered step toward each other. Dating, and thinking of introducing family.

Laura felt ready for it.

CHAPTER ELEVEN

Gidds' return from Arenrhon coincided with Laura's weekly family meal with Sue and the kids. Laura was not given to making announcements about her sleeping arrangements, but thought the meal a good opportunity to shift to semi-publicly dating, and so warned Julian there'd be an extra guest. She was fairly sure her son would be a little surprised but not especially upset when he saw who it was: it had to have been a good ten years since he and Cass had given up hoping Laura and Mike would get back together.

The plan had been for Gidds to arrive early to help with preparation, and this time he arrived at her door exactly on time, with a small overnight case in one hand, and a box of a Kolaren treat called keffet balanced on the other.

Laura took him to bed.

Not at all sensible, but very satisfying, and, after all, it had been the better part of a week since they'd seen each other. Besides, she only had him for the night: he would be leaving again almost immediately, to take his daughters away for the weekend. She only wished she'd thought to have him arrive even earlier.

"Fortunately I'd done most of the dinner prep already," she said, not inclined to get up immediately. "I think we can spare a few more minutes and still be able to safely pretend that we've just been exchanging mild pleasantries and asking how our days have gone."

"The truth would perhaps suggest that I've lost any ability to focus on the task at hand," Gidds said, though with an entirely pleased note to his voice.

Laura smiled, tracing a finger along his collarbone. "You're very distracting." Then, carefully, because she was still disinclined to rush anything, she added: "Though that distraction makes it hard to see you, sometimes. And I'm trying very hard to see you clearly, Gidds."

He understood her. The sheer natural intensity of the man increased to the point where she felt dizzy, and he responded with a bruising kiss, although did not follow up with declarations. He knew—had no doubt in his Sighted way known from the night of the hailstorm—that a part of her kept pulling away from him. He was not going to push the pace beyond what she found comfortable, although she had a strong suspicion he wanted to. Sight Sight talents were given to certainties.

Since dinner guests were imminent, they managed to postpone further indulgence in favour of a quick shower. Here Gidds paused to examine a large yellow-green blotch down her left thigh.

"You've had it treated."

"Yes. Being related to a clutch of Sight talents does cut down on the space for quiet stoicism." She smiled ruefully at the memory. "Kaoren was frowning at me the moment he walked into the room, and Sen was almost distressed, insisting I sit down. Cass sent Ys for a very useful salve, and extracted a promise to come with them on the school shuttle the next morning so I could visit a KOTIS medic. Then she took over cooking."

"I see where Cassandra learned her habit of not informing anyone when she is upset or hurt. What is 'stoicism'?"

Laura explained as they dressed, and they returned to the kitchen well before anyone arrived to wonder at the abandoned crepe batter.

"Did you have to report yourself for spending the night with me, as Kaoren was obliged to with Cass?" she asked, taking bowls of fillings out of the refrigerator, and giving Gidds those that didn't need to be heated.

"I had myself taken out of your family's supervision chain," he said. "And made a private report that would not have been necessary if I were not a KOTIS officer. While there is not quite the same strict management around Cassandra now that the crisis has passed, there will always be a level of control regarding interaction with both her and Liranadestar, and that washes over to you."

Too dangerous. Too valuable. Laura didn't particularly like that KOTIS literally had a committee monitoring developments with her family, but she understood it. Her daughter and granddaughter could be used to reshape reality.

"What happens when Lira, almost inevitably, pushes back on that?"

"Isten Notra has recommended continuing to give her as much freedom as possible without sacrificing security concerns," Gidds said. "Fortunately the decision to allow her to remain with the Ruuel Devlins has proven to be a good one, since they are a steadying influence on a personality which is considerably more volatile than Cassandra's. But she has been testing her limits—most recently by attempting to stymie the Kalrani set to be her security detail."

"Does she try to leave school grounds?"

"No. She doesn't wish to put herself in danger, only demonstrate her opinion of KOTIS."

Lira, in the days of old Muina, had been kidnapped and used to power a machine that had almost destroyed her world, and left her in a state that was not quite dead or alive. Even though Muina's current inhabitants did not fully understand the machinery involved, it was not in the least surprising that Lira wanted to avoid any possibility of the same thing happening.

"Mum! Guess what, I—" Julian, galloping at his usual pace down the stair, checked at the sight of Gidds, who was wearing his uniform minus the jacket, and in the process of putting bowls of filling on the table. But Julian simply switched to Muinan to say: "Hi Tsur Selkie. Hey, are we having crepes? How much grated cheese is there?"

"Feel free to top it up," Laura said, pushing a covered bowl toward him. "What am I guessing?"

"Wouldn't be guessing if I told you, would it? What have we got to drink? Can I put some spider milk on?"

"If you can manage to heat it without spreading it over everything this time," Laura said, smiling at him.

"Spider milk?" Gidds repeated, carefully sounding out the English phrase Julian had dropped into his question.

"It's just what we call the juice of those Taren dozai fruit," Laura explained. "Once we saw what it came from."

Dozai juice, when heated, tasted like syrupy coconut milk, and the fruit resembled coconuts—if you replaced thick brown coconut husk with fragile white filaments.

"They just *say* it's a fruit," Julian said, opening and closing cupboard doors with as much noise as anti-slam hinges would allow. "Nothing's going to convince me there's not something with too many legs laying those things."

"These spiders are large?" Gidds asked.

"Only in nightmares," Laura said, and waved a spatula at Nick and Alyssa, as they arrived. "There's plenty of them about on Muina, though on Tare the closest seems to be what are called ferat. Although ferat are much larger than Earth spiders." Ferat were eight-legged things twice the size of human hands, and a powerful reason never to venture into the few 'natural' caves remaining on Tare.

"Are we having spider milk?" Sue asked, following Alyssa. "Do you have any of the flavouring that tastes like pistachio left?"

"Maybe," Julian said, emptying the carton of dozai juice into a saucepan and remembering—this time—to put the lid on before setting it to heat. "The zingy flavours are way better."

"Where's Maddy?" Laura said, watching Alyssa and Nick exchange a quick glance before murmuring their hellos to Gidds.

"Taking off her skates," Sue said, giving Gidds a wide, highly entertained grin. "No interplanetary crisis this time?"

"I usually avoid them," Gidds replied, with his usual equanimity.

Sue: *I can never decide if he's the most literal man in the universe, or secretly funny.*

Laura did not have a response for this, and instead said: "So the copies have arrived?" as Maddy belatedly trotted through the patio doors.

"Yes, and they even managed to get the size right," Maddy said, energetically depositing herself wrong-way around on one of the dining chairs. "My feet have gotten bigger, but they made a couple of different pairs around my size. Now all we need is the ice." She glanced at Gidds, plainly not altogether sure who he was, but switching to Muinan to say, with the long halts that showed she was repeating phrases sounded out to her by the interface: "Do you have an Ice talent, mister? We could freeze Aunt Laura's pond and I could try out my skates."

"Too small," Alyssa said, even as Gidds shook his head. "You'd run right into the edges, Maddy. Wait until tomorrow afternoon."

"You're the one who wants to make sure you're not totally out of condition when bunches of people aren't around."

"Tomorrow afternoon?" Gidds said in Muinan, his expression suggesting a mild revelation. "For a half-kasse after the end of the school day?"

"We're using the school swimming pool," Alyssa said, eyeing him cautiously. "It's still too small, but it'll do to show Maddy's friends she really can skate. Though the whole thing's turning into a total circus, with half the school and every second Setari squad inviting themselves along."

"Including at least one of the Kalrani, I suspect," Gidds said. "It's rare Haelin postpones one of our outings."

"You're Haelin's dad?" Maddy asked, brightening. "We started at Pandora Shore on the same day. We're only in a couple of the same classes, though, because mostly she has Kalrani lessons. Our feet are the same size, so she's going to try out my skates when I get tired."

Gidds seemed to follow the tangle of English and Muinan easily enough, and said simply: "Thank you for allowing that."

Laura paused in turning out crepes to rescue a near overflow of spider milk, then listened in mild appreciation as Gidds began to ask about skating, and Alyssa opened up over the technicalities of producing a rink on Earth, and how much or little the double edges of the blades needed sharpening. Gidds maintained his usual relaxed but upright posture, listening far more than he spoke.

It wasn't until the crepes were near-demolished, and the spider milk all gone, that Julian moved from casting Gidds brief sidelong glances onto a small experiment.

"Hey, Tsur Selkie," he said. "What would you do if I went to the moonfall tomorrow night?"

Pandora's moonfall was a weekly event centred on the ruins of the old Muinan town that had been the settlement's starting point. It was actually a process to draw the teleport system's energy source, 'aether', from the Ena, and was spectacular to look at, with glowing mist seeming to rise toward the moon. But aether—although it had something of a healing effect on Muinan citizens—also acted very much like alcohol. The planetary government had quickly had to set access regulations in place.

Gidds response to Julian's question was a straightforward: "Nothing."

"I can at least tell you what *I'd* do," Laura said, annoyed. "Which would start with reminding you that you need to be legally an adult."

"Yeah, but that was a hint, Mum," Julian said, with a suggestion of a shrug.

"Did you pass the technically-grown-up exam, brat?" Sue asked. "No fair beating me there."

Laura joined the spate of congratulations that followed Julian's nod, although it was very odd to now have both her children possessing a wider range of rights than she had. Especially since there was more than an Earth year to go before Julian turned eighteen. But she wasn't going to let him off trying to draw Gidds into this particular boundary test, looking at her son steadily until he ducked his head.

"Some of my guild from *Red Exchange* live in Pandora, and they finally got to the head of the queue to go to the moonfall," Julian explained. "Corezzy said if I passed I could go as his guest, and since most people wear masks to control the aether intake a bit, I thought it would be fun to go and not have people know who I was."

Laura's immediate reaction involved a firm decision to spend some time with Julian in-game in order to do some initial vetting of this 'Corezzy'—or anyone else inviting her teenaged son to go get drunk. Moonfall attendance might be thoroughly monitored, and the interface something of an in-built policeman, but it was not as if the Triplanetary was without crime or bad intentions.

Gidds, meanwhile, responded informatively: "Tsien Faluden, who is currently managing Arcadia's security arrangements, would likely assign two Setari to accompany you. They would, of course, need to wear Exclusion Suits, to prevent the aether from affecting them."

Julian's response to this prospect was as enthusiastic as could be expected. "Hard pass."

"Which is your primary objective?" Gidds asked. "To experience moonfall, or to meet your friends without the burden of identity?"

Julian blinked at Gidds' phrasing, and Sue—watching with an amused smile—said: "A bit of both, I'd bet."

"Moonfall is easier," Gidds told them. "Since you could ask to visit one of the undeveloped platform towns. They are all monitored, but many have no settlements, and it would be easy to arrange a visit with less intrusive security." He looked across at Laura. "Or a family outing."

Laura glanced at Sue—and carefully only at Sue—then said: "I admit I'm curious. I don't think I'd care to copy Cass' experience of passing out in the centre of town, but the images look amazing. A walk through one of the towns before the aether concentration rose too high might work."

"Sounds like fun," Sue said easily. "I'm in. Provided I can ever pass this stupid adulthood exam."

"But what about me?" Maddy protested. "I can't do that exam, but I want to go and see what it's like too!"

"You were double-dipped in aether the whole of the first month you were here," Alyssa said, with just the faintest frown. "You know what it's like."

"It doesn't count when you're sick. I don't even remember that. Besides, I want to *look* at it."

"She could wear one of those Exclusion Suits," Nick said, mildly. He turned to Gidds. "If they have any in her size."

"They do. I will process a request for you."

They moved on to dessert then, and ate the star-shaped keffet, a chewy, jellified citrus pulp, while Maddy interrogated Gidds on the details of Kalrani training.

Sue: *Do I get to call him your boyfriend now?*

Laura: *Unless you prefer 'gentleman caller'.*

Sue: *I wonder what he'd look like in a natty morning suit and a monocle? But, okay, you've had the meet-cute, the hot-and-heavy, and set him before the family to admire.*

What comes next? The ex-wife turning up with a spanner to throw in the works? Or the Big Misunderstanding?

Laura: *Neither, I'd hope. Spending some time with his daughters.*

Sue: *No more wibbling?*

Laura shrugged at that, and Sue smiled, and gripped Laura's hand in brief, silent encouragement. Laura had to admit she was feeling optimistic. And the next month would at the least involve a great deal of being ruined for other men.

Although it was the afterwards that she was beginning to look forward to most. She liked to touch him when they were curled together, both too replete for it to be sexual.

"Are you going to join the crowd to watch Haelin try out Maddy's ice skates?" she asked much later that night, after the exertion, the lingering shower, and the comfortable positioning beneath sheets.

The faintest shake of his head. "The Setari and Kalrani won't be able to be fully at ease if I'm there. And Haelin— even now my behaviour with Haelin and Allidi is examined for hints of favouritism. That will be why she didn't tell me just why she wanted to delay the outing I had arranged with her."

Of course. The Principal's daughters: considered privileged, no matter how impartial he strove to be.

"It bothered your Sights. Not to know."

"Yes. It's rare that they don't tell me things they know might trigger a Sight reaction. But it is important for me to demonstrate a decision not to ask when information isn't volunteered. Although, on that subject..." He slid his hand down her arm, and linked fingers. "Is the tension that rose around the discussion of the moonfall something you can tell me about? You were annoyed at Julian, but deeply worried for Nick."

"Yes." Laura grimaced, then sighed. "There's no secret to any of that. Well, not on Earth. Sue handles it far better than I, which is typical of Sue. She is...well, you can't miss that she's a very vibrant person, but she's also had more than her share of hurdles. She started out full of music, you know. Ever since she was tiny she'd play anything and everything she could get her hands on, but particularly the violin. Almost didn't need lessons. But she started going deaf when she was eight. She stuck with music for quite a few years, but lost almost all the high pitches, and then the lower ranges faded, and hearing aids only helped a bit. When she was fourteen she put down all her instruments, and hasn't picked them up since."

"Even though that has been corrected now?"

"She's been listening to a lot of music since we came here—Muinan and Terran—but she hasn't gone near any instruments. Back when her hearing loss was shifting from moderate to severe, she took up photography instead. And proved to be extremely good at that as well, making quite a reputation for herself, particularly with landscape photography. She was on assignment in Western Australia—wildflower season—when she met Nick and Nick's dad, Sam Dale."

Laura lay silent, thinking back to first impressions and happy years. Gidds waited, rubbing a thumb on the palm of one of her hands, and eventually she went on.

"They married about two days after they met. Sam's a writer—non-fiction books with a sideline of articles—and they ended up collaborating on a lot of things: Sue doing the photography for the articles he wrote. Nick is his mirror image, in looks and personality. Laconic-ironic, I think of it. Nick was ten when Sue and Sam married, and he took to Sue right away. She adored him. Everything was great."

The kind of life people envied. Shared interests. A beautiful home. Frequent international trips.

"The Dales had been in a car crash when Nick was just little. Nick came through unhurt, Sam was injured, and Maria—Nick's birth mother—was killed. Sam had been driving, and he fell apart for the better part of a year afterwards, then pulled himself together for Nick. But he'd been left with chronic pain, and when Nick was fifteen it flared up badly. He self-medicated with alcohol—something he hadn't touched since that year after the accident—and..."

Laura faltered, stomach twisting. Then she remembered just how Gidds would be experiencing this tale, and started to draw back, murmuring an apology.

Gidds stopped her. "I am more than capable of shifting myself, if there is something I can't face," he said firmly.

Laura sighed, but then gripped his hand. "One night—past midnight—I got a call from Nick. He was at the hospital. Sue had a fractured skull. Poor kid, he had to tell me how she got it."

Laura could not stop herself reliving that midnight trip to the hospital, Cass and Julian in tow because they were too young to leave behind and Bet and Steve had been out of town. Nick in the waiting room, outwardly composed, but shivering, constantly shivering, no matter how hard she hugged. Finally being allowed to see Sue: small and bruised and so very still.

"Sue left the marriage after that. Even if Sam had managed to keep himself sober—which he didn't—there was no way to come back. She wanted custody of Nick, but his maternal grandparents won that argument: Sue could only manage to get him for family trips. After the divorce, Sam tried to dry out—to stop drinking—but couldn't, and has struggled a great deal with depression ever since. When Nick was eighteen, which is legal adulthood in Australia, he moved back in with his father. And that...helped Sam."

"The boy had an eye injury," Gidds said. "When Cassandra visited your family through the Ena."

"Yes. Nick pulled Sam out of the hole, but he couldn't move him away from the edge. And when Sam relapses, he lashes out blindly at whoever's in reach. Doesn't even seem to recognise them. But we failed completely to convince Nick to put his own well-being first. He wasn't even going to come here, despite he and Alyssa being so close, and I know for certain he's worried about how Sam is holding up because he's no longer there with him. I'll never forgive Sam for hurting Sue, but I am grateful for the moment of clarity that made him push Nick through the gate to Muina."

"And you fear the boy might become distressed during a moonfall?"

"I don't know. Nick faces situations relating to alcohol with complete aplomb. He'll even accept a drink to be social, but I've never seen him finish one. He never gives any hint he's bothered by anyone drinking around him, but we worry about him."

"I will arrange for Exclusion Suits for all of you, then," Gidds said. "It will allow you to experience a moonfall at its height, and control your exposure."

Laura thanked him, but searched his expression at the same time. "Will you find yourself being accused of favouritism because of your relationship with me?"

That brought out his flicker of a smile. "Not beyond those who would criticise me for breathing. I would be more likely held to account if I didn't arrange something like this. Don't underestimate who you are. The debt owed to your daughter is literally impossible for us to repay, because she allowed us to use her to regain our home world, and to save ourselves. Cassandra is the reason we are alive."

His expression had become very still, although his voice remained clear and steady as he went on: "And, when she was trapped in the facility that was the source of our problems, I am the person who gave the order to detonate charges rather than continue to try to rescue her."

Laura had known that already, although she'd not thought about it in quite those terms. It had obviously been weighing on Gidds.

"So you did," she said. "I don't know how I would have felt if she hadn't lived through that, but when the decision is between everyone definitely dying including Cass, or Cass alone possibly dying, I'm fairly sure she and I have similar views." She paused, because his expression had remained very still and shuttered. "It would have made every difference if Cass had died. But, so far as I understand that situation, setting off those charges saved her life, even if the entire building did drop on her head in the aftermath. I've neglected to thank you."

She raised their joined hands and kissed his fingers, and knew he would feel the certainty that lay behind her words. And perhaps even her clear awareness that Cass and Laura's own positions on this world—where her daughter had the gratitude of millions, but was not allowed to leave—was more complex than it appeared on the surface. It was very fortunate indeed that Cass wanted to stay.

Laura watched Gidds struggling not to fall asleep, and thought about Sue's five years of marriage, and her own ten. They had been happy, and then things had changed, and there was no guarantee things would not change with Gidds. They would grow together or grow apart, and she had no way of knowing which it would be until they lived it.

Admittedly, Gidds' complications might involve interplanetary politics. Would her attempts to promote ties with Earth cause him problems? Would KOTIS' plans for Cass drive a wedge between them?

Laura closed her eyes, refusing to get drawn into worrying through all the worst possibilities. She would get to know the man better. She would enjoy it.

She really was enjoying this.

Chapter Twelve

"No, I'm not surprised at all," Cass said. "Something similar happened when, oh, I forget which of the documentaries I subtitled it was, but there were horses. I got asked about it, produced some images from the Olympics—show-jumping and dressage and whatnot—and suddenly half Muina desperately wanted to re-enact *National Velvet*."

"Are there no horses in all the Triplanetary?" Sue asked, leaning around Laura.

"Not on Tare or Kolar. They did find some herds on Muina, but they were the short, fat pony type of horses. And really unfriendly, though I gather some Kolaren smallholder has actually managed to bribe a few into letting her pat them. Don't mention that you can ride, Aunt Sue, or you'll have her sitting at your feet."

"I *like* people sitting at my feet," Sue remarked. "All my horses have come pre-bribed, though."

"Fortunately I could just tell everyone I'd never even been on a horse, and they left me alone," Cass went on. "Alyssa isn't going to have a moment's peace after this."

They all paused as Alyssa, who had been making slow circuits of Pandora Shore's ice-filled indoor swimming pool, leaped into the air, executed a single twist, and landed neatly. Everyone who had been allowed in to watch the preparation—two teachers, the Arcadian contingent, and assorted senior Setari—promptly applauded.

Shaking her head, Alyssa skated to the end of the pool where Laura, Julian, Cass and Sue were standing on specially-laid rubbery matting behind a pair of benches.

"I'm so totally out of condition."

"Show off for five minutes and then offer someone your skates," Cass advised.

"I need to be ready in case Maddy tries to—" Alyssa began.

"Even if she tries to do a handstand, we'll be surrounded by Telekinesis talents. She's not going to get hurt."

Alyssa looked doubtful, then sighed and sat on the nearest bench, looking around the generously-sized hall at the various Setari who were settling down in the modest bleachers, and then at the semi-translucent fence that had been grown around the pool to give new skaters something to hold on to.

"All this just so Maddy can make a point with a couple of kids in her class."

"All this so Zee can try it out," Cass said, nose wrinkling. "She's the driving force behind things actually happening. Though Mara's helping it along because she bet Zee that she could stay upright longer than Zee could. Why do you think most of the skates they made are in adult sizes, and all the senior Setari are here?"

"Not sure I'd invite all my friends—and a bunch of schoolkids—to watch me on skates for the first time," Sue said.

"I think the gorgeous, naturally-athletic psychic will survive publicly falling on her ass," Cass said, grinning. "Besides, Zee's one of the Telekinesis talents, so I don't think for a moment she'll actually *fall.*"

"But using a talent will count for losing the bet," said a throaty voice behind them, and Laura turned to appreciate Zee's husband, Nils, who was exactly as described in Cass' diaries: a 200-proof combination of beauty and sensuality that raised the temperature of every room he entered.

Cass smiled at him, unabashed, and said: "I would never have helped with that translation app if I knew it meant I'd have to stop snarking about people in English."

"Who needs translation when your expression makes everything so clear?" Nils said, tweaking her nose.

Cass swatted him away, then waved at further new arrivals, including Zee and Mara. "Are you going to try?"

"Apparently," Nils said, eyeing the waiting line of skates with a mischievous quirk of his lips. "I must admit dancing on knives is almost as unexpected as your melted rock spouts."

"Skating's a bit more common," Cass said. "Here comes the horde: we'd better go snaffle some seats. Good luck Alyssa!"

"I'm going to need it," Alyssa said, dubiously eyeing Maddy's class streaming through the door, although she brightened when Nick came in with Maddy.

Cass had similarly lit up because Kaoren had appeared with Ys, Rye, Lira and Sen, and Mara's husband and two older sons as well. They settled into the bleachers next to the cluster of highly amused Setari, and listened as Alyssa—her voice transmitted to the audience through the interface—began to set out basic ice etiquette and safety while Nick helped her three tall students with their skates.

Rather than watch the show, Laura studied her daughter as she answered additional questions from Kaoren and her children. Content, settled, and unlikely to cause KOTIS difficulties. Not precisely in a gilded cage— Cass had made a deliberate and clear-eyed choice to stay on Muina—but Laura wondered if it was possible for her to not look at every treat, extravagant or small, and think of it as 'placation'. Kaoren's position was no less complicated, especially since he would be more aware of the apparently fractious internal politics of KOTIS, and the debates over how Touchstones were to be managed.

How much of a conflict of interest Laura represented for Gidds she could not guess.

Reminded, Laura studied Maddy's class, and spotted Haelin easily: not only because she was one of the few in Kalrani uniform, but because she was sitting relaxed but upright, with her hands neatly arranged on her knees. Too cute.

Quite possibly because of her Sights, or because she had also been paying attention to Laura, Haelin turned her head and they looked at each other. Laura smiled faintly at the girl, but was saved from any awkwardness by Maddy, finally permitted onto the ice. Maddy promptly sped around the pool, then reversed the direction she was facing and did a circuit backward, smiling triumphantly at her classmates while she did so. Haelin joined in the applause, apparently pleased. Zee, Nils and Mara, in the meantime, were clutching the circling wall.

It would not do to go too much longer without a proper meeting with Gidds' children. Even without Sight Sight the girls might be hearing rumours through the KOTIS gossip channels. Speaking of which...

"Did you want to go with us on this trip to witness a moonfall, Cass?" Laura asked. "I know you had more than enough aether early on, but we've worked out a way around that."

"Yeah, Kaoren said Tsur Selkie had agreed to line up Exclusion Suits for you. They didn't even have those a couple of years ago, but they had to figure out a way to deal with looking after people who kept heading into the platform towns during moonfall and passing out."

There was no hesitation at the mention of Gidds. It seemed either word hadn't reached Cass, or she was going to follow Julian's lead and not ask questions. Which, frankly, suited Laura, who didn't have all her answers yet.

"I want to go," Lira said, from where the kids sat in a line on the lower tier of the bleacher.

"Can we?" Rye asked, looking from Cass to Kaoren and back again.

"They wouldn't have told us about it if we couldn't," Ys commented, but then seemed to recall herself and added: "But I would like to too, please."

As they discussed technicalities—and a timeframe that now did not depend on passing adulthood exams—Laura reached back and touched Julian's foot. He had gone quiet as soon as they'd reached Pandora Shore, and Laura could not help but contrast his silence with the chatty boy who had interrogated Gidds a short week ago. Was it just his bashfulness around pretty girls, or had Gidds' presence last night been more of a shock than Laura had expected?

Laura: *Muina has enhanced reality gaming locations— and a few nightclubs—that disguise identity. You could be thoroughly anonymous if you still wanted to meet your guild friends—and any minders would be a lot more inconspicuous.*

Julian: *Knowing my luck, they'd assign Siame to me.*

Siame, Kaoren's delicately pretty and highly disconcerting sister, had recently been made captain of her own Setari squad—for all she was only a few months older than Julian. With the Ruuel plethora of Sights, she was one of the people Julian avoided most assiduously.

Laura: *I think her squad's going to be assigned to Tare soon. Maybe wait until after she's left?*

Julian: *You'd let me go?*

Laura: *I don't technically get a say in it any more. Now that you've passed that exam I can't even monitor your school work or do half the parental rights related things the interface used to let me do. I'd prefer it if you didn't try to ditch your minder, but I don't expect you to give up every freedom just because it's easier on KOTIS. Though if you do go to a nightclub, think about inviting Nick and Alyssa along.*

Laughter drew her attention back to the ice. There she saw Zee and Mara holding hands for balance, while Nils spiralled gracefully around them, as adeptly as a lifelong skater. He sped to the far end of the pool and turned into a jump, twisting five-six-seven times before landing feather-soft and coming to a halt in the very centre of the pool. Here he bowed to the jeers and applause, then finally set himself down on the surface of the ice, and promptly fell over.

"He has superb control," Kaoren remarked. "That level of fine, complex movement is far harder with Levitation than Telekinesis."

"What happened with the boy who was trying to juggle rocks the other day?" Sue asked, as Alyssa skated over and showed Nils how to stand up without the assistance of any psychic talents.

Shar, who had been watching the skating intently, glanced first at his father, Lohn, who didn't seem to have heard the question, then answered himself: "He has promised not to use his talents unsupervised, and might keep his word if he can resist being goaded."

Lohn heard that, and responded with a puzzled frown. "Why did Sema feel he had to prove he could enhance his connection to the Ena? It wasn't common on Nuri, was it?"

"No, but Nurans—possibly because we travelled unprotected through deep-space—have shown a greater capacity for increasing our talent strength that way," Shar replied. "There's..." He hesitated.

"There is a belief that 'true high Nurans' are naturally adept at focusing their connection to the Ena," Kaoren finished for him.

Shar nodded, and rubbed the back of his neck. "On average Nurans are stronger than either Tarens or Kolarens, and we have usually trained our talents, though not as intensely as the Setari. When we can also achieve the enhanced power that comes from focusing the link to the Ena...it is something to hold on to, that strength."

Pandora Shore was a complicated school. It had been built to accommodate the strongest psychic children who had survived the destruction of Nuri, and then had added the relatives of the senior Taren Setari who had taken land grants in the islands to the west of Pandora. The next wave to be included were the children of wealthy citizens and officials immigrating from Tare and Kolar, most of whom had only minor, untrained talents, but who required a school with extra security. And now Kalrani, whose natural strengths had been honed to their highest pitch, outmatching the original students.

A wide mix of cultures and social backgrounds, in other words, and the Nurans one of the largest groups in the school, and yet—with less than ten thousand survivors on all of Muina—also the most negligible politically, and furthest behind in the Taren-based education system. Understandable that there would be a push among the Nurans to prove their worth in other ways.

"Stupid," Ys said, not turning around.

Shar glanced at her back, then smiled wryly and said to Lohn: "I don't think the idea of 'true high Nurans' will come to anything—there's too many inconsistencies over who actually manages to focus their connection to the Ena. Those who were members of the Great Houses are being pushed to prove themselves, but I think—hope—they'll all get tired of it soon. He paused again, then said: "Perhaps this will distract everyone. Do you think they made any of the knife-boots in my size?"

Not making several dozen pairs of skates had definitely been an oversight, judging from the fascinated attention of Maddy's class. Since she still tired quite quickly, it was not long before Maddy called down Haelin and another girl, and took a break while they tried on the two pairs that had been made for her.

Laura checked Gidds' schedule and saw that while he was still working, he was using the colour code that indicated 'interruptions permitted', so she sent him a text.

Laura: *I'm not sure I have the rights to record this, but can you see what I'm looking at?*

The complex rules for what could or could not be recorded or transmitted over the interface meant that

Haelin would very likely appear as an outline, but Laura still included a link to her 'visual input' in hopes Gidds would be able to watch Haelin take her first steps onto the ice.

Gidds: *You're in an image-restricted area, but I can by-pass.*

Laura kept her attention on Haelin as the girl glided along beside the outer wall, one hand on the translucent surface for balance. She was an athletic child—no surprise if she'd been learning Setari combat techniques—who looked like she'd grow up quite tall. After only a little time clutching the wall, she allowed her forward momentum to take her toward the middle of the pool, arms held out from her sides.

Gidds switched to voice communication, asking questions about learning to skate. It was truly fantastical to share a companionable chat with a man while allowing him see through her eyes. That was the world Laura now lived in. She would never stop appreciating the wonders every new day brought her.

"*I have a feeling Alyssa's plans to join KOTIS are about to be thoroughly derailed,*" Laura sub-vocalised.

"*There will certainly be others wishing for lessons,*" Gidds replied. "*Although it's difficult to predict how long the enthusiasm will last. On that point, Allidi and Haelin are interested in sampling* Red Exchange. *If they enjoy it, would you be comfortable with them joining our next session?*"

"*We could form our own band,*" Laura said, amused by the idea.

"*We could.*"

The response came heavy with unspoken meaning. Laura felt the weight of it, but the moment to respond passed when Haelin, who had picked up a little speed, tried to stop herself and tripped, falling forward. The neatness of her landing hinted at her combat training, and she was back up on her skates almost immediately.

"Don't use the toe pick to try to stop yourself," Alyssa instructed, gliding over to demonstrate correct technique. Haelin listened intently, and tried again, smiling when she succeeded.

"*She's a quick study.*"

"*Yes.*"

Outright pride in his mental voice, and as they continued to watch he told her of Haelin's love of sport, and her disappointment that she was unlikely to be able to raise her Telekinesis to the point where she could participate in Tare's most popular sport, Tairo. It was clear to Laura that he did not often speak to people about his daughters: that need to not show favouritism had gagged him.

"All right, Mum?"

Cass had noticed her abstraction. That blow to the chest sensation struck Laura all anew, to have her daughter here, being worried about *her*.

"Just thinking about how lucky I am," she said, squeezing Cass' hand. "And how I've been most considerate not mentioning the number of times you went down to the skating rink with Alyssa."

"Hey, if Nick can wriggle out of showing his beginner-level moves, I can too," Cass objected. "I never got past figure eights anyway."

This produced a lively debate that did not budge Cass in the slightest, and Laura listened with half her attention, while settling a gaming date with Gidds. He and his daughters would be in the southern hemisphere city of Meziath—a remarkable place of ruins beneath trees the size of giant redwoods—but that would be no bar to a virtual meet-up.

"*Do the girls get to spend much time with their mother?*" Laura asked, tentatively. She still wasn't sure if the woman had moved to Muina.

"*Allidi and Haelin have had no contact with their mother for over twenty Taren years,*" Gidds replied, without noticeable hesitation, but with an inordinate amount of precision to the words. *"When we ended our marriage, Elezin broke legal ties with our daughters as well."*

"You can...divorce your children on Tare?" Laura asked, failing to keep the shock from her mental voice.

"The laws came about following the rise of machine-assisted gestation," Gidds replied. *"It is uncommon but not unknown for them to be employed during the dissolution of a marriage. And Elezin is not the only person who chose complete separation when KOTIS took their children."*

He paused, and Laura was suddenly quite sure that he was searching for words, that his calm had briefly failed him.

"I am the reason the Setari program exists," Gidds went on, finally. *"I disliked intensely the decision to continue the program through conscription, but I couldn't argue against the logic. As the Setari grew in strength, my Sight suggested they would produce the results KOTIS sought. That lives would be saved. Elezin—her Sight told her that the program was a death sentence."*

"Sight Sight can be that contradictory?"

"Sight Sight gives knowledge and certainty not omniscience. I can be certain your hair is brown, but this morning you brushed it and it was green. Neither colour is wrong in the correct context."

"You mean you were looking at it from different angles? But—" Laura stopped, not knowing when Gidds had met his ex-wife.

"When Allidi was six—the age mandated for conscription—the senior squads had only been venturing into the Ena for a Taren year, but were already proving very successful at preventing incursions into Taren real-space. Elezin saw in this the start of an endless cycle of attrition, of Setari sent into the Ena to fight the same Ionoth until error and ill luck finally killed them." He paused. *"And that was exactly the situation we faced. The Setari,*

when we found Cassandra, were a dam cracking before a rising flood."

"But very handy to have around once Muina had been unlocked," Laura pointed out. Then, very carefully, she added: *"This didn't become obvious to your wife until Allidi was due to become a Kalrani?"*

"Our marriage's crisis point was my refusal to find a way for Allidi to be passed over," Gidds replied. He was fully in command of himself again, his tone only factual. *"Elezin and I saw each other more clearly then. I was someone who would not find a special exemption for my own children. Elezin was someone who had expected no other possibility."*

"That must have been incredibly difficult for all four of you," Laura said at last.

"It added to Allidi's burden. Haelin does not fully remember her mother, but Allidi had rejection layered on top of separation when she started as a Kalrani. Elezin...her choice was at least in part because she knew she would not be able to hide from Allidi and Haelin's Sight her absolute certainty that the Setari Program would kill them, but she of course could not explain that to our daughters."

"Do you—now that the crisis is over, and the Program has changed so much, do you think their mother will want to see them?"

"It's possible. But she has not thus far."

And it had been years. Laura surprised herself by feeling intensely sorry for this unknown woman, who had chosen a clean break from her own children.

"Thank you for telling me, Gidds," Laura said, keeping her mental voice quiet and clear. *"I would have hated to have said something entirely insensitive when I met them."*

"They are stronger than I am on the subject," Gidds said.

In an outright change of subject, he moved to talking about taking the girls to different parts of Muina, and the progress of settlement. Laura asked questions, and watched Haelin, and thought about the parents of children conscripted into the Setari Program.

Some of the Kalrani had died. Even before becoming Setari there had been accidents, tragic and impossible to predict, and what argument about the greater good could ever change what it felt like to trace a line from your choices to a dead child? And then to set your own children on potentially the same path?

Of course, Gidds had faced first-hand the urgent need to deal with the tears into the Ena. *Partially eaten.* That was more than a physical fact. The Ena had eaten Gidds' life, swallowed him up. He had still been a child himself when KOTIS first sent him there to try to find solutions, and clearly held himself responsible for all that followed. What had the past couple of years been for him, with the urgency gone and the rest of his life to discover?

No point denying that he was working on fitting Laura into that future. Meeting with his daughters would be the biggest step they'd taken so far, although a virtual family outing seemed slightly less challenging than a proper meeting—not least because the girls' Sights would not be quite so large a factor.

Chances were high that Allidi and Haelin would prefer their own mother back in their life, rather than someone new and unknown. Trying to build a relationship with them would be far more challenging than playing grandma with Cass' brood.

Laura wasn't running in the other direction, but she found herself most definitely nervous. A sign, she supposed, that she'd moved past wibbling and now really hoped that she could make things work with Gidds.

They still only knew each other at a surface level. But she would not let herself run away: she wanted this, wanted to know him fully, for them to truly trust each other. She wanted to believe in belonging with a Serious Soldier.

CHAPTER THIRTEEN

Laura's workroom opened off the southern side of her bedroom, and had the best ground floor view of Braid Meadow. The outside wall, in keeping with the rest of the house, was a single curving window, fitted with an equally curving bench. A sink and a mass of shelving, cupboards, and places to hang tools filled the other walls, but because of the room's generous size it did not feel cramped or crowded.

When she'd first arrived on Muina, with only a tiny wallet of her favourite crafting implements tucked in a pocket of her backpack, Laura had felt overwhelmed by all the empty possibility of the workroom. She'd added a divan to the nook at the eastern end, and a plushy woollen rug to the floor, but the place hadn't really felt like hers until she'd had several projects under her belt, and accrued pots of paint, spools of wire, and all manner of cloth, leather and thread. Fortunately Pandora had a thriving artist's community, and she'd had no trouble sourcing materials she was skilled with using—and samples of unfamiliar goops, clays and foams to try out.

To fill the day before meeting Gidds and his daughters, she was working on models of Romana-Angharad and Ruvord, each facing their first teszen. The last few years she'd been experimenting with unjointed wire frame and air-dry pieces—foam-light statuettes much larger than the gothic palm-sized dolls that had been such a reliable source of income. The larger, more expensive pieces hadn't been such easy sales, but she loved the amount of detail she could lavish on them.

For the *Red Exchange* characters she was trying out a slow-drying Taren polymer clay which gave her a heavier but still slightly-flexible result. She'd completed the basic forms earlier in the week, and now dived into the fine detail layer, appreciating that even on a grey, drizzly day she had plenty of natural light to work with.

Lira: *Can I come visit, Unna Laura?*

Laura: *Of course.*

Laura glanced at her internal clock, a little surprised. Nearly lunchtime. Hadn't Cass arranged to take the kids into town?

Double-checking that all the clay was properly sealed, Laura visited her bathroom, and then headed to the kitchen for a drink and to meet her granddaughter.

"Would you like something to eat?" she asked, when Lira paused at the patio door to wipe her feet.

"No thank you, Unna Laura."

Lira hadn't bothered with an umbrella or coat for the trip up the hill, and stood damply in the doorway. Even from the kitchen bench, Laura could see her eyes were red-rimmed.

"Go dry off a little," Laura recommended.

Lira wordlessly obeyed, and Laura started putting together a light lunch that could be easily shared if the girl changed her mind.

Laura: *Cass, are you still going into the city for lunch and shopping?*

Cass: *We're about to leave. Have you changed your mind?*

Laura: *I'm still overwhelmed from the last cavalcade. Is there a reason Lira's not going?*

Cass: *She headed up there, did she? We had a storm over her ditching her Kalrani guard. I wasn't planning on more than asking her to be a little more considerate, but things always seem to escalate with Lira, especially since the latest round of 'will she fade away'. I wouldn't have punished her except she tends to push or kick furniture when she's angry, even though we've told her it's a bad* idea, and today we ended up with baby bottles everywhere. So no shopping trip.

Laura: *Can I shower her with treats and generally spoil her?*

Cass: *If you want. We didn't tell her to stay in her room or anything, so there's no problem with her hanging out with you. If you're in the mood to entertain her, I'll let her security detail know they can stay snug in the guard house.*

Laura: *I'll give her a project, then.*

Cass: *Thanks, Mum. See if you can put her in a good mood for the aether trip tomorrow.*

Lira, when she returned, appeared to have spent more time washing her face than drying the rest of her.

"What did you think of the ice skating?" Laura asked, choosing to ignore dramas altogether.

Lira dropped heavily into a chair. "It's pretty, but it would be a lot of work. Can you knife dance, Unna Laura?"

"No. Roller skates, yes, ice, no."

"Rol-ler?" Lira sounded out the English word carefully.

"Shoes with wheels on the bottom. You can't jump on them in the same way as you can ice skates, but they're fun to zoom about on. And there's a sport you can play on skates."

Laura quickly ran through the mass of movies and TV shows she'd brought from Earth and had converted to the Muinan file system, but couldn't off the top of her head think of one that included a roller derby, so settled on *Xanadu*, and pulled out a few clips.

Lira absently picked at the plate of food while she watched, then said: "Do you have to sing while skating?"

"Only in musicals," Laura said, and wondered if Cass had introduced her kids of Disney, or if she was avoiding the princess theme given the class issues Nuri and old Muina seem to have shared.

"Do you want to see my latest project?" she asked instead, and was pleased when Lira brightened immediately, and headed straight for the workroom.

Laura triggered the door so that it opened as the girl arrived. "I'm working on a model of my character in a new game I've been playing," she explained, as Lira inspected the two partially-complete figures.

"What are their names? Are you being both of them?"

"No, this is mine," Laura replied, picking up the female model and reviewing her progress. The face had come out well—very reminiscent of Lalla Ward—and the hands were expressively posed. "Her name's Angharad. The other is my friend's character, Ruvord."

"Do you always make figures from the games you play?"

"Often. It's like taking a picture to remember them by. Though I left my previous ones in storage with your Great-Aunt Bet when I came here, since I didn't have room for them in my bag."

"Great-Aunt," Lira repeated. "Does that mean 'Big Aunt'?"

Laura smiled, and explained while rolling out and shaping some clay for the clothing detail.

Lira listened attentively, then made a face. "This is a stupid language," she said—demonstrating a tolerable command of it. Daily breakfast lessons had had an impact.

"It's known for its contradictions. But I like all the shades and complications. Words that mean three things, names that have history."

"Does your name mean something?"

"Laura comes from 'laurel', which is a kind of tree that symbolised honour and victory."

"Do you have a secret name too, like She does?"

"A secret name?" Laura repeated, surprised. 'She' was Cass, whenever Ys or Lira were angry with her. "What's Cass' secret name?"

"Eloise."

"Oh, her middle name?"

Tarens didn't go in for middle names, and Nurans and Old Muinans ran their 'House' and personal name together—so Lira's full name was Liranadestar because she had belonged to House Destar, just as Sen was Sentarestal of House Restal. Ys and Rye had been only Ys and Rye until Cass and Kaoren had adopted them, and there were worlds of rank and privilege issues tied up in this naming system. It was not only out of Australian habit that Cass called Sen and Lira by shortened names.

"My middle name is Rose," Laura said. "Which is a type of flower that grows on both Earth and Muina, though Earth has a few thousand more varieties."

"Your name is Tree Flower and you like plants." Lira smiled for the first time. "That is very silly."

Laura stroked the girl's thick hair. "I'll have to name one of my characters Tree Flower one day. It's nicely literal. Now, would you like to work on something as well? I'll be meeting my friend in my game in an hour or so, but there's time enough for me to show you how to use this type of clay."

"Can I try the game?" Lira asked, eyeing the Ruvord figure speculatively. "What is it called?"

"*Red Exchange*," Laura said, sending a link while admiring the girl's unerring instinct for the nuances of 'friend'. "I don't see why not. Do you need me to help you make an account?"

Lira might have been born in a pre-industrial culture, but she'd clocked up a couple of years of heavy interface use, so this offer earned only a scornful negative, then some absent nodding as Laura told her which island to start on, and where to meet later. Laura watched her curl up on the workroom divan. There would be no long download delay—most of the games Laura had played on Muina had taken only a few minutes before they were playable.

After a pause to adjust the room's temperature a notch higher, Laura sent a message to Gidds.

Laura: *Would there be any issues with Lira joining us for today's game?*

Gidds: *None occurs to me. She will know Allidi and Haelin a very little from Kaoren and Cassandra's wedding.*

Laura: *I'll see you soon, then.*

Gidds had actually been the celebrant for Cass and Kaoren's wedding—something Laura hadn't managed to notice on multiple viewings of the event's recording, so busy had she been staring at Cass. After meeting Gidds she'd gone back to look for him, and forgiven herself for not noticing the few side-on glimpses. But she should have remembered that voice.

Before returning focus to her models, Laura sat for a while watching her granddaughter. The girl's usual haughty mask relaxed into a small frown, and then an absorbed expression that Laura suspected meant she'd reached character creation. When she let her guard down she looked younger than her thirteen years.

Lira had spent a very long time alone and afraid. She hardly ever let her guard down.

Since Laura had no solution to public speculation about the lifespan of a girl brought back from the not-quite-dead, she returned to working on Angharad's starting outfit, but only made a little progress before it was time to pack away for the day. After tidying up, she touched Lira's shoulder, murmured that she would be logging in, and then climbed the loops of the spiral stair up to her roofline window seat.

CHAPTER FOURTEEN

A girl called Rose was dancing with a tiny flying sea serpent in the fountain on Porphery Mountain. The sea serpent was blue and silver, with trailing scalloped fins. The girl strongly resembled a slightly-older Ys: an interesting choice given how very different the two girls were. Deciding the name was a compliment, Laura waved until the girl splashed over, the serpent disappearing from view.

"Look, Unna Laura." Rose-Lira held out her hand to display an Ouroboros brand in the centre of her palm. "Its name is Nimenny. I'm splashing because Nimenny likes it."

"That was quick!" Lira had obviously had no trouble with her first teszen. "Mine was very grumpy, and doesn't seem to like anything at all."

"You sound very funny, Unna Laura. Isn't it strange how our voices come out all different from how we've said them?" Lira was looking about. "I don't see your friend. Isn't he coming?"

"I'm a little early," Laura said, hiding a smile at the unabashed curiosity. "I'm glad you're here. He's bringing his daughters for me to meet, and now I won't feel quite so outnumbered."

"How many daughters?"

"Two. You've met them before: they came to your Mum and Dad's wedding. Allidi and Haelin."

Rose-Lira's head came up, her eyes round. "Is your friend Tsur Selkie?"

"That's right."

Lira's amazed delight turned to suspicion. "His daughters are Kalrani."

"They are," Laura agreed readily. "I'm a little nervous to meet them, really."

"Why?"

"They're both Sight Sight talents. And...let's just say I want to make a good first impression."

Laura's strategy worked: Lira was diverted back to the fascinating discovery that Unna Laura had a special friend.

"Why do you need to meet them in this game? They live in Pandora."

"They're visiting Meziath at the moment. Gidds travels a lot, and the game lets me spend a little more time with him. Besides, I like games."

Laura spotted Ruvord-Gidds then, and raised a hand in greeting. With him were a pair of girls who stood almost equal to him in height—like Lira they'd chosen the upper age limit allowed for minors playing the game—but not closely resembling his Ruvord. Named 'Dakal' and 'Zenneth', they were long-limbed, elegant and graceful, and gazed at her with cool interest.

Laura had not been able to avoid fretting over meeting Gidds' daughters, not least because their Sight Sight meant any nerves, minor irritations, and false enthusiasms would not necessarily be private. She had decided the most she could do was be forthright and friendly, and hope for the best.

Because it mattered whether they liked her. It would matter to Gidds. It mattered to Laura.

Wondering how much of this was clear to the girls through the filter of the game, she smiled at them and said hello. "You'll have to tell me which is Allidi and which Haelin, I'm afraid."

"I'm Allidi," said 'Zenneth'.

'Dakal' said: "Haelin," and then looked from Gidds to Laura: "Should we use our proper names or the game names when talking to each other?"

"The game names when other people are around, I guess," Laura said. "Though I gather so many people pretend to be Cass and her family any slips of the tongue are likely to be dismissed."

"I met one who was being me," Lira said. "She didn't sound like me at all, but a few people seemed to believe her." From the face Lira made, it had not been a complimentary impersonation.

"Li—Rose has already contracted with her first teszen," Laura told the others. "If you've collected a mission for us, Ruvord, we're all ready to set out."

Gidds nodded. "We'll be taking the airship to Mris."

"I know where the docking platform is," Haelin said, shedding cool reserve to bounce a little.

"Then lead the way," Gidds told her, hanging back as she obeyed so that he could walk with Laura.

"Hello," she said quietly.

He brushed the back of her hand with his fingers. Such a small thing to leave Laura glowing with outright pleasure, simply because he wanted to greet her with that touch even though it would give him vertigo.

"What are you doing in Meziath?" Lira asked, trailing the sisters with a certain amount of reluctance.

"Looking," Haelin replied.

"We're touring all the towns on the teleport network," Allidi added, carefully polite. "In one of them, perhaps, we'll keep a house to go to during longer holidays."

"Oh, a summer house," Lira said. "Cassandra talks about getting one of those every winter, though she hasn't yet."

"What would it be called when it's winter where the house is?" Allidi asked.

Lira shrugged, and three pairs of eyes immediately turned to Laura. Sight Sight need to know in triplicate. Mildly amused, Laura explained the difference between a house you visited to get away from the heat of summer, and a holiday house—that presumably would be located where it was summer during Arcadia's winter.

"So Cassandra is using the word wrong?" Allidi asked.

"I suspect deliberately changing the meaning," Laura said. "Do you like Meziath?"

"Yes," said Allidi.

"No," Haelin said, glanced at her father, and continued: "It's not terrible, but I don't like being at the bottom of the trees."

"Everything feels a little loomed-over there, doesn't it?" Laura said.

"Like standing with grown-ups," Haelin said absently, then pointed. "Look, the airship's already at the dock. Let's run!"

They ran, an effortless thing in the game, although their avatars still took on plummy hues and panted. Laura laughed as they flung themselves aboard the gondola just as the mooring ropes were cast loose, and cheered Lira, who was last to make the leap.

"Well done," she said, hugging the girl. "Even in the game it's still scary jumping a gap like that."

"I would have fallen a long way," Lira said, gazing interestedly over the railing of the gondola. "What is Mris?"

"An island a little closer to the main point of damage," Gidds told her and—since Lira obviously hadn't spent any time on the game's backstory—explained how a strange object had fallen from the sky and struck the island of Ramara, and a burning miasma had rapidly spread, fracturing the land so that most of the island had vanished beneath in-rushing water. Mris was starting to see small spots of this corruption.

There were other passengers, most of whom directed only disinterested glances their way, but one pair listened to Gidds' explanation as attentively as Lira. Laura smiled at the way he shifted so that they would be able to hear him more easily.

The trip between islands was barely long enough for Gidds to set out the basics, and then they were spilling out of the gondola onto a mooring platform above a walled town, clattering down wooden stairs, and heading straight out into orchards.

Laura, as ever, thoroughly enjoyed the chance for a scenic walk and this was particularly lovely: long rows of trees, the sweet-sharp scent of fruit ripening in sunshine, and strange drooping...were they insects or birds? White gossamer puffs of down that could well be dandelion seeds, except that they would whir off whenever anyone strayed too close. She was glad to see Allidi and Haelin drop some of their formality and join Lira in trying to get close enough to see one properly. Gidds caught at Laura's fingers again, and she smiled at him, knowing he was pleased.

"Do you think they have a teszen, Unna—Angharad?" Lira asked, trotting back. "But we're not hunting new teszen at the moment, right?"

"I expect if we met one we could ask it to lend us its power," Laura said. "But no, we're here to find damage to the island and try to repair it. Look for..." She paused, and then pointed in the direction that the downy puffs had fled. "I think what we're looking for might well be over there."

The puffs had gathered in great numbers around a collection of grey dimples that interrupted the neat grass stripes separating the rows of trees. The puffs perched in branches, or spiralled in small clouds above each dimple, and although the air smelled sulphurous, it wasn't until Laura was standing nearly on the rim of the nearest that she understood that they must be attracted by the rising heat.

"It's called 'grey scar'," Allidi told Lira, pointing to watermelon-sized pocks spreading from the edge of the dimples. "We should be able to close the little ones on our own, but we'll have to work together to get the bigger holes to go away."

"Nimenny knows what to do," Lira said confidently, and proved it by holding her hands out toward the nearest pock mark and conjuring a swirl of water. In moments the grey-black patch had been erased, smoothed out to the healthy brown of rich, fertile earth.

Laura, who now had two novels' worth of backstory to draw upon, concentrated on the paw print branded onto her wrist, and asked the kirr-tut teszen to lend its strength. All the teszen were aligned to a series of elemental wheels—a combination of the typical water strong against fire and weak against ice configuration, but intersecting with 'sharp' and 'fast' and 'silk' and other complexities. A kirr-tut was aligned to bone/fast, and when Laura asked for aid it flickered into existence and seemed to fill in a pockmark by scratching surrounding dirt into it.

The larger dimples of the grey scar were not so easily dealt with, since they required carefully timed elemental combinations, and reacted to attempts to close them with little jolts of force and gusts of rotten-egg miasma that had to be shielded against, blown away or dodged.

It was a tricky form of combat, and far harder to master than clicking through skill buttons, but it was not too long before the last of the dimples closed over, and only healthy earth remained.

"We did it!" Lira cheered, then sat down. "I feel tired even though I'm really just lying down."

"That took a lot of concentration," Laura agreed. "I think we scared all the puff balls away, too."

"What is this?" Haelin asked, using the toe of her boot to expose a dully-glinting object buried in the soil.

"Melted glass, perhaps?" Laura suggested. "I know you're supposed to get crafting materials as a reward for repairing damage."

Haelin nudged to expose it further, then picked up an elaborately whorled blue-green object that resembled a blown-glass decanter.

"Musical instrument?" Lira suggested. "Like a horn to blow through?"

"Dzo, there's something..." Allidi began.

'Dzo'—short for 'dzozen'—was an equivalent of 'dad', and she turned to Gidds, who responded with a nod, and his brief smile.

"Too hasty," he told Haelin. "It is a trap, not a reward. I can feel it waiting to trigger."

"Don't try to put it down," Allidi added. "I think that's what sets it off."

"*Not* crafting material?"   Haelin shot Laura a reproachful glance.

"I wasn't warned of traps at the Hall of the Weaver," Gidds said, ignoring a sudden jut to Haelin's lower lip. "Is there any mention in the books you've been reading, Laura?"

"Nothing. I think I'll ask Julian—he's been playing a lot more than I have."

Laura: *Hey kiddo. In* Red Exchange, *what do you do with weird bits of glass left behind when you clear grey scar?*

Julian: *Gems, Mum. Get them made into necklaces and they'll boost your teszen's strength.*

Laura: *Not gems. Something like a vase or a glass horn.*

Julian: *! Is it kind of bruise-coloured? Send me a screenie.*

Laura obediently emailed him an image of 'Dakal' and her whorl of glass.

Julian: *Star Claw! OMFG, Mum, where are you? Give me your map coordinates.*

Laura: *So demanding. So unexplainy.*

It was surely Laura's imagination that brought her Julian's exasperated cry all the way from his bedroom.

She read the detailed response that followed, and then told Haelin: "You've thrown Julian into a welter of excitement. This is apparently a rare item that will trigger a major event. Still, unfortunately, a trap. He says to not give it to anyone else, or leave the immediate area. Both will trigger it."

"What kind of event?" Haelin asked, brightening.

"The corruption will try to make a serious incursion on Mris. In the form of..." She paused, then read: "...tentacles of ultimate doom. When it appears, players will come frantically running from all the islands, because if it's not beaten back, Mris will start to break apart. Being first on site gives the greatest chance of gaining some very nice rewards. Julian's guild—ah, band—is asking very nicely for us to tell them where we are, and for you try to hold off triggering the event until most of them are here."

Haelin was a 'psychic psychic', and had spent several years training to fight semi-real monsters, but she was still a youngster who plainly found the idea of sending a wave of players running most gratifying.

"If they can help me not get killed that would be good, too," she said.

"All right," Laura said, and relayed the map coordinates. "Julian says it will only be a few minutes— few joden—before the first of them reach us, but it will be at least a quarter-kasse before there will be enough of the band here to start. The best thing to do is to stay very still."

"So we just stand around?" Haelin asked, more in token protest than annoyance.

"We were ready for a break anyway," Gidds told her. "Go to the bathroom if you need to—we will probably be very busy in a few minutes."

"*Dzo*." A whole world's dignity and reproach in a single syllable.

Lira, who had been idly poking the fresh dirt where the Star Claw had been uncovered, said: "Does Julian have a secret name as well, Unna Laura?"

"Alexander." Anticipating Sight Sight this time, Laura went on to explain middle names once again.

"May I ask you a question about your family name, Tsa Devlin?" Allidi asked, in her calm, direct way. "I'm not certain if it is an impolite question in Earth culture."

Laura nodded, and was not surprised to be asked whether 'Devlin' was her own family name. Muina, Tare and Kolar were all matrilineal, and she could see where Allidi might be confused. Laura was only glad Gidds had explained a little about his own family's situation, allowing Laura to avoid awkward return questions.

"Devlin is Cass' father's family name. I kept it in part because having the same family name is less confusing for schools." Laura grinned. "And because Cass objected strongly when I suggested she and Julian could swap to my family name."

"Why?" Lira asked, very interested. "What is it?"

"Jiglea." She pronounced it Jeg-lee-ah, as her father had. "Originally from a country called Romania. The problem being that English speakers, reading it, would pronounce it 'jiggly', which is, ah, duni, in Muinan."

Three pairs of eyes widened. Gidds kept his response to a barely audible: "Ah."

"They used to call us the Jiggly Sisters, when we were at school," Laura said. Which had been far more apposite for Sue and Bet, but Laura had hated it just as much.

"Cassandra Duni," Lira said reverently.

"Lira Duni," Haelin offered, and produced a flicker-smile the very image of her father's.

"No."

Lira's response held more than a hint of thunderstorm, so Laura reached for a quick diversion.

"Did Cass ever mention what 'selkie' means on Earth?"

Sudden, fixed attention was answer enough, but before Laura could go on there was a shout from above.

A half-dozen golden birds swooped low, and a cluster of people leapt to the ground. None of these were Julian's 'Space Ninja', but one was 'Corezzy', whom Laura was particularly interested in meeting. The avatar, at least, was that of a young man in a blue Adonis mould.

"Thanks for waiting!" said another player, an equally muscular young woman called 'Tzatch'. "I'm leader of the *Sky Wing.*" She nodded generally to Laura's group, then went on directly to 'Dakal'. "It'll be a few joden before enough of us are here. I can talk you through some strategies, but chances are high you'll get caught by the emergence whatever we do."

"It seems pretty harsh to have something like this lying around the new player areas," Laura commented.

"It's a lucky find, really it is," Corezzy put in. "The person who triggers the Star Claw—well, there's only been two before in the game, but each time the trigger got a powerful teszen out of it. And it made the teszen who fought the corruption node stronger, which explains why we all came scrambling here."

"What would happen if I just threw it as far as I could?" Haelin asked.

"No-one's tried that, yet. You can if you want, but I don't think it will help."

Laura was not surprised to receive a channel request from Gidds, and when she accepted she found all three Selkies in channel.

"*We will be extremely distracted without an explanation,*" Gidds said.

"*What happens if the need-to-know aspect of Sight Sight triggers and you can't get an answer?*" Laura asked, curious.

"*Nightmares,*" Haelin said. "*And feeling cross, and not being able to settle. And seeing things that remind you of it* everywhere. *Sometimes the answer puts itself together. Sometimes it itches for years.*"

"*Sounds frustrating,*" Laura said, bringing Lira into the channel because she could see 'Rose' frowning at her. She mightn't have Sights, but Lira was very socially intuitive.

"*This is a seal,*" Laura continued, showing them an underwater sequence from one of the documentaries Cass had spent the last few years translating.

"*Tedan,*" Lira said. "*They sometimes come out onto rocks near Kalasa.*"

Another animal that could be found on both worlds? But the Kalasan tedan would be in a freshwater habitat. And now was not time for further distraction.

"*Selkies are mythological beings that are seals in the ocean, and shed their skin on land to assume a human form,*" Laura said briskly. "*I can look to see if I have a selkie tale among the books I brought with me, and translate it for you. There are quite a few different traditions, but they tend to be quietly tragic stories.*"

And quite a lot of them involved some seriously problematic consent issues, which Laura wished she'd thought about before using the name as a diversion. She'd talk to Gidds about that first.

Fortunately Sight Sight seemed to be satisfied for the moment, as Allidi politely thanked her, and Haelin went back to asking Tzatch questions about surviving the Star Claw.

In short order nearly four dozen members of the *Sky Wing* band gathered—Julian's 'Space Ninja' arriving and offering a wave and a second glance at 'Rose'. Tzatch, clearly an experienced guild leader, briskly divided her band members into groups with designated tasks and alternate roles for 'when the plan inevitably falls into the sea'.

This settled, she turned back to Laura's small group, but only to shrug. "Every little bit of damage counts, but your defences are all at baby levels. It's up to you how much you want to mix in, but—well, we'll revive you once it's over."

At least it wasn't a permadeath game. Laura glanced at Gidds to see how he was taking relegation to the sidelines, but found 'Ruvord' surveying arrangements with a clinical air. He noticed her gaze and produced his flicker-smile before turning to Haelin.

"It will be very boring if I am caught for the whole time, Dzo," Haelin said.

"We will observe from a safe distance, and then focus on assisting you."

"When you throw the Star Claw, run in the other direction," Allidi advised.

Gidds nodded his agreement, then led Laura, Allidi and Lira along the neat rows of trees so that they could watch without their view being blocked.

Sky Wing had arranged themselves similarly, leaving Haelin-Dakal standing alone, looking very small but entirely self-possessed. At nine, she could only have been training as a Kalrani for a few years, but the Setari program was extremely intensive and disciplined, and Sight Sight talents definitely tended toward confidence.

Did being Gidds' daughter help, or simply add pressure?

Haelin certainly maintained her cool when Tzatch gave the signal. She swung her arm, hurled the Star Claw in the direction of the main cluster of *Sky Wing*, and then dashed directly toward her father.

The whorled glass horn spun end to end and—Laura was watching closely—stretched and changed shape as it did so. Haelin, although she moved at the maximum speed the game would allow, had no chance to escape the expanding twists and whorls.

Purple and shimmering, the Star Claw bloomed and grew, opening into something similar to a sea anemone or a cactus dahlia: hundreds of narrow 'petal' tentacles curving up and around a protected centre. That, no doubt, would be where Haelin's Dakal would be.

"*I can't even* see," Haelin said, still in the channel where they'd been discussing names.

"*Trying to fight your way out might earn you upgrades for your teszen, though,*" Laura pointed out. "*You certainly can't miss from the inside.*"

"*Wouldn't miss anyway,*" Haelin grumped, but without real annoyance.

"Move further back," Gidds said, and they retreated as the 'petals' grew ever-larger, the ground sinking beneath them, and the nearest trees tumbling sideways.

Members of *Sky Wing* were already attacking the bruised starburst of a flower, but Laura was not surprised to see their initial efforts have no visible impact. An encounter designed to be a game-wide event would likely require enormous numbers of players. Tzatch clearly knew this, and was merely testing possible strategies.

Veteran of more than a few large, imaginary battles, Laura guessed the Star Claw would likely phase through vulnerabilities—most likely connected to the elemental wheels—but there was no obvious signal such as a colour change to indicate the shift. She asked Gidds if he could see anything.

"It's definitely changing vulnerabilities," he said. "There doesn't appear to be a visual signal."

"Nimenny can tell," Lira said, shifting her weight from foot to foot, then added over the interface channel. "*It doesn't hurt to be stuck in there, does it?*"

"*No.*" Haelin's response was brief, dismissive. But then, in a slightly altered tone, she added: "*I'm in a jelly bubble. I think it works like a shield. I guess I'd just exit the game if it hurt.*"

Laura glanced at Gidds, and he gave her the faintest nod. That had been a deliberate choice to reassure, then. Only nine, Haelin had still recognised and effortlessly responded to the anxiety that lay behind the question of a girl who had once been cruelly trapped.

Sight Sight. So helpful, so disconcerting.

And so very much a factor in her future. She sent Gidds a direct message.

Laura: *You look like you're enjoying yourself. I was worried that things like this would feel too much like the massive ionoth attacks to you.*

His flicker-smile made an appearance.

Gidds: *In part it's because there are so many excited players. Even though they're not physically here, it's impacting Place and Sight Sight. The combat doesn't bother me—simulations without injuries are merely challenges.*

Laura: *I'm glad.*

Gidds: *Would you like to come with us next week? A two-family outing?*

Laura hesitated, glancing at Allidi.

Gidds: *They will enjoy a larger group.*

Laura wondered, but expected it was worth trying. Cass would be off on a visit to her in-laws, but mixing Julian and Sue with Allidi and Haelin would be a significant step, while being less awkwardly 'Sight Sight Duo faces off with potential Wicked Step-mum'.

But first, a rescue.

CHAPTER FIFTEEN

"Lira's so taken with this game you played that I think I'll put off trying it out," Cass said, studying the helmet of her Exclusion Suit.

"That makes sense?" Laura lowered her own helmet over her head, and twisted to lock it into position.

Cass grinned. "It does, really! She was hugging it a bit to herself, you see. *Her* game with Unna Laura. I don't want to stick my big nose in and take some of the shine off her new toy."

"How would you do that?" Laura asked, startled. "She likes you, Cass—really, she does."

"Oh, yeah. But in a 'naggy older sister' way, at least when I've been telling her to behave. You're the first person that I've seen her really take—oh, I don't know how to put it—'ownership of', maybe. At school she talks about 'my Unna Laura' very matter-of-factly."

"This indulgent grandma gig is paying off."

"I guess so!" Cass sealed her Exclusion Suit, and her voice came out strangely echoing through the clear panels of the helmet. "But it's really been a big step forward. Lira has such a complicated relationship with the idea of parents, and belonging, and who has authority over her. Not because she's some snobbish Lantaren princess, or whatever, but because she's realised that even the people who raised her—the ones she was stolen from—were simply controlling and making use of a Touchstone."

"And she applies that to you and Kaoren?"

"On and off. I might be in the same situation as her in a lot of ways, but Kaoren and I choose to work for KOTIS. And KOTIS is...well, there's a lot of factions, and plenty of people pushing to have her spend days on end telling them everything about Muina in the past. But she was kept so sheltered and controlled that she can't answer most of their questions—not good, since she hates feeling ignorant—and there are a lot of bad associations, so even the mildest session gives her days of nightmares."

Cass walked to the window of the room in the KOTIS building where they were preparing for their aether excursion, and looked out over the ruins of the ancient town that lay outside.

"They're fairly sure Lira made all this, you know. Not the buildings, but getting the teleport network to work, and maybe even the system that causes moonfall and refines aether. She doesn't know for certain—her whole life before being kidnapped involved being periodically plugged into psionic amplification machines without any explanation. Used to shape reality without any input of her own. Until finally someone put her in a machine with no intention of her getting out again."

Cass' voice was angry and sad—and perhaps shadowed with the awareness that KOTIS was exploring the possibility of eventually plugging Cass into a few machines. Laura gripped her daughter's shoulder through the strange, slippery material of the suit.

"At least, with your collection of monitors and oversight committees, you can be sure there'll be plenty of warning, and probably a year or two of public debate and dispute, if they do go that route. Interested as they are in creating more teleportation platforms, no-one here wants to risk setting off the disasters and instabilities that cost them Muina in the first place—and the delays will give you lots of opportunity to leave the Triplanetary in your dust."

"I guess. I get caught up in worry sometimes—I need to stop that." Cass rapped lightly on her own helmet. "We totally look like we're wearing spacesuits."

"We do! I feel very classic sci-fi in this."

"I wonder if they'd work in vacuum?"

"Doesn't seem likely they'd be designed for the pressure difference," Laura said, admiring herself in the mirror. Streamlined, but undeniably spacesuit-like, the Exclusion Suit would generate a shield field to prevent the moonfall aether from reaching them.

She started to go on, but noticed Cass was looking down and to her left, which Laura had learned many people did when they were talking over the interface, so she waited until Cass looked back at her with an apologetic grimace.

"Sorry, Kaoren's Mum wanted to make a change to our schedule. Visiting the Ruuels always ends up being hectic."

"Do the kids get along with Teor?"

"Most of the time. She and Paran are really pretty cool—super-smart and creative. Sen likes them a lot, which is always a good sign, and they're fantastic with Rye. I was worried about Ys for a while, but I eventually figured that she and Teor positively enjoy trying to get the best of each other. Teor's still trying to convince Kaoren to stop being a Setari, though, and she finds the way Lira chops and changes hobbies frustrating. She doesn't push, but she wants to, and Lira picks up on that. It's not really a problem except when Lira's stressed out like she has been lately."

Laura, testing out the impact of the suit's weight on her walking, paused.

"Why not let her come with me and Sue this weekend?"

"On this exploration trip you've wangled? Mum, they wouldn't let her go without extra guards."

"We get security either way, don't we? Shall I ask if it's possible, and see what they say?"

"Mm. Well, it's worth thinking about—Rye has managed to make Lira appreciate country walks more than she used to, and Areziath in spring would definitely be worth it. We've only been once, and that was in summer. I wonder if I can manage to rearrange things without offending Teor?"

They headed out to check the kids' progress, and found a fully-suited Ruuel Devlin complement, with Kaoren checking that everyone's helmets were fully locked and active.

"Is this the line for the auditions for *Lost in Space*?" Sue asked, joining them with Julian, Alyssa, Nick and Maddy in tow.

"That would imply we don't know the way home," Laura said. "How about *The Jetsons*?"

"Mm, possible I suppose, though a bit iffy on the gender roles. There's not too many family-in-space stories are there?"

"*The Jetsons* weren't in space, were they?" Cass asked, then added to Kaoren: "We're talking about Earth vidshows."

Descriptions of *Lost in Space* and *The Jetsons* kept everyone occupied as they trooped out of the building, meeting up with their security escort, and a trio of KOTIS scientists who were researching various aspects of moonfall. The lead scientist, Isten Sydel, introduced his team, and then led the way from the KOTIS building back into the small town due to witness moonfall.

Called Dulesza, the town sat on an isthmus in Muina's tropical zone. It had been designated for research rather than housing, and so the single KOTIS building, along with occasional scanners and excavation sites, were the only visible impact of Muina's resettlement. The rest was vines and vivid flowery bushes and stone buildings with empty doors and windows.

"The platform towns were almost certainly constructed within a short period of time, and occupied for a bare few years before the disaster," Isten Sydel said, as they climbed a steep road between near-identical white, blockish buildings. "Their locations do not appear linked to any pre-existing sites, and—while there are some adaptations for terrain—they all share the same square, patterned-roofed houses, a minimum of four watch towers at the outer boundaries, and a centrally located amphitheatre." He paused at the entrance of Dulesza's amphitheatre, looking not down into it, but back the way they had come: "This is undoubtedly one of the most spectacular locations."

True. Dulesza rose in tiers above a broad lake, the water currently transitioning through vivid shades of blue as the afternoon progressed toward evening. Above, a handful of enormous gulls drifted almost motionless, while a cloud of smaller seabirds dipped and swooped among the rocks scattered just beyond the shore.

"Give it a few blue domes and it could be Santorini," Sue said, lifting her favourite scanner to a better angle.

"Santorini with sea monsters," Laura said, for she had glimpsed something scaly and looping and large moving where the birds dived and darted.

She and Sue shared a glance, bright and marvelling, for the sheer wonder of being on a whole new planet. A comfortable paradise with constant reminders that this was not Earth: from the strange creatures mixed among familiar animals, to the moon slowly cresting the horizon.

Named Esune, it appeared a touch larger, and had a bluer tint compared to Earth's Luna, but these faint differences receded behind a dark 'bullet hole' with a trailing tear that made the moon look like it had been shot with a comma.

Laura couldn't look at Muina's moon without being overwhelmed by enormities. Not merely by the loud statement that this was Definitely Not Earth, but because part of that comma in the sky was due to Cass. The hole had appeared at the same time as the disaster that had made Muina uninhabitable. The trailing tear during the close call that Cass had barely escaped two years ago.

Noting another of the scientists darting a fascinated glance at her granddaughter, Laura moved so she could drop comforting hands on Cass and Lira's shoulders. Two girls, very different, but both Touchstones who had been fulcrums for the events that had left those lunar scars. The sheer scope of their potential occasionally left Laura gasping, but also wishing there was more she could do to protect them.

The vigilant attendance of an entire squad of highly trained psychic space ninjas—Sixth Squad today—were a reminder that there was plenty of protection about. But physical safety was only one layer, and Laura was entirely determined to be someone who would spoil and hug and be glad of all her family, not for the things they could do, but for their own selves.

"The amphitheatre arrangement speaks to a design philosophy prioritising efficiency and multipurpose function," Isten Sydel continued, as they at last turned away from the view. "The primary purpose of these towns is undoubtedly the refinement of aether. But that single process channels that aether to the Ena stabilisation pillars, the teleportation platforms, and, we are coming to surmise, to heating and lighting the towns themselves, although that system appears inactive. Since aether has restorative aspects, even the use of an amphitheatre as the power collection point suggests that this is, in fact, a kind of hospital or wellness centre."

He paused as one of his team, almost bouncing, said: "Given how very beneficial aether is on a cellular level—to the point where we're seeing rejuvenation in older subjects—these settlements may have been intended for privileged residents. Or perhaps simply health retreats. The population of the planet certainly exceeded the capacity of the platform towns."

There was an enormous amount of Not Looking at Lira going on. Too much to hope that Lira hadn't noticed, wasn't aware of the mute pressure for her to dredge her memory and speak up about past visits to similar villages, and any dropped titbits of overheard conversation. But Lira, mouth compressed, only stared at the ground, and it was surely no coincidence that Kaoren now stood between his daughter and the hopeful scientists.

Laura couldn't entirely blame them—it must be eternally frustrating to have a witness to the thing you were investigating and be told to keep away. Fortunately Isten Sydel was obedient to his no-doubt strict orders, quickly shifting to ushering them along the upper rim of the amphitheatre to a wide platform.

"This location is ideal for observing the beginning of aether generation, both at the centre of the amphitheatre and across a large swathe of the pattern-roof dwellings. We've established that the generation process does not commence until the sun is no longer visible, which gives us fifteen joden or more to wait."

Kaoren and Cass began to ask questions about the kind of experiments the research team were conducting. Recognising deliberate distraction, Laura linked her arms with her two older granddaughters and moved with them to a handy knee-high ledge that made a useful seat.

"I feel like I'm in one of my favourite stories," she said, squeezing their hands. "Walking through mysterious ruins, witnessing ancient marvels. I'm going to have a thousand adventures in my dreams tonight."

"Which stories?" asked Ys, ever the voracious reader.

Laura glanced at her internal ebook collection, and pointed Ys to *Catseye* as a starter, then added: "Although most people in stories have a rather uncomfortable time of it, while I'd prefer my story free of people shooting at me, or toothy carnivores sniffing out my path."

"Is it still an adventure if it's safe?" Ys asked, dubious.

"I think so. We're in an exciting new place, about to witness a marvel. What about that doesn't feel like an adventure?"

"I don't know 'marvel', Unna Laura," Sen said, wriggling onto the ledge next to Lira.

"It means 'amazing'," Maddy said, squishing in on Lira's other side. "Things that make you leave your mouth open and go 'ooh!'."

"Like cakes," Lira said, in a mild shot across Sen's bows that the younger girl didn't acknowledge.

"Do you feel you're having an adventure, Maddy?" Laura asked.

Maddy nodded emphatically. "And there *are* toothy monsters, just down there," she noted, pointing to the now deeply-shadowed rocks.

"Not monsters," Rye said, tucking himself onto the last inch of the ledge. "Those are zatrals. They eat water weed."

"I bet they're still pretty toothy," Laura said, and led the conversation further into the safely neutral topic of local wildlife, and the not-so-local creatures that could be found outside the relatively safe zones around the platform towns.

Sue: *What happened to Serious Soldier? I thought he was meeting us here.*

Laura: *Minor crisis at Kalasa.*

Sue: *Story of his life, from the sounds of it. Are the cancellations getting to you?*

Laura: *I figure it's a bit like being married to a doctor or a police officer. Never quite off-duty, so last-minute rescheduling is to be expected.*

Sue: *Ooh, the M-word. Haven't heard you go there before now. When are you telling Cass? Did you tell her who organised our weekend trip?*

Laura: *I told her a friend had invited us. Somehow, telling Cass feels like a point of no return. Not that I'm going out of my way to hide it from her either—I thought I'd be having an interesting discussion tonight on the topic of Mum Sex, but I guess not. There's no hurry. I mightn't be wibbling anymore, but I don't see a reason to rush through the getting-to-know-you stage. I've yet to see how he behaves when annoyed, or even noticeably under stress.*

Sue: *Hard to push off-balance isn't he? Maybe he's a robot! What would you do if you discovered circuitry?*

Laura: *Well, I already know he's fully functional...*

Sue and Laura both burst out laughing, and only laughed harder at Cass' demand to know what was so funny. Laura hugged her daughter, their helmets knocking together.

"Things that would make you go 'ew'," she said, giving Cass one last squeeze.

Letting go, she caught a faint shift in Kaoren's expression, and guessed that he, at least, knew exactly where Gidds Selkie spent his nights. And, obedient to Sight Sight etiquette, he would not tell tales to Cass, but leave Laura to make her own announcements.

No doubt recognising her comprehension just as effortlessly, Kaoren offered Laura a sudden, warm smile. Entirely approving. Laura smiled back, and then said: "I think—is it starting?"

Modern Muinans did not yet know what role the moon played in the refinement of aether. But it certainly played some part, for it was only when the light of the moon fell on the complex medallion patterns etched into the whitestone roofs that aether was produced.

At first there was only the faintest haze, hanging like a summer mist above each of the rooftop circles and the much larger pattern located in the centre of the amphitheatre. This thickened, brightened, and began to drift downward: a glowing, heavier-than-air gas that then defied expectation by beginning to flow *upward*.

Laura forgot everything else. The fabric of another dimension was being woven before her eyes into a light that healed, and powered teleporters, and had the potential to do so much more, if only they understood how to use it.

"Magic," Sue breathed, as the amphitheatre began to swim, a bowl of light dominated by a shimmering central column. "Mana, even. If I soak myself in the stuff, do you think I could learn to be a space mage?"

"I gather you're more likely to be unconscious," Laura said, then added to Isten Sydel: "Can we go down there?"

They could, of course. That was the point of the visit, and the reason for the Exclusion Suits. Aether was apparently as much radiation as mist, and it was not enough to simply wear a gas mask. Only suits that generated a barrier shield would allow them to move through aether unaffected.

Laura walked into light.

After a period of straightforward amazement, she deactivated the suit and, opening the helmet, inhaled a cold, tingling mist that ran warm butter through her bones. A gentle sense of wellbeing made her sigh. Her life really had become the stuff of dreams.

But, not minded to finish the outing unconscious, she sealed the suit again and turned to see her sister closing up her own helmet, her own gaze fixed on Nick, who was walking hand-in-hand with Alyssa.

Laura: *He looks happy.*

Sue: *He is. But he's always been able to make the best of wherever he is.*

For a moment Sue's own naturally-upbeat attitude slipped, and an ache rose in her eyes. To throw your heart and soul into someone, and have them taken away, left a deep, abiding mark. The wound might heal, circumstances might improve, but the scar remained.

Sen had run up to Nick and Alyssa and was pretending to ice skate through the billowing light. Adorable, but Laura had learned enough of Sen by now to know that she would react to unhappiness by trying to comfort or distract. Of course, so would Sue and Laura.

"So, have you made a decision yet, Alyssa?" Sue asked, as she crossed to the pair. It had only taken a day after Alyssa's brief skating tutorial for offers of something more permanent to roll in.

Alyssa groaned. "Is it bad that I've been trying not to think about it?"

"Procrastination is good," Sue said, positively. "Maybe even smart, since you might spark some kind of bidding war."

"That sounds—" Alyssa shook her head.

"I think it's the idea that they'd go and build an entire skating rink just for Lyss to teach in. And the amount of money they're willing to pay..." Nick shook his head slowly. "I can only do the basics and they're still waving ridiculous amounts at me."

"The value of scarcity," Laura said. "Is it that you don't think you'd like teaching?"

"That would probably depend on the brat-quotient in the class," Alyssa said. "But I think it's more there seems to be an expectation that I can train people to Olympic level. I couldn't even make the State finals."

"So tell them how far you think you can take them," Sue said, shrugging. "It's not like anyone—except maybe Zee, who I'd believe anything of—could get to your level in less than a bunch of years. And by that time maybe they'll really have found the deep-space route to Earth, and can import top-tier coaches."

"At which point the exorbitant salary will drop," Nick noted. "I guess we should make hay, etcetera."

"What about joining KOTIS?" Alyssa asked.

"We can do that later."

Alyssa hesitated, then nodded. "You're right, of course. I think it's the idea of being the one in charge that's scaring me." She put a hand against her helmet, smiling wryly. "It's stupid to feel like a fake, isn't it? And at least, if we go with Pandora Shore's offer, we'll be covered by the school's security and won't have to worry about that complication."

She glanced at the upper level of the amphitheatre, and Laura managed to stop herself from following the line of her gaze, knowing that Sixth Squad would be there, similarly suited, but alert and unfailingly on duty. There were around two dozen squads, counting Kolar and Tare's, and despite Laura's best efforts of memory, everyone outside First, Second and Fourth Squad tended to blur into interchangeable black-clad figures.

"Even if I'd planned to do more than sample aether, that would be off-putting," Alyssa said. "I keep thinking how dull it must be for trained monster-hunters to play bodyguard."

"I expect seeing moonfall close up is a nice treat for them," Laura said. "Since trained elemental talents aren't allowed to get drunk, they would usually have to stay well away from any free-floating aether."

"Good point."

"I wonder if untrained elemental talents have the same restrictions?" Sue said. "A Fire talent could do plenty of damage, even if they weren't at pillar-of-flame level."

As this question was settled via Kaoren, Laura looked about for Julian, and for a moment couldn't see him. But then she saw his outline before the central column of light and, coming closer, was surprised to see that he, too, had resealed his suit.

"Not going to demonstrate your new adult status?"

"By zonking out in front of everyone?" Julian shot his sister a disgusted glance. "That's just what Cass thinks I'm going to do. I should moon the guy in charge just to make her feel she was right."

"The ten minutes it'd take you to get that suit off would take the fun out of it," Laura said, trying not to laugh. Sibling rivalry hadn't gone away, no matter what else had changed.

"Maybe. But then she could tch at me for months. She'd like that."

"I know this isn't as fun as it would be going with your friends," Laura said, offering up an apologetic smile.

"Bleh. I probably wouldn't have gone. Too much risk that they'd find out who I am. And then it'd be all weird and stuff. Maybe I'll go to that avatar café to meet up with them."

"I can see why you like that guild, though. The Star Claw went down neatly, and Haelin's very happy with the new teszen she got out of it."

"Who?"

"One of Gidds' daughters. You'll meet her this weekend."

Julian briefly showed the whites of his eyes, but he only said: "I thought you were playing with Cass' kids."

Laura was starting to suspect that the topic of Mum Sex was going to be more challenging than she expected, but they were both rescued from further attempts by Cass, who came to ask if they wanted to follow the aether down as it drained toward the teleport platform below the amphitheatre.

"Not that we'll see much except glowy mist. And make sure you don't actually get on the platform, or you'll end up back in Kalasa."

"Tell us something we don't know," Julian said.

"Wouldn't put anything past you, brat," Cass said, and they traded amiable barbs until the sheer wonder of the moonfall caught up with them again, and the three of them stepped together into the rising pillar of light and held each other's hands and stared through the vivid glow at the moon, in all its fractured glory.

Awkward conversations could wait. Today, they were together in wonder.

CHAPTER SIXTEEN

In the nature of careless wishes, Laura's desire to see how Gidds dealt with stress was gratified the day before their weekend trip. She woke, not long after midnight, feeling strangely cold and oppressed and, shifting, saw Gidds sitting on the edge of the bed. In the bare light of the stars, Laura could make out no detail, so she raised the room lights to a dim partial visibility.

His back was rigid.

This was such a contrast to Gidds' usual composed calm that for a moment Laura just blinked at him. What had happened?

Thought caught up with astonishment, and Laura realised that of course he must be talking to someone over the interface. Not wanting to interrupt what was probably an important conversation, Laura rose and slipped on her robe before heading out to the kitchen to make something to drink.

She had barely poured out when Gidds came out of the bedroom, shrugging into his uniform jacket. She lifted a mug of perfectly-warmed spider milk enquiringly, and was pleased when he accepted it.

"I'm sorry for waking you, Laura," he said. "There is a situation at Liriath."

He was still...not visibly angry, but very tense, and somehow remote. Locked down.

"Is it something you can tell me about?" she asked, as he drained the mug.

"A group of children overdue at their homes, with no location trace visible through the interface. A sibling confessed that they'd discovered a cave system in the hills south of the city, and gone exploring. The caves appear to be extensive, and the children must be far enough in that the rock is blocking any signal from their interface uplink. A number of Kalrani were in Liriath for a training exercise, and their supervisor volunteered them for the retrieval." His jaw tightened. "They, too, are now non-contactable."

"Are these caves outside the Ionoth-clear zone around the settlement?" Laura asked, biting down on sudden horror. All the platform towns were kept free of Ionoth by powerful constructs called 'ddura', but the vast majority of Muina was still considered too dangerous for unarmed travel.

"They are on the edge of the ddura's range. But there are also native predators, and adapted Ionoth."

Laura hesitated, for she was still negotiating an understanding of his Sights, and how much her own feelings might distract or interrupt much-needed focus. That sense of separateness that was very much a part of him was particularly to the fore just now. But then she stepped forward and wrapped her arms around him.

"I'll hope for the best result for the search, then."

The right decision. His arms closed around her, fierce and tight, and he let out his breath as if the contact had helped. Then he brushed her cheek with a kiss, and was halfway to the door before she even caught the faint hum of an approaching flyer.

Laura drank her spider milk slowly, activated the cleaning unit, and returned to her bedroom, but only to dress and walk down to the bottom of the hill, leaving the path to head directly to the island's stony shore.

The dark water breathed cold, but Laura had not held back on layers, and was not troubled by the chill as she sat herself down on one of the large rocks.

Impossible not to imagine horrors. Children in caves of teeth and claw. Parents waiting with rising dread for news of the vanished, and every hour feeling like days, like months.

Laura could picture that all too well.

Nor did she wonder at the strength of Gidds' reaction. Students sent in without preparation. And civilian children who must surely bring to the forefront of his mind one terrible day long ago, when a dimensional tear had opened and death had swarmed through.

Sinuous, with bone-white claws and a ridge of razor scales, those Ionoth had been small, not much larger than cats. But their numbers and their ferocity had seen them cut effortlessly through an entire residential district of one of the beehive Taren cities. Gidds had been very young, and those things had killed his family, and...

Partially *eaten.*

Laura shuddered, and closed her eyes. The situation might not be as desperately bad as that. And he would have told her if Allidi or Haelin were involved. But still...

A faint rattle of stone made her stiffen, but it was followed by a small cough, and so she activated the interface proximity display. It showed Maze, making his way down to her from the path above. He, too, would have taught some of the missing Kalrani, and no doubt was itching against the constraints of guard duty.

"I'm just accepting there's no chance of sleeping," she said, when he reached her.

"Not worth trying," he agreed. "I can watch what's going on, but that just makes it more difficult to not order someone out to take my shift so I can go help the search. Pointless of me. They've deployed two full squads, both with strong Path Sight talents, so it won't be long before they're found."

He sat down on the rock nearest hers, and for a time they waited in silence. Then Maze said: "Have you ever been out on the lake at night?"

"In one of the boats?"

"In the canoes. It's become a favourite indulgence for Alay and I. And is a very good distraction."

"Sounds like just the thing."

To their left, the lights of the docks came on—the conveniences of the interface were innumerable—and Laura found herself gently wafting through the air toward it, for the conveniences of Telekinesis talents were equally boundless. She almost asked Maze to forget the canoes and play Peter Pan instead, but flying took energy and concentration for him, and so she held her tongue.

Cass had accumulated quite a collection of watercraft since her move to Arcadia. There was an expansive boathouse to shelter the equivalent of the family car, and multiple racks of canoes. Laura watched appreciatively as Maze wafted one of these into the water, and nodded her thanks when he held it steady so she could step in.

There had been many family trips onto the lake in the past few months, and so Laura was relatively practiced with paddling. Gliding out of the light into inky nothing was something very new, however.

"Head west—the water is usually smoothest there."

Laura followed the rhythm of his strokes, her thoughts already stolen by the sky. The lake was not so still tonight that it offered a mirror reflection, but an echo of the stars' expanse was still caught in the slight chop. Miles from the steady glow of Pandora, with only a few small points of light from the surrounding islands, Laura skimmed beneath a million suns.

But even glory could not keep frayed nerves still, so Laura sought refuge in conversation.

"They worked out Earth and Muina are in the same galaxy," she noted. "A different spiral arm, with the galactic core between us."

"Near neighbours," Maze said, and there was something in the tone of his voice that made her turn to try to see him, floating a short way behind her.

"What is it?"

"They've found two of the Kalrani, and one of the missing children. The boy had fallen down a shaft. His friends went for help, and most of the Kalrani went on to track them, leaving two to bring the boy to the surface. They encountered...sounds like an adapted Ionoth."

Adapted Ionoth were the result of creatures from the Ena surviving long enough on Muina to reproduce. The guardian ddura construct often did not seem to recognise these offspring as alien to the planet, and did not eradicate them during its sweeps.

"The Kalrani held it off, thankfully," Maze continued. "Some injuries."

But one predator made others likely, and the still-missing had been heading back to the entrance.

"The Kalrani do have a strong Telekinetic with the group that's still missing," Maze said, unhappily. "But this was a Sights training trip, and multi-Sighted talents rarely have strong elementals. And three are Place Sight talents: even if they're not physically attacked, this kind of thing is the worst kind of stimulus."

"I gather not many Place Sight talents make it through Setari training."

"Usually eliminated in the first few months of evaluation," Maze said, restively. "Only those with the most resilient core are trained to increase the strength of that talent. And even the most formidable are vulnerable in ways that other Setari simply are not."

And they had been sent into a closed-in, dread-filled ordeal. Fear and pain imprinted on stone itself.

"I've read a little about the Tasken Outbreak," Laura said, carefully. "How hard is this going to be for Gidds?"

Maze's response was a long silence, until the lapping water seemed to jangle by contrast.

Finally: "He never shows it, but we all know he wears every injury, every loss. He's gone in with the squads himself today, which is going to mean he's hit with Place impressions directly, and then he'll work with the Kalrani afterwards, trying to ease the impact on them."

"He's still that central to the Setari, even though the crisis is past, and he's being assigned to so many other things?"

That prompted the briefest cough of laughter. "Oh, yes. The reason we are here, and the reason we survived. Our first trainer, and in the early years the first to take us into the Ena. For every Setari, he is the one we have hated, just a little, and tried to impress, to live up to. Our captain of captains. That's never going to change, no matter what he's assigned to. Besides, he still conducts much of the Sights training."

"Hated?"

"It's a complicated relationship. I've definitely had occasions where I've resented him for—for the *standard* he set, as much as anything, and at times for the simple fact of the Setari. But mostly we've been glad of him, because his judgment has been all that stood between us and disaster so many times. I wouldn't quite say it's a parental relationship, except perhaps with Kaoren, but we have burned to prove ourselves to him—and would protect him with our lives."

The words were forthright, honest, exposed. Laura was startled: she'd seen the way the Setari stood straighter around Gidds, but she'd assumed it was a parade-discipline reaction.

"Did it start out that way? He must have been quite young when you were recruited."

"He would have been, I don't know, forty-seven, forty-eight? Certainly less than fifty. I remember we called him 'the boy in charge', so our impression of him was definitely not of an adult. I have some scans stored up from that time, and it's always a shock to look and see him not even old enough for Ena missions under the current system."

Taren years. You could make your attempts on the adulthood exam from fifty, so Gidds would have been just a little older than Julian when he'd transitioned from being the first Setari to training the next generation.

"I've been surprised to not be featuring on the gossip channels lately," she commented.

"Ah, well, most of the upper command chain in KOTIS is very strict on privacy. Personal arrangements definitely are not considered general release reports. And I'm the one who organises Arcadia's security detail. You might have noticed it's always the senior squads here lately. Watching wide-eyed."

Laura laughed, and felt faintly reassured. The gossip would come, of course, especially if they did progress to the point of making things official. First stages were long past. Gone was the simplicity of feeling flustered, of exploring a mutual attraction, of scratching an itch. There was nothing light about the way she felt when thinking about Gidds, the awareness of his absence, the comfort of his presence. They were starting to knit together, to consolidate attraction into belonging. And, yes, the deeper the strands of their lives intertwined, the more the potential for hurt grew. Not simply that his interest could wane, but the kind of pain she felt now, born out of her inability to shield him from his past, and from the weight of a thousand duties.

"They have the rest," Maze said then, and his voice was a mix of relief and dismay. "Some injuries among the Kalrani, but not serious. One of the missing children is dead, the other two critical."

At almost the same moment, a text appeared in her interface.

Gidds: *All Kalrani recovered. One fatality among the explorers. I will be some time, Laura.*

Laura: *Come back here when you need to sleep, whatever time of day.*

Because he would have nightmares. She knew he would have nightmares—*she* would have nightmares, and she stood only at the very fringe of events.

Gidds: *I will.*

Bare text could not truly carry emotion, so it was Laura's imagination that supplied a thousand layers to two simple words. She squeezed her eyes shut briefly, then tipped her head back to gaze at the universe.

oOo

Laura hadn't meant to go to sleep, but her mind slipped away during a visit to one of her most reliable comfort reads, and when it swam to the surface the day had jumped from mid-morning to early afternoon.

Gidds was with her. She turned, working not to wake him, and saw exhaustion writ as clearly as bruises on his sleeping face.

If he was having a nightmare, Laura could not tell. She couldn't remember any of her own, and as her eyes drooped again she hoped they would stay away, but her subconscious was not so kind, and the second time she woke it was necessary to struggle from a tangled morass involving Cass and Julian and caves. This time she was alone.

Hoping her dreams hadn't cut short Gidds' rest, Laura washed her face and tidied impressively tangled hair while checking her messages and then the proximity display. Gidds and Julian were together: an unusual development. Whenever Gidds was in the house, Julian had shown a marked increase in his tendency to only come down for meals. Curious, she went in search of them, following Gidds' measured, beautiful voice out to the pool. Julian said something in response, then looked around at her step.

Sunset, slanting over Braid Meadow, bathed the back patio with light, but that could not be the reason her son's cheeks were so pink.

He didn't seem upset, however, merely saying: "I'm doing dinner, Mum. Won't be long."

"Fondue again?"

"You know you love it."

He took himself off to the kitchen, which was not very far away, but proceeded to make sufficient noise to cover any conversation. Amused, Laura smiled at Gidds, who was in full uniform, and managed to look as impeccably crisp as ever, despite the shadows still sketched in blue beneath his eyes.

"You need to head back already?" she asked, snugging herself into his side.

"I've been and returned," he said, drawing her down to sit on the cup-shaped whitestone bench she'd recently had grown. "I'll spend some more time with several of the Kalrani tomorrow morning, before we head to Areziath. Just visualisation exercises, but they help a great deal." He glanced toward the kitchen, and a lighter note entered his voice as he added: "In all manner of situations."

Laura blinked at the idea of Julian doing anything as meditative as Sight talent visualisation exercises, but then realised that Gidds would be perhaps the best person to ask about trying to avoid embarrassing Sight and Place Sight revelations.

She leaned against his shoulder. "How useful of you. Perhaps he'll stop vanishing whenever Siame visits the island."

"Many people can never be comfortable around Sight talents," he said, serious once more. "The diminished privacy, the broken nights, the need to seek places of quiet: it grows wearisome."

"You're the one who looks tired," she pointed out, curling fingers through his. "Does—does it help you at all to talk?"

"Offer you descriptive words about the instructor who thought missing children a useful training exercise?" He lifted their linked hands, regarding them gravely. "But you mean Tasken. In truth, I don't fully remember it. I was only eight—around three in your years. I dream about it on bad days, which I'm used to managing. It helped me a great deal to be able to come here. Arcadia is very calming in Place, and you draw my thoughts away from old wounds."

"Do my nightmares bother you?"

"They wake me. I watch them sometimes." He reached across to stroke a few strands off her cheek, then shared a log of her, asleep, the space above her full of jagged tracery.

"You keep a lot of scans," Laura said, not discomforted since she had taken a few of her own, when Gidds had been asleep.

"Because my Sights are often used for evidentiary matters, my role requires me to retain full logs. It is not quite as formal as the level of monitoring Cassandra suffers, but is similar."

"Does it bother you?" Cass absolutely hated the mandatory log kept of every single thing she did, for all it could only be accessed under the strictest protocols.

"There have been occasions when it has been used as a tool against me," he said. "And times when I have been so glad to have one of my life's spare, precious moment preserved." He showed her a day, not so very long ago, and then kissed the fingers of their joined hands.

That led to more kissing, nicely filling the short time before Julian called them in for fondue, and a discussion of the public response to the Liriath incident.

"Increasing the amount of active monitoring might prevent other deaths," Gidds said in response to Julian's questions, "but I doubt that the proposed changes will go through. The Kolaren contingent barely accepts the invasive aspects of the interface at the most basic level of monitoring."

"What's the most basic level?" Julian asked, twining strings of cheese.

"The system reports if an exclusion boundary is crossed, or physical condition requires intervention."

"They'd have to be tracking you and checking on your physical condition to be able to tell that's changed, wouldn't they?"

"Yes. It is not actively observed, and no records are kept, however. Today's incident triggered no alerts because the settlement boundary was not crossed, and no medical crisis occurred before the signal was blocked. The at-minimum change proposed is that signal loss triggers an alert."

"What's so bad about that?"

"The argument is against an incremental slide to active monitoring. There are many who passionately believe the Taren system of monitoring has already been taken too far."

"Can you really get programs that shut your interface off?"

"Location masks. Primarily used to cover romantic assignations, from my observation."

"What? How boring." Julian waved his fondue fork at his own face. "I'm on the next step up from basic monitoring, right? What would happen if I activated a location mask?"

"A security detail would be despatched to your last known location, acting on the assumption that a kidnap attempt was underway," Gidds said. "All available scanners would be used in an attempt to image-match for your face. Depending on distance and response time, it is possible all active transport would be temporarily suspended."

"*Cool.*"

"Not quite the appropriate reaction, Julian," Laura said, but with a helpless smile.

"Once you had been located, attention would turn toward whoever had supplied you with the mask," Gidds went on, unperturbed. "They would likely suffer penalties."

"Take the fun out of it, why don't you?" Julian asked, but without rancour. "Hey, Tsur Selkie, how come you don't wear a nanosuit? If you were one of the first Setari?"

"Those weren't developed until the senior squads were due to become active. I do wear one when I'm leading Ena training sessions." His smile made its momentary appearance. "The unformed suits remind me of the duct cleaner, and I find myself curiously disinclined to be in contact with it."

Since the viscous sludge that crawled out of the air-conditioning ducts to absorb dust was widely referred to as 'yanner'—'snot'—Laura could understand a reluctance to *wear* the stuff.

"Does nanite goop retain Place impressions?" she asked.

"I've rarely encountered that. Clothing often does, but the process of being reformed and repurposed appears to disrupt Place."

They wandered into a comparison of Place Sight and what was called psychometry on Earth, trying to decide whether psychometry could be very weak Place Sight.

"It sucks that no-one except Cass got to be psychic or a Touchstone or whatever," Julian said. "They scanned all our brains and said that we've got the same synaptic structures as people here, but none of us have been able to do anything fun."

"Except visit multiple planets, and play in virtual worlds," Laura noted.

Julian grinned. "Yeah, I guess. And Nils takes me flying sometimes, which is way cool." He paused, glancing sidelong at Gidds, then saying to Laura: "Next weekend maybe I will go to that café to meet some of my band from *Red Exchange*. I've been working on not sounding Australian when I talk."

"I wonder if they'll think you're someone trying to pretend to be you?" Laura mused. "Your friends seemed to be good players." And, in Laura's estimation, relatively young. A meet-up—especially with some guards in the background—shouldn't be anything to worry about.

"Tzatch and Corezzy have applied to join the same bit of KOTIS that Nick and Alyssa were going to sign up for," Julian said, with another glance at Gidds. "Apparently it's hard to get in."

"Very competitive," Gidds agreed neutrally.

Julian paused, then shrugged and began collecting plates. "You all should join our band, because it would totally be the best laugh, one day years from now, to tell Tzatch who she kept ordering around."

"I think the plan is to form our own band," Laura said. "But perhaps we can meet up for another event some time."

"Spoilsport," Julian said, piling plates on the cleaning unit and starting for the stairs. "See you, Tsur Selkie."

"Remember you're getting up early," Laura said.

"Tell that to Aunt Sue!" Julian called, and crashed up the stairs.

Gidds didn't seem to be bothered by Julian's ideas for amusing revelations. "You said he had been bullied after Cassandra's disappearance?"

Laura nodded. "The worst were a couple of boys he thought were the best of his friends. Being able step back and devote himself to games has been a good break for him, but I'm glad he's starting to want to meet people around his own age."

"Did you also regret not having a strong talent?"

She laughed. "Doesn't everyone think it would be wonderful to be able to fly? Can you fly? I don't even know your full talent set."

"Low level Telekinesis," he said, making his glass lift briefly from the table. "Place, Combat and Sight Sight, and Speed." He rubbed a hand across his eyes, then added: "I would have enjoyed flying, but hit my limit very early."

He looked like he was close to hitting a more ordinary limit, and she told him so.

Gidds nodded. "I have a meeting—interface-only—in a few joden, so I'm trying to stay awake. Then, I fear, I will make a very boring guest for you."

"Perhaps I'll watch you dream," she said, with a faint smile. Then, longing to do something to help lift some of the shadows from his face, she stood and held out her hand. "Before your meeting, maybe you could show me what my workroom looks like in Place?"

Making Gidds Selkie catch his breath had become a main source of Laura's 'spare, precious moments'. And this time she'd even remembered to start a log so that, during times when she needed a captive fragment of joy, she could watch him go still, so completely focused on her.

"I would be glad to," he said, and his beautiful voice was husky.

He took her hand, and she led the way, reflecting wryly that it said something about her that showing Gidds her workroom felt more momentous than the sex.

"I've been guessing that the door probably signals 'private'," she said, as they reached her room.

In response, he shared her the feed of his vision, and the plain white door was suddenly stitched over with silver tracery. Not quite bars, or chains, or ghostly boards, but a mass that held something of all these things, and which quite clearly warned intruders away.

Laura laughed, almost embarrassed by how truly she'd spoken. "My art supplies are the one thing I'm very organised about, and I was always having to lock the kids and the cat out, or find everything in chaos. And, when we were children ourselves, Sue and Bet would take positive joy in creeping up behind me. So I'm in the habit of keeping the door shut."

She opened it, and watched Gidds' face rather than his feed as he caught his breath for the second time in a handful of minutes.

Her own eyes showed only two stools side-by-side before an empty workbench, and a window looking out onto grey evening. Laura was very particular about wrapping and storing current projects, and putting her tools away, so there was nothing else of note from this angle. But Gidds' feed showed her a room filled with a riot of whorls and spirals, scrolls and arabesques.

For a moment Laura could only blink, overwhelmed by layer upon layer, but then sorted out two distinct sets of patterns. One, the blue of a twilight sky, covered the whole of the room, though concentrated most around Laura's favourite spot at the bench. The other was less widespread, but darker, stronger: vivid threads woven through the larger skein.

"We've rather painted the room in silver and gold, haven't we?" Laura said, awed and delighted. "Does everyone make different colours?"

Gidds shook his head. "Liranadestar has been spending time here? It looks like she has been using her abilities."

"We've been making models of our characters from *Red Exchange*," Laura explained. "Do...do you mean that Lira might have been making a version of her character in the Ena, as well?"

"Creative activities have been shown to leave a more marked imprint," Gidds said. "But it is not something we have tested in any depth with Cassandra." He took a step into the room. "There is a great sense of belonging here. Both yours and Liranadestar's."

Laura flushed, shaken by a strange mixture of pride and tenderness. She had had numerous thoughts about abruptly becoming 'Unna Laura' to so many children, but foremost among them had been a desire to live up to the role.

"I find myself desperately wanting to protect people from the things that have already happened to them," she said.

The time until Gidds' meeting was conveniently filled by a demonstration of the interesting patterns produced during extended bouts of kissing. And then, after a meeting and a shower, she did watch him sleep for a while, and replayed the log of the patterns they had made together, in her workroom.

For all the pain Place Sight brought him, it filled Gidds' life with wonder. And she was fitting into that, less clumsily than she had feared.

When the opportunity presented, who would not want to live such an extraordinary life? Like learning to fly, it was something Laura could not help but embrace.

CHAPTER SEVENTEEN

"So this place is going to be on a river instead of a lake?" Julian said.

"What makes you say that?" Laura asked absently, casting an eye over Lira and Julian to ensure that all sensible precautions for a day out in the sun had been taken.

"Because it's called Areziath, Unna Laura," Lira said. "River City."

"I thought 'river' was 'Avez'," Laura said, picking up one of the backpacks weighted down with lunch.

"Arez," Lira said firmly.

"In Old Muinan, Mum," Julian said, grabbing his backpack. "Come on—we'd better go make sure Aunt Sue isn't still in bed."

But Sue had Nick, Alyssa and Maddy to haul her out of her Pikachu onesie and into some semblance of order.

"Come on, slowpokes!" she called, waving from further down the path. "Laura, you need to overcome this habit of always showing up late."

Laura offered her sister some rolled eyes, then said to Julian: "If you've managed to add Old Muinan to your accomplishments, along with beating me to adulthood, I'm going to have to seriously think about getting up earlier to make up lost ground."

"The trick is to stay up all night, Mum. Or just asking Lira."

"Ask Lira what?" Sue asked.

"What Areziath means."

"River City. According to Muinapedia."

"Hey, we weren't going to look it up beforehand," Laura protested.

Sue shrugged. "I didn't look at any pictures. Just checked the bugs and heat factor. Southern hemisphere, spring, but a bit more temperate than the Pandora region. If it gets snow at all, it'd only be a light dusting, and we'd be well past any spring melt."

Since this was barely more than Gidds had already told them, Laura relaxed and instead waved to the trio of black-clad Setari waiting at the docks. Zee, Mara and Alay had most likely already been involved in performing surveys of Areziath during the initial months of Muina's resettlement, but all three of the senior Setari greeted the small expedition with bright smiles and no sign that they resented their years of training and incredibly deadly skills being wasted on guard duty at a picnic.

"All I know is that Areziath is beautiful, and an unusual example of the platform towns," Laura said, in response to a question from Alay. "Gidds thought I'd like it, but suggested I not look it up."

"Maze loves it," Alay said. "And visiting without any idea of what to expect—especially at this time of year—is an excellent idea. There's a good deal of debate over what to do with the site...but I won't go on. You'll see soon enough."

"It's so special that we had a little competition to see who got this assignment," Mara said, with a meaning grin at Laura.

To watch wide-eyed? Laura smiled wryly, finding she wasn't bothered by their warm curiosity.

The arrival of their transport distracted her from further reflection. This was a small aircraft known as a tanz: a highly manoeuvrable vehicle that always made Laura think of the space shuttle as if designed by Batman.

It settled into the water just off the end of the dock, and they walked across the wing to board, with Laura revisiting her perennial bemusement about military transports being used as taxis for her family. That was likely not even due to Gidds, but instead because of Lira, so valuable and so potentially dangerous.

And currently sitting with her head bowed, expression distracted. Of course, she'd visited Areziath before, and knew what to expect, but she'd seemed to enjoy the idea of another visit—and the fact that Laura wanted to be surprised by what it was like.

Squeezing her granddaughter's hand, Laura sent a text.

Laura: *Feeling okay?*

Liranadestar: *I'm just checking on Nimenny, Unna Laura.*

Laura: *You're lucky your Nimenny is so much less grumpy than my Kirr-tut. Would you like to go on another group quest with us tomorrow?*

Liranadestar: *Maybe.*

Laura left it at that, not wanting to do anything to push the girl away from *Red Exchange*. Cass had noticed a sharp decrease in Lira's nightmares since she'd started playing, and so adventures with 'Nimenny' would not be complicated by the prospect of stealth Kalrani bodyguards.

On the flip side, Laura had to wonder if there had been a committee meeting or two about the relative dangers of Touchstones who became devoted to computer-generated water spirits. As virtual pets went, the teszen were light-years from Tamagotchi.

Literally. Literally light-years from Earth. She would never quite get over that.

The trip to Pandora's old town was brief and direct, with the tanz dropping them directly into the amphitheatre, allowing the shortest of walks to the teleport platform. A green-suited security detail was waiting to ensure no onlookers pressed too close, but as they disembarked Zee, Mara and Alay still shifted from relaxed and chatty to alert and focused. Laura was fascinated by the change, and the reminder that these three personable and friendly women were some of the most dangerous people on the planet, quite capable of swatting attackers like flies. Their training had been intended for killing monsters in the Ena, but they were more than equal to human threats—and over-eager fans, which was all they faced now, with a ring of spectators at the upper rim of the amphitheatre waving and calling out names. Mostly the three Setari's, ironically, but also Lira's and—to Laura's immense and carefully hidden amusement—Julian's.

He might be growing into his father's gawky, stork-like figure, but Julian's features were even and pleasantly attractive when not quite so crimson, and he had accrued a not-insubstantial fan club. Though, as he had repeatedly pointed out, having a fan club for being someone's brother didn't really count.

Their Setari escort ushered them below the amphitheatre to a simple round room with an unassuming white platform in the centre. This activated as soon as they had all filed on, replacing one round room with a second, almost identical, the only visible difference a sign that switched from 'Pandora' to 'Kalasa'.

It was entirely impossible for Laura to make this trip without a burst of wonder at actual, real teleportation platforms, and a lurch of distress because Cass had been the one who'd discovered the function of the platforms—a development that had left her trapped in Kalasa, hunted by monsters.

Laura always looked at the wall opposite the entrance, searching for signs of the gap that had allowed Cass to escape capture, but the patch was seamless. Repairs were underway all over Kalasa since, after considerable argument, the decision had been made to restore the ancient city rather than preserve it in the fractured state in which it had been found.

Having imperfectly followed some of the debate, Laura knew there were practical reasons for making use of Kalasa, but could not help but wish it could be left untouched. A whitestone city filling a valley protected and concealed by an ancient and still-functioning forcefield, it truly was an abandoned ruin out of Forerunner legend.

But KOTIS—recruiting a massive team of archaeologists—had moved in and, after years of cataloguing, were now cleaning and patching, decently dealing with the bodies of the long-ago fallen, and cautiously making the place habitable, because Kalasa was the place all the teleport platforms linked up: a planetary Grand Central Station.

Since Laura's last visit, the technicians had finished restoring the arching fountain that soared above the teleportation platforms. A curving and elegant tripod structure, it would produce a vertical drop into a blue-tiled pool at the very centre of the city, though no water fell as yet.

"The devices team refuses to allow installation of a conventional pump," Alay informed Laura. "As much as possible they're aiming to restore the original systems, which is quite a challenge when we barely understand them."

Laura was looking about for Gidds, surprised to not find him waiting at the fountain as planned. While last-minute demands on his time were something she now expected, he was punctilious in keeping her informed of delays, and she'd expect him to be even more particular for their first almost-public date. Had something happened that–?

But no, there he was, walking with Allidi and Haelin from the direction of the city gate.

Sue: *Ooh, civvies. Fit snug, don't they?*

Laura: *Indeed.*

Sue: *Do you think he'd do a few push-ups if I asked nicely?*

Laura: *I think he would smile at you if you asked him that.*

Sue: *You mean "Ah yes, humour"? Pfui.*

Laura: *After a couple of decades of students, I suspect that's a built-in response.*

"A side-trip to view the tedan," Gidds explained, when the three Selkies reached the main group.

"'Tedan'?" Sue echoed.

"Freshwater version of seals," Laura explained, and then introduced Allidi and Haelin.

The two girls responded with calm self-possession. It was one of those times when Laura felt challenged when faced with Sight Sight, knowing that chances were high that they would see she felt a little anxious, fretting over nothing. Perhaps she should ask Gidds to teach her a few Sights exercises as well.

"Laura's been giving you selkie stories, has she?" Sue asked.

"Just one. About a girl who met a man who was really a tedan," Haelin said, then glanced at Laura and added: "Are they all sad stories?"

"Mostly. If you could dance in the sea, it seems almost inevitable to miss it when clumping about on land."

"Hm," Haelin said, and then crossed to Alyssa and began to ply her with questions about the planned skating rink, Allidi following along behind.

In their position, Laura would also have found ice skating infinitely more interesting than parental partners, and so she suppressed an impulse to push for their attention, instead taking the opportunity to briefly brush her fingers against Gidds'. Still, it was difficult not to think about the distance between indulgent grandma and wicked stepmother. She had been quickly accepted by Cass' children, but the situation she was facing with these two girls was one that left her full of questions about belonging.

Getting way ahead of yourself, Laura.

As they started into the building housing the Areziath platform, she put complexities aside and smiled at Gidds. "I feel like I've accidentally changed your relationship to your own name."

"I have been thinking about that story a great deal," he admitted. "And contrasting the tedan's movements with my swimming ability. Swimming is not common on Tare, and I only learned relatively recently."

Picturing him learning gave her one of those flashes of hilarity that she knew by now he would see, so she smiled apologetically and said: "It's a useful skill to have when moving to a planet covered with lakes."

They reached the platform, and stepped from one hemisphere to the other with no effort at all, and Laura gave herself up to a burble of anticipation. Going to a beautiful place she'd never seen. Of course, all that met her eyes was a round white room, blandly identical except for the location sign, and perhaps the faintest shift of temperature. And when they headed up, it was to yet another amphitheatre, this one beneath a pale, thin sky.

"Why is it you've only settled five out of the fourteen pattern-roof towns?" Sue asked Gidds.

"We were in danger of tripping over our feet," he told her. "There needs to be a period of consolidation and balancing before any further expansion. Nor do we necessarily want to build cities at every one of the platform locations."

"Definitely not Areziath," Zee said, shifting briefly from her ultra-professional guard stance. "Or, at least, it would have to be managed sensitively."

"Nothing here until we understand its purpose," Gidds said, deliberately mysterious, and took Laura's hand firmly as they climbed the stair.

She regarded him with faint amusement, knowing that he was anticipating the moment she saw the town. But she was glad she'd resisted the temptation to look the place up beforehand. What could be so special? Yet another whitestone town, but presumably in a particularly dramatic setting?

"What's that weird sound?" Maddy asked. "Is that rain?"

"What?" Alyssa asked, then lifted her head. "Oh, I hear it."

"Kind of...whirry," Maddy said.

"Maybe it's robots," Julian said, on an eager note, but then almost fell over backward as a formless amoeba blotted the pale sky above. Constantly changing shape, it crossed over the amphitheatre, abruptly reversed direction, and was lost to sight.

Sue had gripped Laura's arm, but now raced up the stair, only to stop dead as she reached the top.

"A murmuration!" Laura said, thoroughly delighted, and added to Gidds: "Sue's always wanted to see one."

"It is a behaviour seen on Earth, then?"

"Oh, yes, although I've never seen it in Australia. I wonder if it's the same species of bird?"

The top of the stair had become crowded with people standing staring, but Gidds deftly manoeuvred Laura sideways, and then she, too, stopped in her tracks and gaped.

The amphitheatre sat on the crown of a lone hill in the centre of large plain. There was, as anticipated, a collection of pattern-roof buildings, but these were confined to the slopes of the hill. Beyond was pearl and silver and milky blues in a mist-shrouded dawn.

"River City," Laura said, with a full appreciation of a very literal name.

The region was all river. Not a driving torrent or lazy rills, but...fretwork. Artificial channels—they had to be— had been cut into the entire sweep of land around the amphitheatre hill, to form a kind of Art Nouveau Norfolk Broads, with shades of a Japanese hanabi, for it was spring in Areziath, and a millennia ago someone had carefully chosen the trees.

Sue: *When Howl took Sophie to the garden in the Waste.*

Impossible not to agree. This was the stuff of purest fantasy. Magic.

Laura: *I would definitely not be surprised to encounter moving castles, talking fire, or a door that leads four ways.*

Sue: *I'm going to spend the rest of the day picturing Serious Soldier moaning about his hair.*

"Teleport platform or door into Faerie?" Alyssa asked, with a catch in her throat that spoke for all of them.

"Can we see it from above, Dzo?" Allidi asked, lifting bright eyes to her father.

He nodded, and Zee said: "Groups of four, please."

She took Maddy, Lira, Allidi and Haelin first, all four of the girls looking delighted, though three not as thunderstruck as the Earth contingent, since they'd all known about Areziath beforehand, but had politely kept details to themselves.

"We don't really know if it's purely decorative, or has some purpose," Mara was saying. "It functions in the same way as the other pattern-roof villages—produces aether each moonfall—but no-one's been able to rule out the possibility that it's more than extreme landscape design."

"There are houses out there," Alay added. "Exactly eleven, and much larger and more complex than the simple, repetitive design of these box structures on the hillside. There might be a lot of theories, but the most likely explanation is this was simply a pretty place for an elite to visit."

"I'm going to stick with it being an outpost of Faerie," Sue said, firmly, and began to circle the rim of the amphitheatre, which had clearly been designed for the purpose of looking out rather than in.

Laura followed a step behind, still holding Gidds' hand, and glad when everyone lapsed back into appreciative silence, for this was a dawn for hush and wonder.

She spotted one of the houses, buried beneath overhanging branches on one of the countless islands. A slender curved bridge connected that island to the next, and Laura was able to pick out occasional sections of a whitestone path, patchily visible beneath undisturbed centuries of leaves turned to mulch, encroaching bushes, and a top layer of fallen petals. Birds were everywhere. Elegant herons. Fat ducks. Sleek divers. Flittings in the bushes. And, above, an ever-changing cloud swirling, darting, turning.

Zee returned with the girls, and took Gidds, Laura, Sue and Julian straight up. Laura gulped because thinking flying incredible didn't stop her stomach from feeling like it dropped to her feet whenever she was being whizzed about. She started to let go of Gidds' hand, but he tightened his grip briefly, and shook his head to show he wasn't bothered, and she found that having something to hold on to helped convince her innards that she wasn't freefalling.

They rose to a point where they could take in the whole of the plain—high enough that it almost felt like a later part of the day—and then Zee tilted them gently forward so that they were hovering 'Superman-style', and could just *look*.

The river really was a river. Laura could see it stretching from their left to their right: a natural flow that only happened to be interrupted by a vast circle of channels in the shape of a tree, all wide spreading branches and tangled roots picked out in shimmering water.

"There's only a single route through," Sue said, eventually. "By land, I mean."

Impressed that she'd been able to work this out, Laura tried to track the path.

"From the amphitheatre, you can walk across the whole thing," Zee said. "It loops all the way through the roots and the branches and returns to the central hill."

"Is anyone studying this?" Sue asked. "Documenting it? I suppose they must be, and there's a million volunteers wanting to help."

"There are multiple studies," Gidds told her. "And opportunities are certainly competitive. However, those vetting the applications may well take your special circumstances into account."

"Cass opens a lot of doors, huh?" Sue said. "Well, I'm not one to stand on principle to the point of idiocy. Nepotism it shall be."

Zee laughed. "Your perspective as a person from an entirely different culture is not so small a factor. And you know we all clamour for copies of the scans you take of the children. I don't know what it is about them that makes for the one image we want to keep of each occasion."

"Framing, mostly," Sue said with a professional's abstraction, gazing at the shimmering scene below.

"Eleven was a significant number in old Muinan society," Gidds offered. "Though whether it has been used here for luck or has greater significance we cannot tell, and until a full study has been made, there will be no construction whatsoever on this site—or even outside its bounds. The research teams are based out of Pandora."

Sue's attention had been stolen by the murmuration, returning from a circuit of the roots of the city. The flight of birds was incredible enough to watch from the ground. Witnessing it from above—and perilously near to within—stunned them to silence until Zee dropped them back to the amphitheatre.

"I think they *are* starlings," Sue said. "Same as Earth, or very similar. Though I thought murmurations were a dusk behaviour for them, not dawn."

As Zee took Nick, Alyssa, Mara and Alay for their turn, Gidds asked the four girls which direction they'd like to walk. Haelin and Lira immediately said opposite directions, and were each seconded by Allidi and Maddy.

"Which do you prefer, Unna Laura?" Lira asked, but Laura was not going to start the day playing favourites.

"I'd say flip a coin—which is how a decision between two choices is often made on Earth—but I don't think any of us would have a coin. I wonder if you have an equivalent of rock-paper-scissors?"

After some explanation she learned that Tare had cloth-razor-stone and old Muina had had spider-snake-bird, but Gidds annoyed his daughters by pointing out that this was not a game you wanted to play against Sight Sight talents, and so they created a makeshift coin, and Haelin won the toss.

Lira was not someone who enjoyed losing, but after a moment's scowl she asked Haelin: "Why do you want to go into the roots instead of the branches?"

"Because that's where trees start," Haelin said, matter-of-factly. "Going the other way would be starting at the end."

"The light comes in at the leaves," Lira countered, though without real heat.

"How long would it take to walk all about this place?" Maddy asked. "Could we do the whole thing?"

"Quite a few days, I'd say," Sue said. "You could maybe walk the edge in a long day, but that path was twisty. Did you notice that there were distinct regions? Blurred by time, but definitely different original plantings."

Zee returned with her last batch, and Laura saw that even the Setari, who had visited Areziath before, were wide-eyed and awed.

"Let's walk without talking—at least at the start," Alyssa said. "It's kind of a place for being quiet."

They started down off the hill: a walk that took a half hour in itself, and made for an eerie progress, for the ruins had been left undisturbed by those who studied them, and the empty doors and windows of the houses gave glimpses into an ancient past, where one day every occupant had died all at once. Whatever the city's purpose in the past, it was a mass grave now.

Yet it was not an oppressive place. Empty, almost lonely, but with no sense of ancient violence. Laura let her breath out in a muted sigh after they had passed the last of the platform-roof houses, and then checked on Lira, who had not precisely lived through that long-ago disaster. The girl's brow was clear, and when she noticed Laura looking she gave *her* a reassuring smile. Kids.

Liranadestar: *Do you think everyone will like the cookies I made, Unna Laura?*

Laura: *If they taste half as nice as they smelled baking, I think they're sure to. Especially after a long walk.*

The entrance to the path was through a stone arch, sadly fractured in several places, but still giving the transition an air of formal commencement. They walked into birdsong, a heady scent of blossom, and the chirrup and whine of insects—fortunately kept at bay by simple sonic devices worn clipped to clothing. Crossing to the second of the countless islands, Gidds sent Laura his visual feed, and a whole extra world of small animals was revealed.

The reverent silence did not last, and they began to point out particular features to each other. Small nests built precariously on the ends of reeds. A turquoise flash as a fishing bird dived. Water thickly layered with blue and white petals. *Otters.*

Laura gripped Gidds' hand at this latest discovery, and his feed showed he glanced at her rather than the ripples in the water. He was enjoying their reaction to Areziath as much as the walk itself. But then he helpfully indicated the direction the otters had headed, and seemed as interested in them as he was pleased by the expression on his daughters' faces as a sleek brown head popped out of the water almost at their feet.

It took all of two hours to reach the first of the structures dotted along the winding path: a rambling house, almost lost beneath a mass of creepers, and a pavilion structure that sat separate, in the point section of a large, teardrop-shaped island.

"Lunchtime," Sue said firmly, and headed for the pavilion.

It was a splendid meal. They spread picnic blankets, shared out dishes, and talked theories—the Setari taking turns to stand on guard. Alay told them some of the details they could not see: the depth of the water, the hidden channels that ensured that there was a cross-flow in places that might otherwise lie stagnant, and the silting that blocked many of them. There was a big push to allow more visitors, but also a counter movement to simply recreate Areziath elsewhere if people wanted to trail about it.

Gidds somehow managed to maintain his upright posture even while sitting cross-legged on a blanket, with a cluster of pink, trumpet-shaped flowers dangling an inch above his head. His daughters imitated him with the ease of long practice, and Laura, noticing her own back was very straight, consciously adjusted her posture. She would never fully understand how a man could be so quiet, and yet have such an impact on those around him. Even Julian was less sprawling than usual.

But it was not an uncomfortable atmosphere, and Laura watched him being happy, while they sampled all the food. Each household had brought a contribution to the picnic, so there was plenty to eat. The cookies were a success.

"Places ending in 'iath' definitely mean 'city', right, Lira?" Sue was saying. "Yet this place can't possibly be intended for a city's population."

"But it is very big," Lira pointed out, with some surprise. "That makes it a city."

"I'd call it a town surrounded by a water park. I wonder whether the otters are local, given that they occur around Pandora as well. Perhaps this was started off as some kind of wetland specimen collection? There's certainly a massive variation of plants."

"Can we explore the house, Dzo?" Allidi asked.

Gidds shook his head. "The research teams have so far catalogued without removing objects, and do not want the interiors disturbed. You can circle the outside of it, if you wish—or take a half-kasse to explore the island. The site map shows areas of use."

Laura hadn't even thought to look for an interface map, and guessed that 'areas of use' was an oblique way of pointing out a set of bushes that had been designated as a latrine area. There she found that the interdiction on building at Areziath did not mean you could not send in floating kiosks containing roomy bathrooms, and so she would not need the trowel she had thoughtfully packed—and could even take a hot shower if the notion struck her. The researchers likely didn't want to introduce an accumulation of human waste to a sensitive site. Or Tarens didn't think much of squatting over a hole. Either way, Laura was grateful for unexpected luxuries.

The island was large, and overgrown enough that when Laura emerged she could not see a single person. Walking to the nearest shore, she settled on a convenient rock and—after sending Sue a suggestion that she check out 'Howl's Perambulating Pottie'—searched the water for more glimpses of otters.

A charming blue and black duck presented itself instead, swimming along the channel and nibbling at waterweed. Laura promptly added it to a collection of scans she was building as a gift for Rye, who—thanks to a stream of subtitled BBC documentaries provided by

Cass—idolised David Attenborough, and diligently catalogued every plant and animal he encountered.

There were quite a few birthdays to prepare for. Sen's was very soon, and Lira's fourteenth. And then it would be not so very long before Tyrian turned one—by the Muinan calendar. By Earth reckoning Tyrian would be one much sooner. Laura would have to–

With a muted 'plup', the blue and black duck vanished. Pulled under. Frozen, Laura stared at the spreading circle of ripples, not sure whether to leap away. It was all too easy to picture something drawn by her movement, exploding from the water in a tentacular frenzy.

Pond weed. Ripples. Nothing.

Laura relaxed, and then murmured: "Et in Arcadia ego."

"Tsa Devlin?"

Laura turned to find Allidi and Haelin dividing their attention between her and the water.

"I was just wondering whether I should move back," Laura said, hoping she hadn't painted herself a coward.

"There's no directed threat," Allidi told her.

"Good to know," Laura said, and then gestured to the rock next to hers, glad for a conversational opener that was less inane than asking if they liked being Kalrani. "I don't really understand Combat Sight. Can you sense all living things, or only those that want to hurt you?"

"Neither," Allidi replied, neatly arranging herself on the rock. "It is an awareness of potential danger."

"Things like worms and most bugs don't register at all," Haelin added, plunking herself down beside her sister, but then making a habitual adjustment to a more arranged posture. "Things that can't hurt you, really, and don't want to."

"Whatever is there is a predator," Allidi said, indicating the now-still water with a faint lift of her chin. "It's not aware of us, and probably would not ordinarily attack creatures our size, but it registers to Combat Sight because there is a potential for danger."

"If we splashed our feet in the water it might bite them," Haelin interpolated. "But it's not going to leap at us."

"Combat Sight tells you all that?"

"It's like coloured static, but without noise, and you can't really see it," Haelin explained—not at all helpfully.

"Something not very dangerous and not interested in us—one of those birds—is barely there," Allidi added. "A grey haze that is hard to even notice. If we made it angry somehow, and it decided to attack us, it would be yellower and a little stronger to see, and we would feel it as a directed threat. Something that could be dangerous, but isn't interested in us would be a green—the more dangerous the easier it is to see. If it decided it wanted to attack us, it would become yellow, and sharper." She paused apologetically. "Those are words to give you some idea. It's not really colours."

"The shape of the experience, but not the taste," Laura said, with a wry smile. "What about if, oh, the pavilion we had lunch in was cracked, and was about to fall on our head. Would Combat Sight notice that?"

"No, it could not have any potential for intent," Allidi said.

"We'd probably see that with Sight Sight, though," Haelin said, shrugging. "What did you say about Arcadia, before you noticed us?"

Laura paused so she could phrase the words as correctly as possible in Muinan. "'Even in Arcadia, there I am.'"

Most Muinans would probably meet this with blankness or mild confusion, and Haelin did precisely that, but Allidi straightened, delicate brows drawing together, and after a distinct pause she said: "Death?"

Sight Sight truly was remarkable. "Has—do you know the meaning of Arcadia?"

"Gelezan," Haelin said.

Laura looked the word up to confirm that Gelezan was, indeed, the equivalent of a rural utopia.

"Yes. On Earth there is a painting—it's about five hundred years old—of people standing in a rural landscape around a tomb. A monument to a dead person. And on it, in a rather old language, is carved what we translate as 'Even in Arcadia, there I am'. There's plenty of debate over what exactly this symbolises—the immortality of art or some such—but on the most basic level it is a reminder that death comes to even the best of places."

"Oh," Haelin said. The younger girl's tone and expression were an unexpected mix of disappointment and frustration, and she sighed deeply before adding: "I wish you would hurry up. Dzo has been waiting so long."

"*Haelin!*" Allidi said, sharply.

"Well it's true," Haelin retorted. "For years and years."

Laura, very confused, said: "We only met a few months ago, you know."

"But it's been forever since you came to Muina," Haelin said. "And we've been waiting and waiting since long before that, ever since Dzo's Sight told him, and, really, you are so very slow."

Laura didn't feel slow. She felt like she was in freefall. It had been little more than a Taren year since she'd first met Gidds Selkie. Yet Haelin had said 'long before' she came to Muina.

What in the world was going on?

CHAPTER EIGHTEEN

Two calmly self-assured Sight Sight talents had been replaced by girls, one glowering at Laura, aggrieved, and the other entirely dismayed.

"She's overstating," Allidi assured Laura, her own face pinched and anxious. "Dzo has—it's the wrong way to put it."

"I—" Laura began, feeling very off-balance. Then she stopped, putting aside her reaction because Allidi looked like she was about to be ill. "Well, this is very confusing, but I gather you're talking about something your own Sights have told you, Haelin? In which case, I suspect you owe your father an apology for telling me things private to him."

"I haven't, really," Haelin protested, but she'd lost her head of steam, and any hint of her usual confidence.

For a moment Laura became very worried indeed, but neither of the girls gave a sense of being *afraid* of their father's reaction. Instead they were behaving as if they'd knocked down some treasured family ornament, and were counting the pieces. Or, more to the point, they were worried they might have cost their father his romance.

Years and years?

"Go explain to Dzo," Allidi said, with a mix of stern command and unhappiness, and when Haelin reluctantly obeyed the older girl turned back to Laura, gathering some semblance of her usual poise to add: "I apologise for her, Tsa Devlin."

The exchange had given Laura a chance to try to put her thoughts into order, and while she couldn't quite put aside a queasy roil of uncertainty, she had no intention of taking that out on this girl.

"I'd like it if you and your sister called me Laura," she said, firmly. "And, Allidi, I'm not someone who—" She hesitated, struggling to translate 'goes off half-cocked' into Muinan, and settled for: "I'm not someone who often leaps before looking. Your father and I seem to be overdue for a conversation, but the simplest thing to do is to have that conversation." She smiled ruefully. "From my point of view, things have been quite fast, not slow at all. I don't quite see why your sister finds that upsetting."

"It's because...you see, it's getting close to the snow season," Allidi haltingly explained, her cheeks flushed. "Haelin wanted to be living...in time for..."

"Winter?"

"The snow fight," Allidi said, with poorly stifled embarrassment.

Laura blinked, then tried not to look too amused. It had become a yearly tradition for Cass and the senior Setari squads to have a friends-and-family snowball fight. Like most semi-public things about Cass, it was widely reported on and imitated, and Laura could quite see how Allidi and Haelin could have built hopes of attending.

"I've been looking forward to that too. Whatever else happens, I'd be glad to have you two on my team." Laura laughed. "I suspect it would give me a distinct advantage."

Allidi did not stop looking upset, but she summoned a smile. "Thank you, Tsa Dev...thank you, Laura."

This was not how Laura had planned to get to know Gidds' daughters, but perhaps it was for the best.

"I begin to understand why there's so much emphasis placed on Sights talent etiquette. It must be quite a challenge to grow up in a family where you can't ever be fully private."

"Sights talents who *aren't* family are harder," Allidi said, and then looked relieved. Gidds had arrived.

He walked a step behind Haelin, as self-contained and unhurried and intense as the first time she'd seen him, come to interview her on behalf of the Triplanetary. Could he really have arrived at that first meeting with an agenda?

"I'm sorry, Tsa Devlin," Haelin said, very subdued. "I was impolite."

"I'll forgive you if you call me Laura," Laura said.

Haelin promptly agreed, but neither she nor Allidi looked entirely reassured. They might not have Place Sight, but evidently Sight Sight—or simple body language—told them that careless words were easier to forgive than forget.

As the two girls departed, Laura studied Gidds' face. Perhaps the tiniest hint of strain, but nothing more. Not that she'd expected that. Where, she wondered, did courtship slipups rank on the list of problems he'd had to deal with that week?

"We haven't exactly had a lot of serious discussions," she said, deciding she wanted to tackle this head-on. "I'm willing to bet that I'm hung about with a few 'don't go there' signs, just like my workroom. But I —" She paused, then said carefully: "Haelin wasn't very clear, but I took the impression that you saw me years ago—I guess it must have been on the log of Cass' visit home on her birthday—and your Sights told you I was the one for you. Or something."

Gidds sat down on the rock his daughters had used, and arranged his hands on his knees, meeting her eyes directly.

"Not quite accurate," he said, in that perfectly controlled voice. "When I watched that log, I saw a woman face an improbable vision of hope fulfilled, and accept that it was true. Not truly remarkable. But when you had been told your daughter could not return to you, that was a struggle for you, and then you said, very simply: 'Live well'. That is what triggered my Sight. You in some manner pictured her doing that—a thousand possibilities in an instant. It left me breathless, wanting to know, to understand...not necessarily what you had been thinking, but you. One of the most powerful Sight Sight reactions I've ever experienced. There was attraction there, but in large part a Sight Sight talent's overwhelming need to understand."

"Which itched for years?"

A sketch of a nod. "It helped that your daughter a number of time created projections of you, and that my role required me to review them. I did so thoroughly."

Laura, remembering how Cass had rewatched her own logs in order to ogle Kaoren, almost managed a smile.

Gidds' expression shifted faintly, no doubt in response to her flicker of amusement, but he went on steadily. "The second year was hardest. When arrangements were underway to bring you here, and meeting you became a real possibility. Sight Sight reactions can be very draining when they are stymied. I was there the day you arrived, but your attention was completely taken up by your family, and I had arranged assignments on Tare and Kolar for the first month, so that I could not be tempted to...hover."

Sensible of him to avoid creepy stalker territory. But still–

"And then you had yourself assigned to do the Evaluation Report on contact with Earth?"

"I was simply the logical person to do that. While it was convenient, it also presented an ethical problem, especially when, after my second arrival at your house, I began to think in terms of being in love with you."

"When I was attractively vomited upon?"

"When you turned dismay into laughter, and returned damp from your shower with that rather thin dress clinging to every curve. And then we simply sat and talked, and it was the same as that first time I saw you. You listened to me, so grave and polite, and sparking with inner fires. It's very...stimulating."

His right hand lifted an inch or so off his knee, but then he dropped it back, and for a moment she could see tension there, before he deliberately relaxed his hands, straightening.

"My Sights didn't tell me to marry you, Laura. I do want that. Marriage, children. Waking up with you. But I already have the thing that is most important to me: spending time with you."

"Children?" she said, startled.

"You don't wish to see what you and I combined could be? I do. But most of all I want to continue to be with you, in whatever way you will allow. What is not clear to me is why knowing I was powerfully attracted before we formally met has dealt you such a blow."

Laura knew she needed to answer this question, but really didn't want to. "I suppose most people would think it romantic," she said, granting herself a brief postponement. "To make such a strong first impression."

Gidds shook his head. "Sight talents are often seen as too invasive. And Sight Sight pushes." He took a slow, deliberate breath. "I cannot be anything but a Sight talent, Laura, or change that my Sights played some role in my desire for you."

There was a pulse leaping in one of his temples, tiny and so revealing. Laura impulsively leaned forward and gripped his partially gloved hand so that he could more easily read her emotions. This wasn't about him, or his Sights, and she wanted him to truly feel that.

Over his shoulder she saw three black-clad figures emerge from the bushes surrounding the floating bathroom. They stood frozen for a moment, then reversed direction, Zee towing Mara by her elbow.

"I'm bad with things that hurt me," Laura said. "I shut them away, or be sensible to a fault, or arrange to not have scenes about them. I did feel a little strange about the possibility that you and I might be together 'because Sight Sight told him to', but I was thrown off-balance mainly because the last few months as I knew them changed and were reshaped by something I didn't know. And that opened an old wound."

She started to let go of his hand, but he firmed his grip, then swapped rocks to sit beside her.

"Utter betrayal," he said, and his voice was very soft. "I could feel that, and I thought it somehow was about me."

"No."

The thought of explaining didn't seem so impossible with him sitting beside her, hand held so firmly. But there was still a constriction in her throat to overcome, to allow her to explain the last time a precious relationship had been so abruptly reshaped.

"On the whole I think it's unhealthy to cling to a marriage that no longer works," she said, voice low. "Everyone changes, and it's far from uncommon to grow apart and move on. That's the kind of thing that hurts for a while, and then you get over it. But moving on while staying is not a kindness."

Gidds shifted but did not speak, and Laura let herself lean against his shoulder.

"I find it very hard to forgive that year," she said, in a small, stilted voice. "A year where I lived a delusion of comfortable marriage with someone who valued me, shared a dozen different interests, who worked and laughed and slept with me, and was happy too. And that person wasn't real, thought me dull, wanted to be with someone else. *Was* with someone else. Which made it a year I wouldn't have participated in, given the choice."

The familiar, sick revulsion washed over her, and she felt Gidds' grip tighten, even though Place Sight would be battering him with remembered nausea. She took deep breaths until it passed.

"Such a shabby way to behave," she said at last. "And history, something I rarely think about any more, but it does mean I react poorly to—well, not surprises. I like good surprises. Just..."

"False foundations," he said.

"Yes." Laura straightened, offering him a wry smile. "That was rather more drama than I usually indulge in. I guess that's what I get for running away from conversations."

"No, this is due to my omission. And I knew certain of Haelin's ambitions, although I didn't expect her to try to push us to them. But she will not be so impolite again, and I cannot be unhappy we've had this conversation."

Laura did feel better. "A little catharsis goes a long way."

Cass had not entered 'catharsis' in her English-Muinan dictionary, and Laura could see Gidds react to the word. Sight Sight.

They took a lightning detour through Greek tragedy—and some kissing—before deciding that the rest of the walking party would surely be tired of tactfully lurking at the other end of the island.

"I have an inspection tour scheduled the day after tomorrow," Gidds said, as they stood. "Dull stuff in terms of my part, but the place has spectacular views and I think you'd enjoy it. Would you like to come along?"

Laura hesitated, but decided she did want to see more of how Gidds behaved on duty. A decorous business trip and pretty scenery mightn't help her settle the question of too fast or too slow, but it would at least distract her.

"Hot or cold weather clothing?"

"Edging toward cooler, but a light jacket should be fine. A long day with a very early start. I'll detail someone to collect you, and arrange for breakfast on the transport."

He added the appointment to her calendar, and then wanted an explanation for why she found that so funny, and so she related a few selected highlights of Cass' diary, particularly the time he'd given Cass an appointment for 'now'.

At the pavilion they found Allidi, Haelin and Lira conscientiously packing the remains of lunch, and talking about *Red Exchange*. All three gave Gidds and Laura evaluating glances, although only Lira extended hers to open consideration.

Apparently satisfied, Lira abruptly leapt for a tangent, saying to Gidds: "Who is it decided I must be followed about at school?"

"The Touchstone Oversight Committee," Gidds replied, not blinking at the sudden change of direction. "Primarily due to the risk posed by Teleportation talents."

"Do the Kalrani get punished when I hide from them?"

"You haven't yet succeeded in hiding," Gidds told her. "The interface shows your exact location at all times. Nor have you been out of range of Combat Sight, which is the primary means of assessing any threat to you. Ducking out of rooms quickly, or blocking doors, only limits line of sight."

"It's more interesting for your security detail when you try to hide," Haelin put in, not necessarily helpfully. "While you're around people, guard duty means not even watching entertainments or playing games. So boring. I'm glad they're only assigning older girls."

"Pandora Shore is easier than in a less controlled area," Allidi said. "But at the same time the students are far more dangerous than the general public. Combat Sight reacts to that." She hesitated, then added: "Can I ask you something?"

Lira, looking frustrated, shrugged.

"Why do you never really try to hide? Create a projection as a distraction? You—Touchstones are so potentially powerful."

"Because then there would be more rules," Lira said, impatiently. "They would not let me go to the school, or put twice as many guards. I am just tired of them being there *all* the time."

"But—" Allidi glanced at her father. "There are Teleportation shields on some rooms, and Combat Sight would reveal any intent to attack among the students.

Can't the guard detail simply stay outside, so long as they can watch the door?"

Lira brightened enormously, and turned a look of burning expectation on Gidds.

"I'm no longer on the Committee," he said. "But I can suggest the compromise to them, if you wish."

Lira wished. Lira stopped short of ordering Gidds to make the arrangements Right Away, but clearly thought it all but settled, and thanked Allidi for the idea. Laura was pleased, but also reminded that having a daughter and granddaughter who were Touchstones mixed poorly with a romance with a KOTIS officer. There was fertile ground for conflict and tension, for while Gidds had very wisely taken himself entirely out of Arcadia's supervision chain, that did not make him any less a person of influence in such matters.

The arrival of the three Setari, Sue, and the rest of the kids provided a handy diversion from the topic, and they decided they would continue along the path until it looped near the central hill, at which point Zee would airlift them to the amphitheatre. Gidds, after a murmur to Laura, caught up with his daughters at the front of the group, clearly having serious conversations over the interface.

Sue, eyeing them thoughtfully, opened a channel to Laura.

"*Our three minders took on a distinct resemblance to sheepdogs for a while there, as if I could fail to have spotted Haelin arriving, figurative cap in hand, to ask for Daddy's forgiveness. And never has a locale leant itself more to me asking if there's trouble in Paradise.*"

"*Not trouble, really. Maybe a pothole in the road to happily ever after. Sight talents really are something to get used to.*"

"*What'd he do? Want me to go kick him in the shins?*"

Laura explained, while wondering if Gidds would let Sue kick him.

"*Love at first Sight Sight, huh? And do you, now you've had a chance to process it, find that romantic?*"

"*I find that I understand Gidds—and his daughters—a little better now. The whole 'years and years' thing just makes me feel pressured. But...*" She paused, thinking about Gidds spending those years wanting to know her better. "*I like his reasons for liking me. I like them a lot.*"

CHAPTER NINETEEN

Laura had never lived anywhere colder than Sydney, and while she was finding the advance of the Pandoran autumn fascinating, it was not nearly so amusing with the addition of pre-dawn rain.

Should have worn a heavier jacket.

But this was only a brief consideration as her patio door slid open, and then it was her turn to step up onto a strut, and settle into the curving seat of a flying machine.

"Skimmers and flitters, oh my," she murmured.

"Tsa Devlin?" the pilot said.

"I'm envying your transportation," Laura told her.

The pilot grinned. "Today, I am envying yours," she said.

Laura started to ask what that meant, but then they rose into the air, and she was too busy gazing appreciatively at the island and the lake, and the view of a sleeping Pandora as they crossed it.

Since Muinan aircraft landed more like helicopters than jets, Muinan airports did not require long runways, and so the whitestone landing zone to the south-east of Pandora was relatively compact. They settled next to a bulky-looking tanz with what seemed like a severe excess of technicians giving it a final check. The pilot helpfully pointed Laura toward Gidds, surrounded by grey-suited technicians beneath the shelter of one of the tanz' wings, and then lifted her agile craft back into the air.

Expecting to have to wait until the cluster of senior technicians had finished giving Gidds' what looked to be several peremptory sets of orders, Laura had to suppress an instinctive step back when they immediately abandoned their discussion in favour of competing to be introduced to her. Fortunately, the flight had a strict schedule, and so she was rescued by the need to board

"I hope I didn't look too overwhelmed," she said on a private channel to Gidds. *"I can barely follow Muinan when so many people talk at once, and I never know what to say when people congratulate me on being someone's Mum."*

"You smiled and nodded in roughly the correct places."

Laura shot him an amused glance, then added: *"Did I hear correctly that the installation we're heading to is named after Isten Notra?"*

"Yes. Its primary purpose is moonfall research, and Isten Notra is heading that team."

"I thought she was heading the teleport network team."

"She is. Muinan installations are so interconnected that Notra is effectively acting as Chief Technician for everything Ena-related. The naming of the base is recognition of the role she played during the crisis, for we certainly would not have come through it without her."

The main cabin of the tanz was organised into two rows of pods divided by a central aisle, and Gidds led Laura to the pair at the very end. She settled into the one on the right with all the pleasure only memories of cattle class could produce, and wriggled a little as the cushions of the 'dentist's chair' style couch moulded around her and a net of safety straps snugged themselves into position. Long-distance tanz gave all passengers their own, aether-proof pods: endlessly comfortable, with bubble-like lids that slid over the top for privacy as well as protection.

"I'll be in conference for most of the flight," Gidds said. *"And there'll be several periods where we won't be able to leave the pods, so only a small meal will be served after launch, and a larger one when we arrive at Sel Notra."*

Laura nodded, but then did a quick search over the interface.

"*Muina would not have come through the crisis without the Setari program you pioneered. But there aren't any bases named after you.*"

He produced his flicker of a smile. "*That lack is not something I object to.*"

"*No? Well, I reserve the right to be highly partisan.*"

This time, instead of smiling, he went still. Then, with complete gravity, he said aloud: "Thank you."

Laura found herself flushing, which was silly of her, but it was impossible not to react when Gidds was at his full intensity. A safety announcement began to play in the interface, and she took the excuse to look away from him to consider the diagram of the tanz, with exits marked, but also the direction that they stay in their pods during emergencies. Flight time would be a little under two kasse—roughly four hours—which, with Muinan technology, could take them to the other side of the planet although the location of Sel Notra base was, entertainingly, not something Laura could look up. Her security classification wasn't high enough.

Secret KOTIS bases. Laura grinned, but—mindful that this was work time for Gidds—only settled back to the vast array of entertainments available over the interface, and ended up reviewing the items she had for sale as 'Tiamat'. She had only made two sales in the months since she'd set up her online store, and though these had been for gratifyingly high prices, it was not exactly a going concern. Still, she didn't have a lot of stock to sell, either, for the elaborate, diorama-style pieces she had been experimenting with took days, even weeks to create. She had the luxury of time.

Laura glanced at Gidds, and then allowed herself to be distracted by a small, bland breakfast, followed by the next book in the series that *Red Exchange* was based upon.

At least, that is, until the ten-joden atmosphere warning.

Startled, Laura frowned at the notice floating as an interface projection ten inches in front of her face, and then turned to stare at Gidds. He was watching her, smiling.

"Atmosphere warning?"

"We have ten joden until movement is restricted. Would you like to see?"

Gidds could hardly look more thoroughly pleased with himself, and Laura had never been so inclined to gape blankly. But then she nodded, and followed him through the doors at the rear of the passenger section, and up a curved stair to an oval area at the top of the tanz that was mainly open, with a few chairs built around the edges. The front was clear of obstruction, however, and as they approached some kind of outer shielding drew back.

Darkness. Stars. And a distant, rounded shape, marked by a comma-shaped hole.

Laura absolutely was gaping now. And then she reached out, and took Gidds' hand. She didn't want to speak, not at first, and found herself taking deep, gulping breaths, as if she'd been running. They'd used up at least half of the ten joden before she managed, in a shaking voice: "Yes, the views are spectacular."

He slid his arms around her, very briefly, and then said: "We cannot linger. The transition from atmosphere is a critical point in the journey, and when we switch to solar speeds we must be in our pods."

Laura was having to work on not crying, and made a quick visit to a restroom to wash her face thoroughly. When she settled back into her pod, she opened a channel with Gidds, but only to say: "*I'm too incoherent to ask sensible questions. Are we really heading to a secret moon base?*"

"*As secret as anything so large can be within KOTIS. Since the chasm was formed during the two attempts to reshape existence, and is clearly linked in some way to the whole aether network, this is considered an important* avenue for research. The secrecy is very temporary, more to keep the planning stage free of any proposals regarding recreational sites."

"*Space resorts!?*" Laura did not consider this a thing to be postponed.

Gidds smiled. "*They will happen soon enough. Since Tare does not have a moon, and our focus has been more on Ena travel than vacuum travel, KOTIS only has experience with small orbital stations. Before we can permit commercial operators on Esune, there is considerable data to gather. Today is the first structural inspection following the activation of the environmental system. If I clear it, then the non-drone occupation stage will commence.*"

As their pod lids closed as a safety precaution, Gidds showed Laura how to access the external cameras of the tanz, and then returned to his meetings while she busied herself with further freaking out.

The moon. The moon, Esune. Space. Stars, brilliant and cold and clear. Muina, vast, and greener than Earth, because the proportion of land to water was roughly equal, and the distribution more even. *Like a vast lattice pie crust*, Laura thought, and fought down a giggle. She was flying from there to the moon.

The contrast to Earth's level of technology had never been sharper. No fiery thrust to escape the gravity well. No discernible change in her weight. No cramped cockpit, or bulky spacesuit, or astronaut nappies. And a four hour trip! She'd read that it took days to reach Earth's moon, though a good portion of that involved deceleration and not turning passengers to mush. But *four hours!*

Laura walked onto a spaceship with no more preparation – less, in fact – than a Sydney to LA flight. With the help of the interface, she found distances and then did some quick calculations and shook her head in awe. Because the Muinans stuck to the Ena for interplanetary travel she'd never really looked into what they were capable of in real-space. Solar system travel was entirely practical at these speeds, and though the other planets in Muina's system weren't exactly colonisation prospects, the Muinans were perfectly capable of sending drones and whitestone nanites, and the raw materials for dome cities.

Sel Notra Base clearly showed this to be true, for as it rapidly came into focus, Laura could see the place was big: a wide central dome surrounded by a ring of whitestone buildings, and then radiating spokes. It sat close to the point where the 'downstroke' of the comma joined the original circle, and Laura eventually gave in to disbelief and—mindful of his meetings—sent Gidds a text.

Laura: *How can this possibly be secret? It has to be visible from the surface of the planet.*

Gidds: *The structure was only formed five days ago.*

Laura: *But...believe me, if anyone planted something like this on the surface of Earth's moon, a half-dozen amateur astronomers would be melting down the internet within the first hour.*

Gidds: *The telescopes most use are interface-enabled. Everyone on Muina has an interface installation.*

Perplexed, Laura stared at him. Then, remembering how she could set her own privacy settings to prevent people taking images of her with interface-enabled devices, she understood. They'd edited it out. The people on Muina literally couldn't see Sel Notra Base, because all the telescopes—potentially everything they saw—ran through the filter of the interface.

It took a long time for Laura to manage to respond.

Laura: *The Triplanetary truly is only two steps from a dystopia.*

Gidds: *One of the reasons we have so many oversight committees. We could so easily slide into nightmare.*

Laura found herself unspeakably glad that he'd said that. That someone with the power Gidds wielded saw the potential for horror in the system he had been raised within. It took her a while to shake off the chill, but it was impossible to resist the rapid approach of an Actual Moon Base. And *landing*, with a light billow of dust that took an age to settle while they waited through the post-flight checks. Then their pod lids lifted, and two green-suited security personnel walked along the aisle distributing helmets.

These were fascinating, with a solid section that curved a little like a hawk's beak pointing up and out over the forehead, providing a frame for a clear substance that could raise up from a heavy-duty ring collar. This gave a reasonably broad area of view, but it wasn't until they were ushered into a shower-like cubicle that Laura realised the ring had a similar function to the control unit of the Setari nanosuits. She managed to mostly not flinch when goo sprayed from the walls, and it was only moments before it formed into an incredibly fine blue-grey coverall that joined up with the control ring of the helmet. It did not strike her as particularly sturdy protection, but Gidds assured her that the suits would hold against full vacuum, although their air supply was very limited without an extra pack. They were simply a precaution in case any environment seals failed during the inspection.

Laura now needed to exercise considerable self-control, as she and Gidds were conducted on a tour of An Actual Moon Base, being handed from senior technician to senior technician as Gidds inspected each of their areas of control in turn—including a kitchen and refectory where they were shown how food would be produced before eating a sample meal.

Laura had never been closer to starring in her own Disney movie, wanting to skip and dance and sing from the sheer joy of An Actual Moon Base. She controlled herself by spending a lot of time peering out of view ports at vistas that 'spectacular' truly undersold.

Her only disappointment was that the gravity was Muinan-standard: artificially generated just as it had been on the tanz. They didn't need to keep their helmets sealed, for the air was perfectly breathable, if a bit swampy thanks to a slight imbalance in the atmosphere system, located in five of the radiating spokes. Great big vats of algae that had been steadily producing oxygen for the last few days, but now needed some balancing.

After she had calmed down just a little, Laura checked Sue's status, saw she was still asleep, and ruthlessly sent an override.

Even with an alarm clock playing in her head, it took next to forever for Sue to respond, and when she did, it was with: *"This had better be good."*

"He took me to the moon."

"Laura, hon, interested as I am in your sex life, I really don't need a daily update. At least not without more interesting details, and at a more reasonable time of day."

"No. You're not listening to me. He took me to the moon. I. Am. On. The. Moon."

"...serious?"

"Serious." Laura shared her visual stream, panning from the current algae bed to the clear curved ceiling, with half of Muina a magnificent spotlight in the sky.

"But how?"

Laura explained, letting all her reaction stream out until Sue said: *"You've started to repeat yourself."*

"I needed to babble."

"Hmph. Well, my opinion of Serious Soldier has gone up several notches. He's not so stick-straight after all, if he's pulled the kind of strings that would have to be involved in taking you along. And just to win some brownie points! I wonder if he could have done that with any old popsy, or if you being Grendel's Sainted Mum made it possible."

"I don't think Cass would appreciate that comparison. Still, it's...something of a revelation, watching the way the technicians behave toward Gidds. A couple are like the Setari, all deep respect and a tendency to stand straighter. Others are this weird mix of dismissive and resentful. They can't go forward with the base until he gives the okay and they're so annoyed and nervous at the same time."

"Maybe you'll give him a bump in the opinion polls. So when's the wedding?"

"Sue..."

"Don't even pretend you're not going to marry him. I know you. And he obviously does, too, inside and out. His deep dark secret turned out to be a couple of years of mooning over your picture—and that totally was a deliberate reference—and you were wavering on heading back to 'burnt before' territory about shacking up with him, so he decides on a big, romantic gesture. Not gifts, not dinner, not even flowers: he's taken you on a business trip. To the moon. Because of all the things it was in his power to do, that's the one that would reduce you to incoherence. Face it, the man knows what makes you tick. Now ask yourself: would you be half so happy without him around?"

Laura didn't respond immediately, then said: *"I don't think I can answer that right now. There's no room in my head for anything except that I am On The Moon."*

"Bosh," Sue replied, succinctly, and broke the connection.

But being in space was a dream come true for Laura, and the next location they visited was especially overwhelming. The central dome: a wide bubble with no floor but the surface of Elune, and no artificial gravity. They sealed their helmets before they went in, just as a precaution, and had to work to stay upright.

"Can I bounce?" Laura asked, long past caring about adult dignity.

"I do not see why not, Tsa Devlin," said the most senior of the technicians, who was apparently Isten Notra's second-in-command.

Laura bounced. She fell over quite a bit, too, and her hair fell all in her eyes and wavered in odd directions, while her suit was smeared with Elunan dust. She had to go get decontaminated afterwards, just in case, but that was just another new and interesting experience.

Mindful that this was actually work for Gidds, Laura had refrained from throwing her arms around him every few minutes, and instead paid rapt attention to the technicians. Her plan was to wait until the flight back to start to try to put into words the things she wanted him to know, but after settling into her couch and delighting in watching take-off, she somehow lost nearly all of the four hour flight back and woke to a half-heard snort and an internal clock which felt like a lie.

But perhaps it was for the best, for when she turned her head to look at Gidds, she found she didn't want to talk at all. She wanted to kiss those delicate temples, and trace that jaw, and—

Gidds turned his head and looked at her, and she would swear for the rest of her life that he went pink. He definitely knew without doubt or ambiguity exactly what line her thoughts were taking, and for all of the remainder of the flight they lay and just stared at each other.

The fortunate privileges of rank meant Gidds had a flyer waiting for them both, and Laura got to sit behind him and the pilot this time, and spent the entire time studying the fine hairs at the nape of his neck, picked out in the tiny dim internal light of the flyer.

It was well into the evening by the time they stepped back onto her patio, and she offered the pilot a barely-held-together smile of thanks, and walked inside.

Then, after an eternity of restraint, she took Gidds' hand.

Laura had never had genuine, clothes-tearing-off sex before. At least one button of her sensible shirt pinged off a wall, and it was to be hoped that Julian didn't emerge from his cave, but Laura did not at that moment care overmuch for the sensibilities of teenaged boys. She and Gidds fell onto her bed and lost themselves in sheer urgency: a short frantic necessity.

"I'd apologise for making your job today very difficult, but I think you brought it on yourself," Laura said at last, panting in the aftermath.

"I underestimated you," he said.

They both laughed like giddy children, and then stopped talking again and just kissed until they could make love a second time, a slow, tender coming together, all bright around the edges with a startled joy that endured even into Laura's dreams when finally they slept.

CHAPTER TWENTY

Rising in the pre-dawn, Laura left a brilliant man tangled in her sheets, and pulled on warm clothes and a beanie before venturing outside.

No leaves on the trees now: the last colour of autumn was lost. Sharp chill spiked her nose, but yesterday's rain had thankfully passed. She followed the path to Arcadia's north-east point, and settled on her favourite seat to watch the dawn, and wait for Gidds.

After a look at his schedule, she had sent him an email containing only a rough electronic sketch of the island, with a single 'x' to mark her seat. He arrived precisely when she'd guessed he would, crisp and correct in yesterday's uniform, and paused beside the bench.

"This place is full of you."

"My favourite spot on the island," she said. "I wanted it to be here."

His eyes went wide, and his face very carefully still, but all he did was sit down. Not interested in stretching the moment, Laura took his hand.

"Gidds. Will you come live with me with a view to getting married some time?"

"I would like that," he said, in a voice that did not waver, but suggested shortness of breath. "Very much."

He look down at their hands, then lifted hers to his lips and kissed the tips of her fingers, closing his eyes as he did so. She took the opportunity to kiss his left temple, and then they lost themselves for a while.

"Maybe we'll even find out what kind of person you and I would make," she said at last. "I've been thinking about that ever since you said it. Though I think, first, some time for our...our current children to adjust."

It was astonishing how right it felt, how no shred of doubt remained. She loved him, and they would make a life together, and deal with whatever came up, and be happy. It was that simple.

Since Gidds' morning schedule was full of meetings, she took him back to the house for an early breakfast, and they agreed to tell their respective families and then meet for lunch to talk about technicalities. Then she went back to her favourite seat and watched the lake for a while, and wallowed in giddy delight.

Cass had already headed off to work, but was also due back before lunch, so Laura decided a midday family meal was a good idea, and sent her an invite and then, when Julian woke, sent him a text.

Laura: *Come down when you're properly conscious.*

Julian had clearly had some presentiment, descending with barely a fraction of his usual noise and speed, and after one look at her face saying: "Do I have to call him Dad?"

"Well, I expect you could call him Gidds, if you wanted to. Or maybe you could call him 'sir', like in old movies." Laura studied his face. "I know it's going to be...different, Julian, but you needn't worry about being stuck with your own personal drill sergeant, or anything like that."

"Nah, it's okay. He's pretty cool. And he's got to be less of a dick than Dad."

"Don't talk about your father that way," Laura said, automatically.

Her lanky son gave her a genuinely puzzled look. "Why do you always do that?" he asked. "Dad treated you like crap. It's a fact. I'm allowed to say it."

"I—" Laura lifted her hands to try to encompass how unfair it would have been to insert her hurt into the kids' relationship with their father, but then gave up. "You are," she conceded. "But let's not spend any time trekking through old swamps. I'm really happy today."

"Yeah, you are," Julian said, hugging her suddenly. "It's been kinda fun and weird all at the same time. I'd even put up with a drill sergeant for that." Then he sighed. "I suppose those girls are going to move in."

"Yes, at least on weekends, and probably whole weeks when their training isn't in intensive phases."

"My growing collection of deadly super-sisters. At least they won't call me *uncle*." Julian made several faces, but then grinned. "Cass is going to go spare. She only figured out there was anything going on this last weekend while we were at Areziath, and me and Aunt Sue had a great time yesterday telling her all sorts of stuff. She looked like she'd been hit by a brick."

But Cass had recovered from any shock by the time she brought Tyrian up for lunch, and simply smiled and kissed Laura at the news.

"So everyone's been belatedly telling me. It's official now?"

"Well, in the Taren-style 'living together with intention to wed' thing, rather than jumping straight to officially engaged. You—you don't mind having a few more Arcadian residents do you?"

"Your house, Mum. So long as you're...do you *really* like Tsur Selkie?"

Laura had to laugh. "I can guarantee that. Why so disbelieving?"

"I don't know. I thought, if you ever married anyone, it'd be someone like Aunt Sue. You know, the way you two talk together. I just can't imagine Tsur Selkie talking like that."

"Lucky I brought Sue along, then."

Cass didn't seem entirely convinced, but said she'd look forward to throwing an engagement party when they made it officially official. And then Gidds arrived with Allidi and Haelin, who were formal and polite, but clearly pleased, and it was not too long before Julian and Cass drew them into a mild squabble over wedding customs, and surnames. And then they all listened in round-eyed disbelief when Laura told them just where Gidds had taken her the day before. It was so comfortable, and familiar, and astonishing, and unbelievable, and...joy.

Sue ambled in an hour or so later, and gave Laura an assessing look, then smiled and hugged her.

"Crossed the Event Horizon, huh? No escape now."

Laura took a deep breath, then nodded. "None at all."

Epilogue

"What a circus."

Bet Wilson agreed with her husband's assessment of the scene outside, but her attention was for their eldest daughter, Kiri.

"I can't believe we're letting you do this."

"I can't believe you're not going with me!" Kiri said, shrugging on her backpack. "Psychics! Spaceships! Alien ruins!"

"But no elves," Steve said. "If only there'd been elves."

They laughed, for Steve did love fantasy far more than science fiction, but the joke didn't change how hard it had been to watch Laura and Sue follow Cass to another planet. And then a year of fielding rumours and dealing with Kiri's relentless campaign to be allowed to go to Muina before the slowly shifting gate between worlds ceased to appear. Bet and Steve had too many ties and commitments to walk away from, but it just hadn't been possible to keep telling Kiri that being fifteen meant she couldn't make a dream come true.

Determined not to miss the opening of the gate, Kiri picked up a package of treats they'd prepared for Sue, then dragged her parents outside to face a street packed with cars. At least a hundred people, Bet guessed, counting faces behind windscreens, along with those who loitered more openly, leaning against fences. Some of them had been there for days, camping in their cars. There was even a police presence, no doubt thanks to complaints from neighbours.

"Be interesting to see what they do if nothing happens," Steve muttered.

"Don't say that," Bet said, managing not to glance toward the Caldwell family, waiting white-faced under the pergola Steve had built in the front yard.

"You'd be too busy coping with my epic meltdown to notice anyone else, Dad," Kiri added.

"A bunch of people are gonna rush the gate," said Bet's second-eldest, Kit, poking his head around his father's bulky frame. "I heard them talking."

Bet exchanged a glance with her husband, and he nodded and headed over to the specially-invited collection of large friends and relatives – most New Zealander expatriates like Steve. Bet checked her watch, and then went to make awkward conversation with the Caldwells, who had sent two of their children to another planet in the hopes of saving the life of their youngest, and had had to wait more than a year to know how to cry.

Doctor Jamandre had also waited, and now sat on the edge of the long front porch with two colleagues. Considering the woman's tense, determined face, Bet thought that she, too, might rush the gate.

Tucked into the corner of the porch beside the doctors was the failed husband collection: Sam Dale and Mike Devlin, along with Mike's remarkably impolite second wife. Bet cast a worried eye over Sam, but he'd managed to clean himself up very thoroughly, though the bloodshot eyes spoiled the impression of established sobriety. Bet doubted Nick would be at all fooled, but at least Sam had made the attempt.

The oldest of the three doctors, a small man with only eyebrows left of his hair, caught her eye and then shifted over to give her room. "You are tired. Sit."

Bet wavered, but the porch had a good view, and she needed to be distracted.

"Thank you, Doctor–?"

"Ehlin. But call me Eberhard."

"I'm Bet." She studied him thoughtfully. "I'm guessing you sit in the sceptic's seat."

He laughed. "Well, 'I want to believe'. But I am by nature suspicious of wild hope. If I hadn't known Jayathri since her residency—for she is a Scully, not a Mulder—then I would have..." He stopped, and considered the occupants of the pergola. "I would have had an investigation launched into the welfare of Maddy Caldwell."

"And after today? Given the gate is only open for five minutes?"

"Well." He shrugged, in an almost embarrassed way, then touched his coat pocket, which crackled faintly. "I wrote them a letter. Put the sceptic aside for a while, and just...begged. Five minutes is more than enough time to send through information. All the next steps in medicine, the breakthroughs that perhaps we would reach eventually, but would make such a difference *now*. Even a few strong hints, a direction." He stopped, shaking his head. "I'm getting ahead of myself. First I need to see with my own eyes that those videos weren't faked."

The videos had been inevitable, and impossible to suppress. This street, a year and a couple of spare months ago, with a much smaller crowd waiting. A front yard party in the middle of the week, except for the way so many tensely scanned the footpath. And then a shout, children pointing down the street at two thin poles with triangles of colour at the end, poking horizontally out of nothing.

Julian had run straight between them, without any hesitation at all, and vanished without even an accompanying 'blip'. And the Caldwells, stumbling, holding on to a too-small child bundled against non-existent cold, had followed, and Bet had not had nearly enough time to say goodbye for real to her two sisters. Family—and a few friends—had recorded it all, from the appearance of the flags, to that last moment, when Nick's father had pushed him and he'd fallen backward into nothing, with only his feet sticking out. The flags had dropped to the ground, Nick's feet had pulled away, and then it was over, leaving the shorn tips of two poles with two green pennants attached to the end.

Bet still had one of them, in the bedroom closet. The other had vanished, and a few months later an analysis of it had been released, showing it was made of polymers available on Earth, and not futuristic at all.

Because of the Caldwells in particular, denial had been a strict policy, but inevitably someone had put up some of the recordings, and rumours had spread, been endlessly discussed on the internet, and a vast variety of people had shown up to ask questions, and receive as they would the family story that they'd just been filming an amateur movie.

But the timing of the next gate opening had been leaked.

People were out of their cars now, and the police had moved forward to keep the street clear. Bet—everyone—stood up, searching for triangles of green.

And then there was...an elf?

She stood directly before the garden gate, sheathed in a gossamer breath of blue dress with a deeply cut décolletage, her hair a fine and shimmering gold streaming about her like a cloak.

And it was glowing. So was the dress, glimmering with silver motes in the afternoon shadows. But the face, though young and endowed with improbable eyelashes, was familiar.

"*Sue?!*"

"Starsha," the vision corrected, then gave her Sue's grin. "Couldn't resist starting this out with a touch of space princess. But business now." She turned, lifted her hands to her mouth to amplify, and shouted: "Make room! Make room! Diplomatic delegation coming through! Thirty people in uniform on their way, entirely peaceful!"

But it wasn't anyone in uniform who stepped through the gate while Sue was making her announcement. Laura heard Nina Caldwell give a strangled gulp, and then a sturdy, curly-haired girl yelled.

"Mum! They're letting me come home! They're letting me come home!"

Matters became confusing as the spectators surged forward, the family brawn formed a wall, the police contingent started to take the whole sideshow much more seriously, and a stream of uniformed people began to emerge from the nothing that led to a different planet.

"Bet!"

"Laura! My god, you look...look..."

"Yes, I'm still not used to it. But there's no time. Steve, Bet, this is Tsaile Nimion, who is in charge of the delegation, and this is Tsa Anar, who is the Triplanetary's official envoy to Earth. Steve, can you start channelling the delegation into the house? Interplanetary relations could do without the mob scene."

Steve laughed, then said: "Can't argue with that. Just tell me, Admiral, is there anything we should know?"

"The shield is down, it's safe to proceed," Laura said, handing him an object that resembled a mobile phone. "Definitely end of the world as we know it territory, though. Here: English-Muinan translator, although most of the delegation are pretty much at conversational level already."

Turning away, Laura searched the crowd. "Doctor Jamandre?" she called, and then led a man in a grey uniform to the cluster of medicos. "This is Islen Peran. He's in charge of the science outreach."

"I think those are Setari, Mum," Kit said, popping up at Bet's elbow to point at a cluster of people in black.

"Tenth Squad," Sue confirmed, emerging from the whirl. "Dual-purpose security and, well, public relations. Real-life psychic superheroes. Come on, we've got a whole minute or so for family business, and we may as well do it somewhere less noisy."

The collection of black-suited Setari had formed a ring around the invisible gate, and were all facing outward. There were more on the other side of the gate, and a sloping hill, and several fantastical flyers. Most of all, there was one man in a blue uniform that Laura particularly wanted Bet to meet.

"This is Gidds," Laura said. "We're getting married tomorrow. I wanted to wait until you could meet him."

Bet knew she did not acquit herself well meeting the striking, self-contained man that Laura—*Laura!*—had decided to marry. There wasn't time for any proper explanations, but Laura pressed a thick envelope into her hand, saying: "Here's all the family news and some pictures. You wait until you see who Sue's dating. Gosh! Now, where's Kiri? Cass did a projection so we know she's coming along."

Kiri was still on the far side of the gate, looking like she was debating dashing past the Setari, and Bet found herself suddenly in tears. Flinging her arms around her daughter, she smoothed her curling brown hair, kissed her cheek, and then let Laura take her through.

Sue whirled up, an ethereal dervish. "Time to white rabbit. Sorry to drop this in your lap, but I'm sure it'll be fun, and probably not a rerun of *Childhood's End*. Here's the last bit, the official start. Press the button, put it on the ground in front of a bunch of cameras, and transmit the result to the world. I hope we all get to see you again sooner rather than later."

It was a good half hour after Sue had dashed back through the gate before matters had calmed down enough for the 'official start'. Then Bet and Steve led a select portion of the delegation out to the edge of the hastily-erected police roadblock, and faced the shouting of the press. In response, she pushed a button, put a small grey dome on the ground, and stood back.

Cass. A hologram of a fit young woman with brown hair worn in a ponytail, with one eye a different colour to the shade she'd grown up with, and a smile that was all Laura's. And then the world changed.

oOo

Transcript of Official Contact Broadcast

Hello, people of Earth! Sorry, I couldn't think of a less clichéd opening.

My name is Cass Ruuel Devlin, and a few years ago I walked through a dimensional portal to a planet called Muina. A lot of stuff happened, and I ended up helping the people here save, well, either a few planets, a large chunk of the galaxy, or the entire universe, depending on what theory you like.

In return, the people of the planets Muina, Tare and Kolar want to open diplomatic relations with Earth, something that's seriously hampered by the gate to Muina only opening once a year for a few minutes. So, as a first step, they...

[Large intake of breath, pause.]

As a first step they're giving you their technology. All the things they know about medicine and physics—and psychics—and nanites and all of that. Because their planets would have been lost by now, if that gate to Earth hadn't opened.

They're sending a delegation to assist in explaining all the information they're giving us...you...Earth. They think a more reliable route to Earth will be found within the next couple of years. And...and, well, there'll be a longer explanation transmitted along with this, so I'll just wish everyone good luck.

Oh!, and if there are any ice skating instructors who want to move to another planet next time the gate opens, and don't mind the possibility of not being able to get back for a while, there's about a billion people here who want to sign up for lessons. And if David Attenborough wants to make some BBC documentaries here, my son would be super happy.

END

www.ingramcontent.com/pod-product-compliance
Lightning Source LLC
Chambersburg PA
CBHW060423180626
46817CB00007B/2640